THE
ISLAND PHARISEES

by

JOHN GALSWORTHY

'But this is worshipful Society.'
King John

HEINEMANN : LONDON

William Heinemann Ltd
LONDON MELBOURNE TORONTO
JOHANNESBURG AUCKLAND

First published in 1904

This edition first published 1970

0 434 28111 5

Printed in Great Britain by
Northumberland Press Limited
Gateshead

PREFACE

EACH man born into the world is born—like Shelton in this book —to go a journey, and for the most part he is born on the high road. At first he sits there in the dust, with his little chubby hands reaching at nothing, and his little solemn eyes staring into space. As soon as he can toddle, he moves, by the queer instinct we call the love of life, straight along this road, looking neither to the right nor left, so pleased is he to walk. And he is charmed with everything—with the nice flat road, all broad and white, with his own feet, and with the prospect he can see on either hand. The sun shines, and he finds the road a little hot and dusty; the rain falls, and he splashes through the muddy puddles. It makes no matter—all is pleasant; his fathers went this way before him; they made this road for him to tread, and, when they bred him, passed into his fibre the love of doing things as they themselves had done them. So he walks on and on, resting comfortably at nights under the roofs that have been raised to shelter him, by those who went before.

Suddenly one day, without intending to, he notices a path or opening in the hedge, leading to right or left, and he stands looking at the undiscovered. After that he stops at all the openings in the hedge; one day, with a beating heart, he tries one.

And this is where the fun begins.

Out of ten of him that try the narrow path, nine of him come back to the broad road, and, when they pass the next gap in the hedge, they say: 'No, no, my friend, I found you pleasant for a while, but after that—ah! after that! The way my fathers went is good enough for me, and it is obviously the proper way; for nine of me came back, and that poor silly tenth—I really pity him!'

And when he comes to the next inn, and snuggles in his well-warmed bed, he thinks of the wild waste of heather where he might have had to spend the night alone beneath the stars; nor does it, I think, occur to him that the broad road he treads all day was once a trackless heath itself.

But the poor silly tenth is faring on. It is a windy night that he is travelling through—a windy night, with all things new around, and nothing to help him but his courage. Nine times out of ten that courage fails, and he goes down into the bog. He has seen the undiscovered, and—like Ferrand in this book—the undiscovered has engulfed him; his spirit, tougher than the spirit of the nine who hurried back to sleep in inns, was yet not tough enough. The tenth time he wins across, and on the traces he has left others follow slowly, cautiously—a new road is opened to mankind!

There is a true saying: Whatever is, is right! And if all men from the world's beginning had said that, the world would never have begun at all. Not even the protoplasmic jelly could have commenced its journey; there would have been no motive force to make it start.

And so, that other saying had to be devised before the world could set up business: Whatever is, is wrong! But since the Cosmic Spirit found that matters moved too fast if those who felt 'All things that are, are wrong' equalled in number those who felt 'All things that are, are right,' It solemnly devised polygamy (all, be it said, in a spiritual way of speaking); and to each male spirit crowing 'All things that are, are wrong,' It decreed nine female spirits clucking, 'All things that are, are right.' The Cosmic Spirit, who was very much an artist, knew its work, and had previously devised a quality called courage, and divided it in three, naming the parts spiritual, moral, physical. To all the male-bird spirits, but to no female (spiritually, not corporeally speaking) It gave courage that was spiritual; to nearly all, both male and female, It gave courage that was physical; to very many hen-bird spirits It gave moral courage too. But, because It knew that if all the male-bird spirits were complete, the proportion of male to female—one to ten—would be too great, and cause upheavals, It so arranged that only one in ten male-bird spirits should have all three kinds of courage; so that the other nine, having spiritual courage, but lacking either in moral or in physical, should fail in their extensions of the poultry-run. And having started them upon these lines, It left them to get along as best they might.

Thus, in the sub-division of the poultry-run that we call England, the proportion of the others to the complete male-bird spirit, who, of course, is not infrequently a woman, is ninety-nine to one; and with every Island Pharisee, when he or she starts out in life, the interesting question ought to be: 'Am I that one?' Ninety very soon find out that they are not, and having found it out, lest others should discover, they say they *are*. Nine of the other ten, blinded by their spiritual courage, are harder to convince; but one by one they sink still proclaiming their virility. The hundredth Pharisee alone sits out the play.

Now, the tale of the journey of this young man Shelton, who is surely not the hundredth Pharisee, is but a ragged effort to present the working of the truth, 'All things that are, are wrong,' upon the truth, 'All things that are, are right.'

The Institutions of this country, like the Institutions of all other countries, are but half-truths; they are the working, daily clothing of the nation; no more the body's permanent dress than is a baby's frock. Slowly but surely they wear out, or are outgrown; and in their fashion they are always thirty years at least behind the fashions of those spirits who are concerned with what shall take their place. The conditions which dictate our education, the distribution of our property, our marriage laws, amusements, worship, prisons, and all other things, change imperceptibly from hour to hour; the moulds containing them, being inelastic, do not change, but hold on to the point of bursting, and then are hastily, often clumsily, enlarged. The ninety desiring peace and comfort for their spirit, the ninety of the well-warmed beds, will have it that the fashions need not change, that morality is fixed, that all is ordered and immutable, that every one will always marry, play, and worship in the way that they themselves are marrying, playing, worshipping. They have no speculation, and they hate with a deep hatred those who speculate with thought. They were not made for taking risks. They are the dough, and they dislike that yeasty stuff of life which comes and works about in them. The Yeasty Stuff—the other ten—chafed by all things that are, desirous ever of new forms and moulds, hate in their turn the comfortable ninety. Each party has invented for the other the hardest names that it can think of: Philistines, Bourgeois, Mrs Grundy—Rebels, Anarchists and Ne'er-do-weels. So we go on! And so, as each of us is born to go his journey, he finds himself in time ranged on one side or on the other, and joins the choruses of name-slingers.

But now and then—ah! very seldom—we find ourselves so near that thing which has no breadth, the middle line, that we can watch them both, and smile to see the fun.

When this book was published first, many of its critics found that Shelton was the only Pharisee, and a most unsatisfactory young man—and so, no doubt, he is. Belonging to the comfortable ninety, they felt, in fact, the need of slinging names at one who obviously was of the ten. Others of its critics, belonging to the ten, wielded their epithets upon Antonia, and the serried ranks behind her, and called them Pharisees, dull as ditchwater—and so,

I fear, they are.

One of the greatest charms of authorship is the privilege it gives to the author of studying the secret springs of many unseen persons, of analysing human nature through the criticism that his work evokes—criticism welling out of the instinctive likings or aversions, out of the very fibre of the human being who delivers it; criticism which often seems to leap out against the critic's will, startled like a fawn from some deep bed of sympathy or of antipathy. And so, all authors love to be abused—as any man can see.

But in the matter of the title of this book, we are all Pharisees, whether of the ninety or the ten, and we certainly live upon an Island.

JOHN GALSWORTHY.

January, 1908.

CONTENTS

PART 1

THE TOWN

PART 2

THE COUNTRY

Part One

THE TOWN

Chapter 1

SOCIETY

A QUIET, well-dressed man named Shelton, with a brown face and a short, fair beard, stood by the bookstall at Dover Station. He was about to journey up to London, and had placed his bag in the corner of a third-class carriage.

After his long travel, the flat-vowelled voice of the bookstall clerk offering the latest novel sounded pleasant—pleasant the independent answers of a bearded guard, and the stodgy farewell sayings of a man and wife. The limber porters trundling their barrows, the greyness of the station, and the good stolid humour clinging to the people, air, and voices, all brought to him the sense of home. Meanwhile he wavered between purchasing a book called 'Market Harborough,' which he had read, and would certainly enjoy a second time, and Carlyle's 'French Revolution,' which he had not read, and was doubtful of enjoying; he felt that he ought to buy the latter, but he did not relish giving up the former. While he hesitated thus, his carriage was beginning to fill up; so, quickly buying both, he took up a position from which he could defend his rights. 'Nothing,' he thought, 'shows people up like travelling.'

The carriage was almost full, and, putting his bag up in the rack, he took his seat. At the moment of starting, yet another passenger, a girl with a pale face, scrambled in.

'I was a fool to go third,' thought Shelton, taking in his neighbours from behind his journal.

They were seven. A grizzled rustic sat in the far corner; his empty pipe, bowl downwards, jutted like a handle from his face, all bleared with the smear of nothingness that grows on those who pass their lives in the current of hard facts. Next to him, a ruddy, heavy-shouldered man was discussing with a grey-haired, hatchet-visaged person the condition of their gardens; and Shelton watched their eyes till it occurred to him how curious a look was in them—a watchful friendliness, an allied distrust—and that their voices, cheerful, even jovial, seemed to be cautious all the time. His glance strayed off, and almost rebounded from the semi-Roman, slightly cross, and wholly self-complacent face of a stout lady in a black-and-white costume, who was reading the *Strand Magazine*, while her other sleek, plump hand, freed from its black glove, and ornamented with a thick watch-bracelet, rested on her lap.

A younger, bright-cheeked, and self-conscious female was sitting next her, looking at the pale girl who had just got in.

'There's something about that girl,' thought Shelton, 'that they don't like.' Her brown eyes certainly looked frightened, her clothes were of a foreign cut. Suddenly he met the glance of another pair of eyes; these eyes, prominent and blue, stared with a sort of subtle roguery from above a thin, lopsided nose, and were at once averted. They gave Shelton the impression that he was being judged, and mocked, enticed, initiated. His own gaze did not fall; this sanguine face, with its two-day growth of reddish beard, long nose, full lips, and irony, puzzled him. 'A cynical face!' he thought, and then, 'but sensitive!' and then, again, 'too cynical'.

The young man who owned it sat with his legs parted at the knees, his dusty trouser-ends and boots slanting back beneath the seat, his yellow finger-tips crisped as if rolling cigarettes. A strange air of detachment was about that youthful, shabby figure, and not a scrap of luggage filled the rack above his head.

The frightened girl was sitting next this pagan personality; it was possibly the lack of fashion in his looks which caused her to select him for her confidence.

'Monsieur,' she asked, 'do you speak French?'

'Perfectly.'

'Then can you tell me where they take the tickets?'

The young man shook his head.

'No,' said he, 'I am a foreigner.'

The girl sighed.

'But what is the matter, ma'moiselle?'

The girl did not reply, twisting her hands on an old bag in her lap. Silence had stolen on the carriage—a silence such as steals on animals at the first approach of danger; all eyes were turned towards the figures of the foreigners.

'Yes,' broke out the red-faced man, 'he was a bit squiffy that evening—old Tom.'

'Ah!' replied his neighbour, 'he would be.'

Something seemed to have destroyed their look of mutual distrust. The plump, sleek hand of the lady with the Roman nose curved convulsively; and this movement corresponded to the feeling agitating Shelton's heart. It was almost as if hand and heart

4

feared to be asked for something.

'Monsieur,' said the girl, with a tremble in her voice, 'I am very unhappy; can you tell me what to do? I had no money for a ticket.'

The foreign youth's face flickered.

'Yes?' he said; 'that might happen to anyone, of course.'

'What will they do to me?' sighed the girl.

'Don't lose courage, ma'moiselle.' The young man slid his eyes from left to right, and rested them on Shelton. 'Although I don't as yet see your way out.'

'Oh, monsieur!' sighed the girl, and, though it was clear that none but Shelton understood what they were saying, there was a chilly feeling in the carriage.

'I wish I could assist you,' said the foreign youth; 'unfortunately ——' He shrugged his shoulders, and again his eyes returned to Shelton.

The latter thrust his hand into his pocket.

'Can I be of any use?' he asked in English.

'Certainly, sir; you could render this young lady the greatest possible service by lending her the money for a ticket.'

Shelton produced a sovereign, which the young man took. Passing it to the girl, he said:

'A thousand thanks—*voilá une belle action!*'

The misgivings which attend on casual charity crowded up in Shelton's mind; he was ashamed of having them and of not having them, and he stole covert looks at this young foreigner, who was now talking to the girl in a language that he did not understand. Though vagabond in essence, the fellow's face showed subtle spirit, a fortitude and irony not found upon the face of normal man, and in turning from it to the other passengers Shelton was conscious of revolt, contempt, and questioning, that he could not define. Leaning back with half-closed eyes, he tried to diagnose this new sensation. He found it disconcerting that the faces and behaviour of his neighbours lacked anything he could grasp and secretly abuse. They continued to converse with admirable and slightly conscious phlegm, yet he knew, as well as if each one had whispered to him privately, that this shady incident had shaken them. Something unsettling to their notions of propriety—something dangerous and destructive of complacency—had occurred, and this was unforgivable. Each had a different way, humorous or philosophic, contemptuous, sour, or sly, of showing this resentment. But by a flash of insight Shelton saw that at the bottom of

5

their minds and of his own the feeling was the same. Because he shared in their resentment he was enraged with them and with himself. He looked at the plump, sleek hand of the woman with the Roman nose. The insulation and complacency of its pale skin, the passive righteousness about its curve, the prim separation from the others of the fat little finger, had acquired a wholly unaccountable importance. It embodied the verdict of his fellow-passengers, the verdict of Society; for he knew that, whether or no repugnant to the well-bred mind, each assemblage of eight persons, even in a third-class carriage, contains the kernel of Society.

But being in love, and recently engaged, Shelton had a right to be immune from discontent of any kind, and he reverted to his mental image of the cool, fair face, quick movements, and brilliant smile that now in his probationary exile haunted his imagination; he took out his fiancee's last letter, but the voice of the young foreigner addressing him in rapid French caused him to put it back abruptly.

'From what she tells me, sir,' he said, bending forward to be out of hearing of the girl, 'hers is an unhappy case. I should have been only too glad to help her, but, as you see'—and he made a gesture by which Shelton observed that he had parted from his waistcoat.—'I am not Rothschild. She has been abandoned by the man who brought her over to Dover under promise of marriage. Look'—and by a subtle flicker of his eyes he marked how the two ladies had edged away from the French girl—'they take good care not to let their garments touch her. They are virtuous women. How fine a thing is virtue, sir! and finer to *know* you have it, especially when you are never likely to be tempted.'

Shelton was unable to repress a smile; and when he smiled his face grew soft.

'Haven't you observed,' went on the youthful foreigner, 'that those who by temperament and circumstance are worst fitted to pronounce judgment are usually the first to judge? The judgments of Society are always childish, seeing that it's composed for the most part of individuals who have never smelt the fire. And look at this: they who have money run too great a risk of parting with it if they don't accuse the penniless of being rogues and imbeciles.'

Shelton was startled, and not only by an outburst of philosophy from an utter stranger in poor clothes, but at this singular wording of his own private thoughts. Stifling his sense of the unusual for the queer attraction this young man inspired, he said:

'I suppose you're a stranger over here?'

'I have been in England seven months, but not yet in London,' replied the other. 'I count on doing some good there—it is time!' A bitter and pathetic smile showed for a second on his lips. 'It won't be my fault if I fail. You are English, sir?'

Shelton nodded.

'Forgive my asking; your voice lacks something I have nearly always noticed in the English: a kind of—*comment cela s'appelle* —cocksureness, coming from your nation's greatest quality.'

'And what is that?' asked Shelton with a smile.

'Complacency,' replied the youthful foreigner.

'Complacency!' repeated Shelton; 'do you call that a great quality?'

'I should rather say, monsieur, a great defect in what is always a great people. You are certainly the most highly-civilised nation on the earth; you suffer a little from the fact. If I were an English preacher my desire would be to prick the heart of your complacency.'

Shelton, leaning back, considered this impertinent suggestion.

'Hum!' he said at last, 'you'd be unpopular; I don't know that we're any cockier than other nations.'

The young foreigner made a sign as though confirming this opinion.

'In effect,' said he, 'it is a sufficiently widespread disease. Look at these people here'—and with a rapid glance he pointed to the inmates of the carriage, very average persons—'What have they done to warrant their making a virtuous nose at those who do not walk as they do? That old rustic, perhaps, is different—he never thinks at all—but look at those two occupied with their stupidities about the price of hops, the prospects of potatoes, what George is doing, a thousand things of all that sort—look at their faces; I come of the bourgeoisie myself—have they ever shown proof of any quality that gives them the right to pat themselves upon the back? No fear! Outside potatoes they know nothing, and what they do not understand they dread and they despise—there are millions of that breed. *Voila la Société!* The sole quality these people have shown they have is cowardice. I was educated by the Jesuits,' he concluded; 'it has given me a way of thinking.'

Under ordinary circumstances Shelton would have murmured in a well-bred voice: 'Ah! quite so,' and taken refuge in the columns of the *Daily Telegraph*. In place of this, for some reason that he did not understand, he looked at the young foreigner, and asked:

7

'Why do you say all this to me?'

The tramp—for by his boots he could hardly have been better —hesitated.

'When you have travelled like me,' he said, as if resolved to speak the truth, 'you acquire an instinct in choosing to whom and how you speak. It is necessity that makes the law; if you want to live you must learn all that sort of thing to make face against life.'

Shelton, who himself possessed a certain subtlety, could not but observe the complimentary nature of these words. It was like saying: 'I'm not afraid of *you* misunderstanding me, and thinking me a rascal just because I study human nature.'

'But is there nothing to be done for that poor girl?'

His new acquaintance shrugged his shoulders.

'A broken jug,' said he; 'You will never mend her. She is going to a cousin in London to see if she can get help; you have given her the means of getting there—it is all that you can do. One knows too well what will become of *her*.'

Shelton said gravely:

'Oh! that's horrible! Couldn't she be induced to go back home? I should be glad——'

The foreign vagrant shook his head.

'*Mon cher monsieur*,' he said, 'you evidently have not yet had occasion to know what the "family" is like. "The family" does not like damaged goods; it will have nothing to say to sons whose hands have dipped into the till or daughters no longer to be married. What the devil would they do with her? Better put a stone about her neck and let her drown at once. All the world is Christian, but Christian and good Samaritan are not quite the same.'

Shelton looked at the girl, who was sitting motionless, with her hands crossed on her bag, and revolt against the unfair ways of life arose within him.

'Yes,' said the young foreigner, as if reading all his thoughts, 'what's called virtue is nearly always only luck.' He rolled his eyes, as though to say: 'Ah, ha! conventions? Have them by all means—but don't look like peacocks because you are preserving them; it is but cowardice and luck, my friends—but cowardice and luck!'

'Look here,' said Shelton, 'I'll give her my address, and if she wants to go back to her family she can write to me.'

'She will never go back; she will not have the courage.'

Shelton caught the cringing glance of the girl's eyes; in the droop of her lip there was something sensuous, and the convic-

8

tion that the young man's words were true came over him.

'I had better not give them my private address,' he thought, glancing at the faces opposite; and he wrote down the following: 'Richard Paramor Shelton, c/o Paramor and Herring, Lincoln's Inn Fields.'

'You are very good, sir. My name is Louis Ferrand; no address at present. I will make her understand; she is half stupefied just now.'

Shelton returned to the perusal of his paper, too disturbed to read; the young vagrant's words kept sounding in his ears. He raised his eyes. The plump hand of the lady with the Roman nose still rested on her lap; it had been recased in its black glove with large white stitching. Her frowning gaze was fixed on him suspiciously, as if he had outraged her sense of decorum.

'He didn't get anything from me,' said the voice of the red-faced man, ending a talk on tax-gatherers. The train whistled loudly, and Shelton reverted to his paper. This time he crossed his legs, determined to enjoy the latest murder; once more he found himself looking at the vagrant's long-nosed, mocking face. 'That fellow,' he thought, 'has seen and felt ten times as much as I, although he must be ten years younger.'

He turned for distraction to the landscape, with its April clouds, trim hedgerows, homely coverts. But strange ideas would come, and he was discontented with himself; the conversation he had had, the personality of this young foreigner, disturbed him.

It was all as though he had made a start in some fresh journey through the fields of thought.

Chapter 2

ANTONIA

FIVE years before the journey just described Shelton had stood one afternoon on the barge of his old college at the end of the summer races. He had been 'down' from Oxford for some years, but these Olympian contests still attracted him.

The boats were passing, and in the usual rush to the barge side his arm came in contact with a soft young shoulder. He saw close to him a young girl with fair hair knotted in a ribbon, whose face was eager with excitement. The pointed chin, long neck, the fluffy

9

hair, quick gestures, and the calm strenuousness of her grey-blue eyes, impressed him vividly.

'Oh, we *must* bump them!' he heard her sigh.

'Do you know my people, Shelton?' said a voice behind his back; and he was granted a touch from the girl's shy, impatient hand, the warmer fingers of a lady with kindly eyes resembling a hare's, the dry handclasp of a gentleman with a thin, arched nose, and a quizzical brown face.

'Are you the Mr Shelton who used to play the "bones" at Eton?' said the lady. 'Ah, we so often heard of you from Bernard. He was your fag, wasn't he? How distressin' it is to see these poor boys in the boats!'

'Mother, they like it!' cried the girl.

'Antonia ought to be rowing, herself,' said her father, whose name was Dennant.

Shelton went back with them to their hotel, walking beside Antonia through the Christchurch meadows, telling her details of his college life. He dined with them that evening, and, when he left, had a feeling like that produced by a first glass of champagne.

The Dennants lived at Holm Oaks, within six miles of Oxford, and two days later he drove over and paid a call. Amidst the avocations of reading for the Bar, of cricket, racing, shooting, it but required a whiff of some fresh scent—hay, honeysuckle, clover —to bring Antonia's face before him, with its uncertain colour and its frank, distant eyes. But two years passed before he again saw her. Then, at an invitation from Bernard Dennant, he played cricket for the Manor of Holm Oaks against a neighbouring house; in the evening there was dancing on the lawn. The fair hair was now turned up, but the eyes were quite unchanged. Their steps went together, and they outlasted every other couple on the slippery grass. Thence, perhaps, sprang her respect for him; he was wiry, a little taller than herself, and seemed to talk of things that interested her. He found out she was seventeen, and she found out that he was twenty-nine. The following two years Shelton went to Holm Oaks whenever he was asked; to him this was a period of enchanted games, of cub-hunting, theatricals, and distant sounds of practised music, and during it Antonia's eyes grew more friendly and more curious, and his own more shy, and schooled, more furtive and more ardent. Then came his father's death, a voyage round the world, and that peculiar hour of mixed sensations when, one March morning, abandoning his steamer at Marseilles, he took train for Hyères.

He found her at one of those exclusive hostelries among the pines where the best English go, in common with Americans, Russian princesses, and Jewish families; he would not have been shocked to find her elsewhere, but he would have been surprised. His sunburnt face and the new beard, on which he set some undefined value, apologetically displayed, were scanned by those blue eyes with rapid glances, at once more friendly and less friendly. 'Ah!' they seemed to say, 'here you are; how glad I am! But—what now?'

He was admitted to their sacred table at the table-d'hôte, a snowy oblong in an airy alcove, where the Honourable Mrs Dennant, Miss Dennant, and the Honourable Charlotte Penguin, a maiden aunt with insufficient lungs, sat twice a day in their own atmosphere. A momentary weakness came on Shelton the first time he saw them sitting there at lunch. What was it gave them their look of strange detachment? Mrs Dennant was bending above a camera.

'I'm afraid, d'you know, it's under-exposed,' she said.

'What a pity! The kitten was *rather* nice!' The maiden aunt, placing the knitting of a red silk tie beside her plate, turned her aspiring, well-bred gaze on Shelton.

'Look, Auntie,' said Antonia in her clear, quick voice, 'there's the funny little man again!'

'Oh,' said the maiden aunt—a smile revealed her upper teeth; she looked for the funny little man (who was not English)—'he's *rather* nice!'

Shelton did not look for the funny little man; he stole a glance that barely reached Antonia's brow, where her eyebrows took their tiny upward slant at the outer corners, and her hair was still ruffled by a windy walk. From that moment he became her slave.

'Mr Shelton, do you know anything about these periscopic binoculars?' said Mrs Dennant's voice; 'they're splendid for buildins', but buildin's are so disappointin'. The thing is to get human interest, isn't it?' and her glance wandered absently past Shelton in search of human interest.

'You haven't put down what you've taken, mother.'

From a little leather bag Mrs Dennant took a little leather book.

'It's so easy to forget what they're about,' she said, 'that's so annoyin'.'

Shelton was not again visited by his uneasiness at their detachment; he accepted them and all their works, for there was some-

11

thing quite sublime about the way that they would leave the dining-room unconscious that they themselves were funny to all the people they had found so funny while they had been sitting there, and he would follow them out unnecessarily upright and feeling like a fool.

In the ensuing fortnight, chaperoned by the maiden aunt, for Mrs Dennant disliked driving, he sat opposite to Antonia during many drives; he played sets of tennis with her; but it was in the evenings after dinner—those long evenings on a parquet floor in wicker chairs dragged as far as might be from the heating apparatus—that he seemed so very near her. The community of isolation drew them closer. In place of a companion he had assumed the part of friend, to whom she could confide all her home-sick aspirations. So that, even when she was sitting silent, a slim, long foot stretched out in front, bending with an air of cool absorption over some pencil sketches which she would not show him—even then, by her very attitude, by the sweet freshness that clung about her, by her quick, offended glances at the strange persons round, she seemed to acknowledge in some secret way that he was necessary. He was far from realising this; his intellectual and observant parts were hypnotised and fascinated even by her failings. The faint freckling across her nose, the slim and virginal severeness of her figure, with its narrow hips and arms, the curve of her long neck—all were added charms. She had the wind and rain look, a taste of home; and over the glaring roads, where the palm-tree shadows lay so black, she seemed to pass like the very image of an English day.

One afternoon he had taken her to play tennis with some friends, and afterwards they strolled on to see her favourite view. Down the Toulon road gardens and hills were bathed in the colour of ripe apricot; an evening crispness had stolen on the air; the blood released from the sun's numbing, ran gladly in the veins. On the right hand of the road was a Frenchman playing bowls. Enormous, busy, pleased, and upright as a soldier, pathetically trotting his vast carcass from end to end, he delighted Shelton. But Antonia threw a single look at the huge creature, and her face expressed disgust. She began running up towards the ruined tower.

Shelton let her keep in front, watching her leap from stone to stone and throw back defiant glances when he pressed behind. She stood at the top, and he looked up at her. Over the world, gloriously spread below, she, like a statue, seemed to rule. The colour was brilliant in her cheeks, her young bosom heaved, her eyes shone, and the flowing droop of her long, full sleeves gave to her poised figure the look of one who flies. He pulled himself up and stood beside her; his heart choked him, all the colour had left his cheeks.

'Antonia,' he said, 'I love you.'

She started as if his whisper had intruded on her thoughts; but his face must have expressed his hunger, for the resentment in her eyes vanished.

They stood for several minutes without speaking and then went home. Shelton painfully revolved the riddle of the colour in her face. Had he a chance, then? Was it possible? That evening the instinct vouchsafed at times to lovers in place of reason caused him to pack his bag and go to Cannes. On returning, two days later, and approaching the group in the centre of the Winter Garden, the voice of the maiden aunt reading aloud an extract from the *Morning Post* reached him across the room.

'Don't you think that's *rather* nice?' he heard her ask and then: 'Oh, here you are! It's quite nice to see you back!'

Shelton slipped into a wicker chair. Antonia looked up quickly from her sketch-book, put out a hand, but did not speak.

He watched her bending head, and his eagerness was changed to gloom. With desperate vivacity he sustained the five intolerable minutes of inquiry, where had he been, what had he been doing? Then once again the maiden aunt commenced her extracts from the *Morning Post*.

A touch on his sleeve startled him. Antonia was leaning forward; her cheeks were crimson above the pallor of her neck.

'Would you like to see my sketches?'

To Shelton, bending above those sketches, that drawl of the well-bred maiden aunt intoning the well-bred paper was the most pleasant sound that he had ever listened to. . . .

'My dear Dick,' Mrs Dennant said to him a fortnight later, 'we would rather, after you leave here, that you don't see each other again until July. Of course I know you count it an engagement and all that and everybody's been writin' to congratulate you. But Algie thinks you ought to give yourselves a chance. Young people don't always know what they're about, you know; it's not long to wait.'

'Three months!' gasped Shelton.

He had to swallow down this pill with what grace he could command. There was no alternative. Antonia had acquiesced in

13

the condition with a queer grave pleasure, as if she expected it to do her good.

'It'll be something to look forward to, Dick,' she said.

He postponed departure as long as possible, and it was not until the end of April that he left for England. She came alone to see him off. It was drizzling, but her tall, slight figure in the golf cape looked impervious to cold and rain amongst the shivering natives. Desperately he clutched her hand, warm through the wet glove; her smile seemed heartless in its brilliancy. He whispered: 'You *will* write?'

'Of course; don't be so stupid, you old Dick!'

She ran forward as the train began to move; her clear 'Goodbye!' sounded shrill and hard above the rumble of the wheels. He saw her raise her hand, an umbrella waving, and last of all, vivid still amongst receding shapes, the red spot of her scarlet tam-o'-shanter.

Chapter 3

A ZOOLOGICAL GARDEN

AFTER his journey up from Dover, Shelton was still gathering his luggage at Charing Cross, when the foreign girl passed him, and, in spite of his desire to say something cheering, he could get nothing out but a shame-faced smile. Her figure vanished, wavering into the hurly-burly; one of his bags had gone astray, and so all thought of her soon faded from his mind. His cab, however, overtook the foreign vagrant marching along towards Pall Mall with a curious, lengthy stride—an observant, disillusioned figure.

The first bustle of installation over, time hung heavy on his hands. July looked distant, as in some future century; Antonia's eyes beckoned him faintly, hopelessly. She would not even be coming back to England for another month.

' . . . I met a young foreigner in the train from Dover (he wrote to her)—'a curious sort of person altogether, who seems to have infected me. Everything here has gone flat and unprofitable; the only good things in life are your letters . . . John Noble dined with me yesterday; the poor fellow tried to persuade me to stand for Parliament. Why should I think myself fit to legislate for the

14

unhappy wretches one sees about in the streets? If people's faces are a fair test of their happiness, I'd rather not feel in any way responsible . . .'

The streets, in fact, after his long absence in the East, afforded him much food for thought—the curious smugness of the passers-by; the utterly unending bustle; the fearful medley of miserable, overdriven women, and full-fed men with leering, bull-beef eyes, whom he saw everywhere—in club windows on their beats, on box seats, on the steps of hotels—discharging dilatory duties; the appalling chaos of hard-eyed, capable dames with defiant clothes, and white-cheeked, hunted-looking men; of splendid creatures in their cabs, and cadging creatures in their broken hats—the callousness and the monotony!

One afternoon in May he received this letter couched in French.

'3, BLANK ROW,
'MY DEAR SIR,   'WESTMINSTER.
'Excuse me for recalling to your memory the offer of assistance you so kindly made me during the journey from Dover to London, in which I was so fortunate as to travel with a man like you. Having beaten the whole town, ignorant of what wood to make arrows, nearly at the end of my resources, my spirit profoundly discouraged, I venture to avail myself of your permission, knowing your good heart. Since I saw you I have run through all the misfortunes of the calendar, and cannot tell what door is left at which I have not knocked. I presented myself at the business firm with whose name you supplied me, but being unfortunately in rags, they refused to give me your address. Is not this very much in the English character? They told me to write, and said they would forward the letter. I put all my hopes in you. Believe me, my dear sir, (whatever you may decide),
'Your devoted LOUIS FERRAND.'

Shelton looked at the envelope, and saw that it bore date a week ago. The face of the young vagrant rose before him, vital, mocking, sensitive; the sound of his quick French buzzed in his ears, and oddly, the whole whiff of him had a power of raising more vividly than ever his memories of Antonia. At the end of the journey from Hyères to London he had met him; and this seemed to give the youth a claim.

He took his hat and hurried to Blank Row. Dismissing his cab

15

at the corner of Victoria Street, he with difficulty found the house in question. It was a doorless place, with stone-flagged corridor—in other words, a 'doss house'. By tapping on a sort of ticket-office with a sliding window, he attracted the attention of a blowsy woman with soap-suds on her arms, who informed him that the person he was looking for had gone without leaving his address.

'But isn't there anybody,' asked Shelton, 'of whom I can make inquiry?'

'Yes; there's a Frenchman.' And opening an inner door, she bellowed: 'Frenchy! Wanted!' and disappeared.

A dried-up, yellow little man, cynical and weary in the face, as if a moral steam-roller had passed over it, answered this call, and stood, sniffing, as it were, at Shelton, on whom he made the singular impression of some little creature in a cage.

'He left here ten days ago, in the company of a mulatto. What do you want with him, if I may ask?' The little man's yellow cheeks were wrinkled with suspicion.

Shelton produced the letter.

'Ah! now I know you'—a pale smile broke through the Frenchman's crow's-feet—'he spoke of you. "If I can only find him," he used to say, "I am saved." I liked that young man; he had ideas.'

'Is there no way of getting at him through his Consul?'

The Frenchman shook his head.

'Might as well look for diamonds at the bottom of the sea.'

'Do you think he will come back here? But by that time I suppose you'll hardly be here yourself?'

A gleam of amusement played about the Frenchman's teeth:

'I? Oh, yes, sir! Once upon a time I cherished the hope of emerging; I no longer have illusions. I shave these specimens for a living, and shall shave them till the day of judgment. But leave a letter with me by all means; he will come back. There's an overcoat of his here on which he borrowed money—it's worth more. Oh, yes; he will come back—a youth of principle. Leave a letter with me; I am always here.'

Shelton hesitated, but those last four words, 'I am always here,' touched him in their simplicity. Nothing more dreadful could be said.

'Can you find me a sheet of paper, then?' he asked; 'please keep the change for the trouble I am giving you.'

'Thank you,' said the Frenchman simply; 'he told me that your heart was good. If you don't mind the kitchen, you could write there at your ease.'

Shelton wrote his letter at the table of this stone-flagged kitchen in company with an aged, dried-up gentleman, who was muttering to himself; and Shelton tried to avoid attracting his attention, suspecting that he was not sober. Just as he was about to take his leave, however, the old fellow thus accosted him:

'Did you ever go to the dentist, mister?' he said, working at a loose tooth with his shrivelled fingers. 'I went to a dentist once, who professed to stop teeth without giving pain, and the beggar did stop my teeth without pain; but did they stay in, those stoppings? No, me bhoy; they came out before you could say Jack Robinson. Now, I shimply ask you, d'you call that dentistry?' Fixing his eyes on Shelton's collar, which had the misfortune to be high and clean, he resumed with drunken scorn: 'Ut's the same all over this pharisaical counthry. Talk of high morality and Anglo-Shaxon civilisation! The world was never at such low ebb! Phwhat's all this morality? Ut stinks of the shop. Look at the condition of Art in this counthry! look at the fools you see upon th' stage! look at the pictures and books that sell! I know what I'm talking about, though I *am* a sandwich man. Phwhat's the secret of ut all? Shop, me bhoy! Ut don't pay to go below a certain depth! Scratch the skin, but pierce us—oh! dear, no! We hate to see the blood fly, eh?'

Shelton stood disconcerted, not knowing if he were expected to reply; but the old gentleman, pursing up his lips, went on:

'Sir, there are no extremes in this fog-smitten land. Do ye think blanks loike me ought to exist? Whoy don't they kill us off? Palliatives—palliatives—and whoy? Because they object to th' extreme course. Look at women: the streets here are a scandal to the world. They won't recognise that they exist—their noses are so damn high! They blink the truth in this middle-class counthry. Me bhoy'—and he whispered confidentially—'ut pays 'em. Eh? you say; why shouldn't they, then?' (But Shelton had not spoken. 'Well, let 'em! let 'em! But don't tell me that'sh morality, don't tell me that'sh civilisation! What can you expect in a counthry where the crimson emotions are never allowed to smell the air? And what'sh the result? Me bhoy, the result is sentiment, a yellow thing with blue spots, like a fungus or a Stilton cheese. Go to the theatre, and see one of these things they call plays. Tell me, are they food for men and women? Why, they're pap for babes and shop-boys! Shure, I was a blanky actor meyself!'

Shelton listened with mingled feelings of amusement and dismay, till the old actor, having finished, resumed his crouching posture at the table.

'You don't get dhrunk, I suppose?' he said suddenly—'too much of 'n Englishman, no doubt.'

'Very seldom,' said Shelton.

'Pity! Think of the pleasures of oblivion! Oi'm dhrunk every night.'

'How long will you last at that rate?'

'There speaks the Englishman! Why should Oi give up me only pleasure to keep me wretched life in? If ye've anything left worth the keeping shober for, keep shober by all means; if not, the sooner ye're dhrunk the better—that stands to reason.'

In the corridor Shelton asked the Frenchman where the old man came from.

'Oh! an Englishman! Yes, yes, from Belfast—very drunken old man. You are a drunken nation'—he made a motion with his hands —'he no longer eats—no inside left. It is unfortunate—a man of spirit. If you have never seen one of these palaces, monsieur, I shall be happy to show you over it.'

Shelton took out his cigarette case.

'Yes, yes,' said the Frenchman, making a wry nose and taking a cigarette; 'I'm accustomed to it. But you are wise to fumigate the air; one is not in a harem.'

And Shelton felt ashamed of his fastidiousness.

'This,' said the guide, leading him upstairs and opening a door, 'is a specimen of the apartments reserved for these princes of the blood.' There were four empty beds on iron legs, and, with the air of a showman, the Frenchman twitched away a dingy quilt. 'They go out in the mornings, earn enough to make them drunk, sleep it off, and then begin again. That's their life. There are people who think they ought to be reformed. *Mon cher monsieur*, one must face reality a little, even in this country. It would be a hundred times better for these people to spend their time reforming high Society. Your high Society makes all these creatures; there's no harvest without cutting stalks. *Selon moi*,' he continued, putting back the quilt, and dribbling cigarette smoke through his nose, 'there is no grand difference between your high Society and these individuals here; both want pleasure, both think only of themselves, which is very natural. One lot have had the luck, the other—well, you see.' He shrugged. 'A common set! I've been robbed here half a dozen times. If you have new shoes, a good waistcoat, an overcoat, you want eyes in the back of your head. And they are populated! Change your bed, and you will run all the dangers of not sleeping alone. *V'là ma clientele!* The half of them don't pay me!' He snapped his yellow sticks of fingers. 'A penny for a shave, twopence a cut! *Quelle vie!* Here,' he continued, standing by a bed, 'is a gentleman who owes me five pence. Here's one who was a soldier; he's done for! All brutalised; not one with any courage left! But, believe me, monsieur,' he went on, opening another door, 'when you come down to houses of this sort you *must* have a vice; it's as necessary as breath is to the lungs. No matter what, you must have a vice to give you a little solace—*un peu de soulagement*. Ah yes! before you judge these swine, reflect on life! I've been through it. Monsieur, it is not nice never to know where to get your next meal. Gentlemen who have food in their stomachs, money in their pockets, and know where to get more, they never think. Why should they—*pas de danger!* All these cages are the same. Come down and you shall see the pantry.' He took Shelton through the kitchen, which seemed the only sitting-room of the establishment, to an inner room furnished with dirty cups and saucers, plates, and knives. Another fire was burning there. 'We always have hot water,' said the Frenchman, 'and three times a week they make a fire down there'—he pointed to a cellar—'for our clients to boil their vermin. Oh, yes, we have all the luxuries.'

Shelton returned to the kitchen, and directly after took leave of the little Frenchman, who said, with a kind of moral button-holing, as if trying to adopt him as a patron:

'Trust me, monsieur; if he comes back—that young man—he shall have your letter without fail. My name is Carolan—Jules Carolan; and I am always at your service.'

Chapter 4

THE PLAY

SHELTON walked away; he had been indulging in a nightmare. 'That old actor was drunk,' thought he, 'and no doubt he was an Irishman; still there may be truth in what he said. I am a Pharisee, like all the rest who aren't in the pit. My respectability is only luck. What should I have become if I'd been born into his kind of life?' and he stared at a stream of people coming from the stores, trying to pierce the mask of their serious, complacent faces. If these ladies and gentlemen were put into that pit into which he had been looking, would a single one of them emerge again? But the effort of picturing them there was too much for him; it was too far—too ridiculously far.

One particular couple, a large, fine man and wife, in the midst of all the dirt and rumbling hurry, the gloomy, ludicrous, and desperately jovial streets, walked side by side in well-bred silence, and had evidently bought some article which pleased them. There was nothing offensive in their manner; they seemed quite unconcerned at the passing of the other people. The man had that fine solidity of shoulder and of waist, the glossy self-possession belonging to those with horses, guns, and dressing-bags. The wife, her chin comfortably settled in her fur, kept her grey eyes on the ground, and, when she spoke, her even and unruffled voice reached Shelton's ears above all the whirling of the traffic. It was leisurely, precise, as if it had never hurried, had never been exhausted, or passionate, or afraid. Their talk, like that of many dozens of fine couples invading London from their country places, was of where to dine, what theatre they should go to, whom they had seen, what they should buy. And Shelton knew that from day's end to end, and even in their bed, these would be the subjects of their conversation. They were the best-bred people of the sort he met in country houses and accepted as of course, with a vague discomfort at the bottom of his soul. Antonia's home, for instance, had been full of them. They were the best-bred people of the sort who supported charities, knew everybody, had clear, calm judgment, and intolerance of all such conduct as seemed to them 'impossible,' all breaches of morality, such as mistakes of etiquette, such as dishonesty, passion, sympathy (except with a canonised class of objects—the *legitimate* sufferings, for instance of their own families and class). How healthy they were! The memory of the doss-house worked in Shelton's mind like poison. He was conscious that in his own groomed figure, in the undemonstrative assurance of his walk, he bore resemblance to the couple he apostrophised. 'Ah!' he thought, 'how vulgar our refinement is!' But he hardly believed in his own outburst. These people were *so* well mannered, *so* well conducted, and *so* healthy, he could not really understand what irritated him. What was the matter with them? They fulfilled their duties, had good appetites, clear consciences, all the furniture of perfect citizens; they merely lacked

—feelers, a loss that, he had read, was suffered by plants and animals which no longer had a need for using them. Some rare national faculty of seeing only the obvious and materially useful had destroyed their power of catching gleams or scents to right or left.

The lady looked up at her husband. The light of quiet, proprietary affection shone in her calm, grey eyes, decorously illumining her features slightly reddened by the wind. And the husband looked back at her, calm, practical, protecting. They were very much alike. So doubtless he looked when he presented himself in snowy shirtsleeves for her to straighten the bow of his white tie; so nightly she would look, standing before the full-length mirror, fixing his gifts upon her bosom. Calm, proprietary, kind! He passed them and walked behind a second less distinguished couple, who manifested a mutual dislike as matter-of-fact and free from nonsense as the unruffled satisfaction of the first; this dislike was just as healthy, and produced in Shelton about the same sensation. It was like knocking at a never-opened door, looking at a circle—couple after couple all the same. No heads, toes, angles of their souls stuck out anywhere. In the sea of their environments they were drowned; no leg braved the air, no arm emerged wet and naked waving at the skies; shop-persons, aristocrats, workmen, officials, they were all respectable. And he himself as respectable as any.

He returned, thus moody, to his rooms and, with the impetuosity which distinguished him when about to do an unwise thing, he seized a pen and poured out before Antonia some of his impressions:

'. . . Mean is the word, darling; we are mean, that's what's the matter with us, dukes and dustmen, the whole species—as mean as caterpillars. To secure our own property and our own comfort, to dole out our sympathy according to rule just so that it won't really hurt us, is what we're all after. There's something about human nature that is awfully repulsive, and the healthier people are, the more repulsive they seem to me to be. . . .'

He paused, biting his pen. Had he one acquaintance who would not counsel him to see a doctor for writing in that style? How would the world go round, how could Society exist, without common sense, practical ability, and the lack of sympathy?

He looked out of the open window. Down on the street a footman was settling the rug over the knees of a lady in a carriage, and the decorous immovability of both their faces, which were clearly visible to him, was like a portion of some well-oiled engine.

He got up and walked up and down. His rooms, in a narrow square skirting Belgravia, were unchanged since the death of his father had made him a man of means. Selected for their centrality, they were furnished in a very miscellaneous way. They were not bare, but close inspection revealed that everything was damaged, more or less, and there was absolutely nothing in which an interest seemed to be taken. His goods were accidents, presents, or the haphazard acquisitions of a pressing need. Nothing, of course, was frowsy, but everything was somewhat dusty, as if belonging to a man who never rebuked a servant. Above all, there was nothing that indicated hobbies.

Three days later he had her answer to his letter.

'. . . I don't think I understand what you mean by "the healthier people are, the more repulsive they seem to be"; one must be healthy to be perfect, mustn't one? I don't like unhealthy people. I had to play on that wretched piano after reading your letter; it made me feel unhappy. I've been having a splendid lot of tennis lately, got the back-handed lifting stroke at last—hurrah! . . .'

By the same post, too, came the following note, in an autocratic writing:

'DEAR BIRD (for this was Shelton's college nickname),

'My wife has gone down to her people, so I'm *en garcon* for a few days. If you've nothing better to do, come and dine to-night at seven, and go to the theatre. It's ages since I saw you.

'Yours ever,
'B. M. HALIDOME.'

Shelton had nothing better to do, for pleasant were his friend Halidome's well-appointed dinners. At seven, therefore, he went to Chester Square. His friend was in his study, reading Matthew Arnold by the light of an electric lamp. The walls of the room were hung with costly etchings, arranged with solid and unfailing taste; from the carving of the mantel-piece to the binding of the books, from the miraculously-coloured meerschaums to the chased fire-irons, everything displayed an unpretentious luxury, an order and a finish significant of life completely under rule of thumb. Everything had been collected. The collector rose as Shelton entered, a fine figure of a man, clean shaven, with dark hair, a Roman nose, good eyes, and the rather weighty dignity of attitude which comes from the assurance that one is in the right.

Taking Shelton by the lapel, he drew him into the radius of the lamp, where he examined him, smiling a slow smile. 'Glad to see you, old chap. I rather like your beard,' he said with genial brusqueness; and nothing perhaps, could better have summed up his faculty for forming independent judgments which Shelton found so admirable. He made no apology for the smallness of the dinner, which, consisting of eight courses and three wines, served by a butler and one footman, smacked of the same perfection as the furniture; in fact, he never apologised for anything, except with a jovial brusqueness that was worse than the offence. The suave and reasonable weight of his dislikes and his approvals stirred Shelton up to feel ironical and insignificant; but whether from a sense of the solid, humane, and healthy quality of his friend's egoism, or merely from the fact that this friendship had been long in bottle, he did not resent his mixed sensations.

'By the way, I congratulate you, old chap,' said Halidome, while driving to the theatre; there was no vulgar hurry about his congratulations, no more than about himself. 'They're awfully nice people, the Dennants.'

A sense of having had a seal put on his choice came over Shelton.

'Where are you going to live? You ought to come down and live near us; there are some ripping houses to be had down there; it's really a ripping neighbourhood. Have you chucked the Bar? You ought to do something, you know; it'll be fatal for you to have nothing to do. I tell you what, Bird: you ought to stand for the County Council.'

But before Shelton had replied they reached the theatre, and their energies were spent in sidling to their stalls. He had time to pass his neighbours in review before the play began. Seated next him was a lady with large healthy shoulders, displayed with splendid liberality; beyond her a husband, red-cheeked, with drooping, yellow-grey moustache and a bald head; beyond him again two men whom he had known at Eton. One of them had a clean-shaved face, dark hair, and a weather-tanned complexion; his small mouth with its upper lip pushed out above the lower, his eyelids a little drooped over his watchful eyes, gave him a satirical and resolute expression. 'I've got hold of your tail, old fellow,' he seemed to say, as though he were always busy with the catching of some kind of fox. The other's goggling eyes rested on Shelton with a chaffing smile; his thick, sleek hair, brushed with water and parted in the middle, his neat moustache and admirable waistcoat, suggested the sort of dandyism that despises women. From his recognition of these old schoolfellows, Shelton turned to look at Halidome, who, having cleared his throat, was staring straight before him at the curtain. Antonia's words kept running in her lover's head: 'I don't like unhealthy people.' Well, all *these* people, anyway, were healthy; they looked as if they had defied the elements to endow them with a spark of anything but health. Just then the curtain rose.

Slowly, unwillingly, for he was of trustful disposition, Shelton recognised that this play was one of those masterpieces of the modern drama whose characters were drawn on the principle that men were made for morals rather than morals made by men, and he watched the play unfold with all its careful sandwiching of grave and gay.

A married woman anxious to be ridded of her husband was the pivot of the story, and a number of scenes, ingeniously contrived, with a hundred reasons why this desire was wrong and inexpedient, were revealed to Shelton's eyes. These reasons issued mainly from the mouth of a well-preserved old gentleman who seemed to play the part of a sort of Moral Salesman. He turned to Halidome and whispered:

'Can you stand that old woman?'

His friend fixed his fine eyes on him wonderingly.

'What old woman?'

'Why, the old ass with the platitudes!'

Halidome's countenance grew cold, a little shocked, as though he had been assailed in person.

'Do you mean Pirbright?' he said. 'I think he's ripping.'

Shelton turned to the play rebuffed; he felt guilty of a breach of manners, sitting as he was in one of his friend's stalls, and he naturally set to work to watch the play more critically than ever. Antonia's words recurred to him: 'I don't like unhealthy people,' and they seemed to throw a sudden light upon this play. It was healthy!

The crisis had now come.

The scene was a drawing-room, softly lighted by electric lamps, with a cat (Shelton could not decide whether she was real or

24

not) asleep upon the mat.

The husband, a thick-set, healthy man in evening dress, was drinking off neat whisky. He put down his tumbler, and deliberately struck a match; and then with even greater deliberation he lit a gold-tipped cigarette. . . .

Shelton was no inexperienced play-goer. He shifted his elbows, for he felt that something was about to happen; and when the match was pitched into the fire, he leaned forward in his seat.

The husband poured more whisky out, drank it at a draught, and walked towards the door; then, turning to the audience as if to admit them to the secret of some tremendous resolution, he puffed at them a puff of smoke. He left the room, returned, and once more filled his glass.

A lady now entered, pale of face and dark of eye—his wife. The husband crossed the stage, and stood before the fire, his legs astride, in the attitude which somehow Shelton had felt sure he would assume. He spoke: 'Come in, and shut the door.'

Shelton suddenly perceived that he was face to face with one of those dumb moments in which two people declare their inextinguishable hatred—the hatred underlying the sexual intimacy of two ill-assorted creatures, and he was suddenly reminded of a scene he had once witnessed in a restaurant. He remembered with extreme minuteness how the woman and the man had sat facing each other across the narrow patch of white, emblazoned by candles with cheap shades and a thin, green vase with yellow flowers. He remembered the curious scornful anger of their voices, subdued so that only a few words reached him. He remembered the cold loathing in their eyes. And, above all, he remembered his impression that this sort of scene happened between them every other day, and would continue so to happen; and as he put on his overcoat and paid his bill, he had asked himself, 'Why in the name of decency do they go on living together?' And now he thought, as he listened to the two players wrangling on the stage: 'What's the good of all this talk? There's something here past words.'

The curtain came down upon the act, and he looked at the lady next him. She was shrugging her shoulders at her husband, whose face was healthy and offended.

'I do dislike these unhealthy women,' he was saying, but catching Shelton's eye, he turned square in his seat and sniffed ironically.

The face of Shelton's friend beyond, composed, satirical as ever, was clothed with a mask of scornful curiosity, as if he had been listening to something that had displeased him not a little. The goggle-eyed man was yawning. Shelton turned to Halidome:

'Can you stand this sort of thing?' said he.

'No; I call that scene a bit too hot,' replied his friend.

Shelton wriggled; he had meant to say it was not hot enough. 'I'll bet you anything,' he said, 'I know what's going to happen now. You'll have that old ass—what's his name?—lunching off cutlets and champagne to fortify himself for a lecture to the wife. He'll show her how unhealthy her feelings are—I know him— and he'll take her hand and say, "Dear lady, is there anything in this poor world but the good opinion of Society?" and he'll pretend to laugh at himself for saying it; but you'll see perfectly well that the old woman means it. And then he'll put her into a set of circumstances that aren't her own but his version of them, and show her the only way of salvation is to kiss her husband'; and Shelton grinned. 'Anyway, I'll bet you anything he takes her hand and says, "Dear lady".'

Halidome turned on him the disapproval of his eyes, and again he said: 'I think Pirbright's ripping!'

But as Shelton had predicted, so it turned out, amidst great applause.

Chapter 5

THE GOOD CITIZEN

LEAVING the theatre, they paused a moment in the hall to don their coats; a stream of people with spotless bosoms eddied round the doors, as if in momentary dread of leaving this hothouse of false morals and emotions for the wet, gusty streets, where human plants thrive and die, human weeds flourish and fade under the fresh, impartial skies. The lights revealed innumerable solemn faces, gleamed innumerably on jewels, on the silk of hats, then passed to whiten a pavement wet with newly fallen rain, to flare on horses, on the visages of cabmen, and stray, queer objects that do not bear the light.

'Shall we walk?' asked Halidome.

'Has it ever struck you,' answered Shelton, 'that in a play nowadays there's always a "Chorus of Scandalmongers" which seems to have acquired the attitude of God?'

Halidome cleared his throat, and there was something portentous in the sound.

'You're so d——d fastidious,' was his answer.

'I've a prejudice for keeping the two things separate,' went on Shelton. 'That ending makes me sick.'

'Why?' asked Halidome. 'What other end is possible? You don't want a play to leave you with a bad taste in your mouth.'

'But that's exactly what this does.'

Halidome increased his stride, already much too long; for in his walk, as in all other phases of his life, he found it necessary to be in front.

'How do you mean?' he asked urbanely; 'it's better than the woman making a fool of herself.'

'I'm thinking of the man.'

'What man?'

'The husband.'

'What's the matter with him? He was a bit of a bounder, certainly.'

'I can't understand any man wanting to live with a woman who doesn't want him.'

Some note of battle in Shelton's voice, rather than the sentiment itself, caused his friend to reply with dignity:

'There's a lot of nonsense talked about that sort of thing. Women don't really care; it's only what's put into their heads.'

'That's much the same as saying to a starving man: "You don't really want anything; it's only what's put into your head!" You are begging the question, my friend.'

But nothing was more calculated to annoy Halidome than to tell him he was 'begging the question,' for he prided himself on being strong in logic.

'That be d——d!' he said.

'Not at all, old chap. Here is a case where a woman wants her freedom, and you merely answer that she *doesn't* want it.'

'Women like that are impossible; better leave them out of court.'

Shelton pondered this and smiled; he had recollected an acquaintance of his own, who, when his wife had left him, invented the theory that she was mad, and this struck him now as funny. But then he thought. 'Poor devil! he was bound to call her mad! If he didn't, it would be confessing himself distasteful; however true, you can't expect a man to consider himself that.' But a glance at his friend's eye warned him that he, too, might

27

think his wife mad in such a case.

'Surely,' he said, 'even if she's his wife, a man's bound to behave like a gentleman.'

'Depends on whether she behaves like a lady.'

'Does it? I don't see the connexion.'

Halidome paused in the act of turning the latch-key in his door; there was a rather angry smile in his fine eyes.

'My dear chap,' he said, 'you're too sentimental altogether.'

The word 'sentimental' nettled Shelton. 'A gentleman either *is* a gentleman or he isn't; what has it to do with the way other people behave?'

Halidome turned the key in the lock and opened the door into his hall, where the firelight fell on the decanters and huge chairs drawn towards the blaze.

'No, Bird,' he said, resuming his urbanity, and gathering his coat-tails in his hands; 'it's all very well to talk, but wait until you're married. A man must be master, and show it, too.'

An idea occurred to Shelton.

'Look here, Hal,' he said : 'what should you do if your wife got tired of you?'

The expression on Halidome's face was a mixture of amusement and contempt.

'I don't mean anything personal, of course, but apply the situation to yourself.'

Halidome took out a toothpick, used it brusquely, and responded :

'I shouldn't stand any humbug—take her travelling; shake her mind up. She'd soon come round.'

'But suppose she really loathed you?'

Halidome cleared his throat; the idea was so obviously indecent. How could anybody loathe him? With great composure, however, regarding Shelton as if he were a forward but amusing child, he answered :

'There are a great many things to be taken into consideration!'

'It appears to me,' said Shelton, 'to be a question of common pride. How can you ask anything of a woman who doesn't want to give it?'

His friend's voice became judicial.

'A man ought not to suffer,' he said, poring over his whisky, 'because a woman gets hysteria. You have to think of Society, your children, house, money arrangements, a thousand things. It's all very well to talk. How do you like this whisky?'

'The part of the good citizen, in fact,' said Shelton, 'self-preservation!'

'Common sense,' returned his friend; 'I believe in justice before sentiment.' He drank, and callously blew smoke at Shelton. 'Besides, there are many people with religious views about it.'

'It's always seemed to me,' said Shelton, 'to be quaint that people should assert that marriage gives them the right to "an eye for an eye," and call themselves Christians. Did you ever know anybody stand on their rights except out of wounded pride or for the sake of their own comfort? Let them call their reasons what they like, you know as well as I do that it's cant.'

'I don't know about that,' said Halidome, more and more superior as Shelton grew more warm; 'when you stand on your rights, you do it for the sake of Society as well as for your own. If you want to do away with marriage, why don't you say so?'

'But I don't' said Shelton: 'is it likely? Why I'm going—' He stopped without adding the words 'to be married myself,' for it suddenly occurred to him that the reason was not the most lofty and philosophic in the world. 'All I can say is,' he went on soberly, 'that you can't make a horse drink by driving him. Generosity is the surest way of tightening the knot between people who've any sense of decency; as to the rest, the chief thing is to prevent their breeding.'

Halidome smiled.

'You're a rum chap,' he said.

Shelton jerked his cigarette into the fire.

'I tell you what'—for late at night a certain power of vision came to him—'it's humbug to talk of doing things for the sake of Society; it's nothing but the instinct to keep our own heads above the water.'

But Halidome remained unruffled.

'All right,' he said, 'call it that. I don't see why *I* should go to the wall; it wouldn't do any good.'

'You admit, then,' said Shelton, 'that our morality is the sum total of everybody's private instinct of self-preservation?'

Halidome stretched his splendid frame and yawned.

'I don't know,' he began, 'that I should quite call it that——'

But the compelling complacency of his fine eyes, the dignified posture of his healthy body, the lofty slope of his narrow forehead, the perfectly humane look of his cultivated brutality, struck Shelton as ridiculous.

'Hang it, Hal!' he cried, jumping from his chair, 'what an old

29

fraud you are! I'll be off.'

'No, look here!' said Halidome; the faintest shade of doubt had appeared upon his face; he took Shelton by a lapel: 'You're quite wrong——'

'Very likely; good night, old chap!'

Shelton walked home, letting the Spring wind into him. It was Saturday, and he passed many silent couples. In every little patch of shadow he could see two forms standing or sitting close together, and in their presence Words the Impostors seemed to hold their tongues. The wind rustled the buds; the stars, one moment bright as diamonds, vanished the next. In the lower streets a large part of the world was under the influence of drink, but by this Shelton was far from being troubled. It seemed better than Drama, than dressing-bagged men, unruffled women, and padded points of view, better than the immaculate solidity of his friend's possessions.

'So,' he reflected, 'it's right for every reason, social, religious, and convenient, to inflict one's society where it's not desired. There are obviously advantages about the married state; charming to feel respectable while you're acting in a way that in any other walk of life would bring on you contempt. If old Halidome showed that he was tired of me, and I continued to visit him, he'd think me a bit of a cad; but if his wife were to tell him she couldn't stand him, he'd still consider himself a perfect gentleman if he persisted in giving her the burden of his society; and he has the cheek to bring religion into it—a religion that says, 'Do unto others!'

But in this he was unjust to Halidome, forgetting how impossible it was for him to believe that a woman could not stand him. He reached his rooms, and, the more freely to enjoy the clear lamplight, the soft, gusty breeze, and waning turmoil of the streets, waited a moment before entering.

'I wonder,' thought he, 'if I shall turn out a cad when I marry, like that chap in the play. It's natural. We all want our money's worth, our pound of flesh! Pity we use such fine words—"Society, Religion, Morality." Humbug!'

He went in, and, throwing his window open, remained there a long time, his figure outlined against the lighted room for the benefit of the dark Square below, his hands in his pockets, his head down, a reflective frown about his eyes. A half-intoxicated old ruffian, a policeman, and a man in a straw hat had stopped below, and were holding a palaver.

'Yus,' the old ruffian said, 'I'm a rackety old blank; but what I say is, if we wus all alike, this wouldn't be a world!'

They went their way, and before the listener's eyes there rose Antonia's face, with its unruffled brow; Halidome's, all health and dignity; the forehead of the goggle-eyed man, with its line of hair parted in the centre, and brushed across. A light seemed to illumine the plane of their existence, as the electric lamp with the green shade had illumined the pages of the Matthew Arnold; serene before Shelton's vision lay that Elysium, untouched by passion or extremes of any kind, autocratic, complacent, possessive, and well-kept as any Midland landscape. Healthy, wealthy, wise! No room but for perfection, self-preservation, the survival of the fittest! 'The part of the good citizen,' he thought: 'No, if we were all alike, this wouldn't be a world?'

Chapter 6

MARRIAGE SETTLEMENT

'MY dear Richard' (wrote Shelton's uncle the next day), 'I shall be glad to see you at three o'clock tomorrow afternoon upon the question of your marriage settlement. . . .' At that hour accordingly Shelton made his way to Lincoln's Inn Fields, where in fat black letters the names 'Paramor and Herring (Commissioners for Oaths)' were written on the wall of a stone entrance. He ascended the solid steps with nervousness, and by a small red-haired boy was introduced to a back-room on the first floor. Here, seated at a table in the very centre, as if he thereby better controlled his universe, a pug-featured gentleman, without a beard, was writing. He paused.

'Ow, Mr Richard!' he said; 'glad to see you, sir. Take a chair. Your uncle will be disengaged in 'arf a minute;' and in the tone of his allusion to his employer was the satirical approval that comes with long and faithful service. 'He will do everything himself,' he went on, screwing up his sly, greenish, honest eyes, 'and he's not a young man.'

Shelton never saw his uncle's clerk without marvelling at the prosperity deepening upon his face. In place of the look of harassment which on most faces begins to grow after the age of fifty, his old friend's countenance, as though in sympathy with the nation, had expanded—a little greasily, a little genially, a little coarsely—every time he met it. A contemptuous tolerance for people who were not getting on was spreading beneath its surface; it left each time a deeper feeling that its owner could never be in the wrong.

'I hope you're well, sir,' he resumed: 'most important for you to have your health now you're going—to'—and, feeling for the delicate way to put it, he involuntarily winked—'to become a family man. We saw it in the paper. My wife said to me the other morning at breakfast: "Bob, here's a Mr Richard Paramor Shelton goin' to be married. Is that any relative to your Mr Shelton?" "My dear," I said to her, "it's the very man!"'

It disquieted Shelton to perceive that his old friend did not pass the whole of his life at that table writing in the centre of the room, but that somewhere (vistas of little grey houses rose before his eyes) he actually lived another life where someone called him 'Bob.' Bob! And this, too, was a revelation. Bob! Why, of course, it was the only name for him! A bell rang.

'That's your uncle;' and again the head clerk's voice sounded ironical. 'Good-bye, sir.'

He seemed to clip off intercourse as one clips off electric light. Shelton left him writing, and preceded the red-haired boy to an enormous room in the front where his uncle waited.

Edmund Paramor was a medium-sized and upright man of seventy, whose brown face was perfectly clean-shaven. His grey, silky hair was brushed in a cock's comb from his fine forehead, bald on the left side. He stood before the hearth facing the room, and his figure had the springy abruptness of men who cannot fatten. There was a certain youthfulness, too, in his eyes, yet they had a look as though he had been through fire; and his mouth curled at the corners in surprising smiles. The room was like the man—morally large, void of red-tape and almost void of furniture; no tin boxes were ranged against the walls, no papers littered up the table; a single bookcase contained a complete edition of the law reports, and resting on the Law Directory was a single red rose in a glass of water. It looked the room of one with a sober magnanimity, who went to the heart of things, despised haggling, and before whose smiles the more immediate kinds of humbug faded.

'Well, Dick,' said he, 'how's your mother?'

Shelton replied that his mother was all right.

'Tell her that I'm going to sell her Easterns after all, and put into this Brass thing. You can say it's safe, from me.'

Shelton made a face.

'Mother,' said he, 'always believes things are safe.'

His uncle looked through him with his keen, half-suffering glance, and up went the corners of his mouth.

'She's splendid,' he said.

'Yes,' said Shelton, 'splendid.'

The transaction, however, did not interest him; his uncle's judgment in such matters had a breezy soundness he would never dream of questioning.

'Well, about your settlement;' and, touching a bell three times, Mr Paramor walked up and down the room. 'Bring me the draft of Mr Richard's marriage settlement.'

The stalwart commissionaire reappearing with a document— 'Now then, Dick,' said Mr Paramor. 'She's not bringing anything into settlement, I understand; how's that?'

'I didn't want it,' replied Shelton, unaccountably ashamed.

Mr Paramor's lips quivered; he drew the draft closer, took up a blue pencil, and, squeezing Shelton's arm, began to read. The latter, following his uncle's rapid exposition of the clauses, was relieved when he paused suddenly.

'If you die and she marries again,' said Mr Paramor, 'she forfeits her life interest—see?'

'Oh!' said Shelton; 'wait a minute, Uncle Ted.'

Mr Paramor waited, biting his pencil; a smile flickered on his mouth, and was decorously subdued. It was Shelton's turn to walk about.

'If she marries again,' he repeated to himself.

Mr Paramor was a keen fisherman; he watched his nephew as he might have watched a fish he had just landed.

'It's very usual,' he remarked.

Shelton took another turn.

'She forfeits,' thought he; 'exactly.'

When he was dead, he would have no other way of seeing that she continued to belong to him. Exactly!

Mr Paramor's haunting eyes were fastened on his nephew's face.

'Well, my dear,' they seemed to say, 'what's the matter?'

Exactly! Why *should* she have his money if she married again? She would forfeit it. There was comfort in the thought. Shelton came back, and carefully reread the clause, to put the thing on a purely business basis, and disguise the real significance of what was passing in his mind.

'If I die and she marries again,' he repeated aloud, 'she forfeits.'

What wiser provision for a man passionately in love could possibly have been devised? His uncle's eye travelled beyond him, humanely turning from the last despairing wriggles of his fish.

'I don't want to tie her,' said Shelton suddenly.

The corners of Mr Paramor's mouth flew up.

'You want the forfeiture out?' he asked.

The blood rushed into Shelton's face; he felt he had been detected in a piece of sentiment.

'Ye-es,' he stammered.

'Sure?'

'Quite!'

The answer was a little sulky.

His uncle's pencil descended on the clause, and he resumed the reading of the draft; but Shelton could not follow it, he was too much occupied in considering exactly why Mr Paramor had been amused, and to do this he was obliged to keep his eyes upon him. Those features, just pleasantly rugged; the springy poise of the figure; the hair neither straight nor curly, neither short nor long; the haunting look of his eyes and the humorous look of his mouth; his clothes neither shabby nor dandified; his serviceable, fine hands; above all, the equability of the hovering blue pencil, conveyed the impression of a perfect balance between heart and head, sensibility and reason, theory and its opposite.

' "During coverture," ' quoted Mr Paramor, pausing again, 'you understand, of course, if you don't get on and separate, she goes on taking?'

If they didn't get on! Shelton smiled. Mr Paramor did not smile, and again Shelton had the sense of having knocked up against something poised but firm. He remarked irritably:

'If we're not living together, all the more reason for her having it.'

This time his uncle smiled. It was difficult for Shelton to feel angry at that ironic merriment, with its sudden ending; it was too impersonal to irritate; it was too concerned with human nature.

'If—hum—it came to the other thing,' said Mr Paramor, 'the settlement's at an end as far as she's concerned. We're bound to look at every case, you know, old boy.'

The memory of the play and his conversation with Halidome was still strong in Shelton. He was not one of those who could not face the notion of transferred affections—at a safe distance.

'All right, Uncle Ted,' said he. For one mad moment he was

attacked by the desire to 'throw in' the case of divorce. Would it not be common chivalry to make her independent, able to change her affections if she wished, unhampered by monetary troubles? You only needed to take out the words 'during coverture'.

Almost anxiously he looked into his uncle's face. There was no meanness there, but neither was there encouragement in that comprehensive brow with its wide sweep of hair. 'Quixotism,' it seemed to say, 'has merits, but——' The room, too, with its wide horizon and tall windows, looking as if it dealt habitually in common sense, discouraged him. Innumerable men of breeding and the soundest principles must have bought their wives in here. It was perfumed with the atmosphere of wisdom and law-calf. The aroma of Precedent was strong; Shelton swerved his lance, and once more settled down to complete the purchase of his wife.

'I can't conceive what you're in such a hurry for; you're not going to be married till the autumn,' said Mr Paramor, finishing at last. Replacing the blue pencil in the rack, he took the red rose from the glass, and sniffed at it. 'Will you come with me as far as Pall Mall? I'm going to take an afternoon off; too cold for Lord's, I suppose?'

They walked into the Strand.

'Have you seen this new play of Borogrove's?' asked Shelton as they passed the theatre to which he had been with Halidome.

'I never go to modern plays,' replied Mr Paramor; 'too d——d gloomy.'

Shelton glanced at him; he wore his hat rather far back on his head, his eyes haunted the street in front; he had shouldered his umbrella.

'Psychology's not in your line, Uncle Ted?'

'Is that what they call putting into words things that can't be put in words?'

'The French succeed in doing it,' replied Shelton, 'and the Russians; why shouldn't we?'

Mr Paramor stopped to look in at a fishmonger's.

'What's right for the French and Russians, Dick,' he said, 'is wrong for us. When we begin to be *real*, we only really begin to be false. I should like to have had the catching of that fellow; let's send him to your mother.'

He went in and bought a salmon.

'Now, my dear,' he continued, as they went on, 'do you tell me that it's decent for men and women on the stage to writhe about

35

like eels? Isn't life bad enough already?'

It suddenly struck Shelton that, for all his smile, his uncle's face had a look of crucifixion. It was, perhaps, only the stronger sunlight in the open spaces of Trafalgar Square.

'I don't know,' he said; 'I think I prefer the truth.'

'Bad endings and the rest?' said Mr Paramor, pausing under one of Nelson's lions and taking Shelton by a button. 'Truth's the very devil!'

He stood there, very straight, his eyes haunting his nephew's face; there seemed to Shelton a touching muddle in his optimism —a muddle of tenderness and of intolerance, of truth and second-handedness. Like the lion above him, he seemed to be defying Life to make him look at her.

'No, my dear,' he said, handing sixpence to a sweeper; 'feelings are snakes! only fit to be kept in bottles with tight corks. You won't come to my club? Well, good-bye, old boy; my love to your mother when you see her;' and turning up the Square, he left Shelton to go on to his own club, feeling that he had parted, not from his uncle, but from the nation of which they were both members by birth, and blood, and education.

Chapter 7

THE CLUB

HE went into the library of his club, and took up Burke's 'Peerage'. The words his uncle had said to him on hearing his engagement had been these: 'Dennant! Are those the Holm Oaks Dennants? She was a Penguin.'

No one who knew Mr Paramor connected him with snobbery, but there had been an 'Ah! that's right; this is due to us' tone about the saying.

Shelton hunted for the name of Baltimore: 'Charles Penguin, fifth Baron Baltimore. Issue: Alice, b. 184-, m. 186- Algernon Dennant, Esq., of Holm Oaks, Cross Eaton, Oxfordshire.' He put down the 'Peerage' and took up the 'Landed Gentry' : 'Dennant, Algernon Cuffe, eldest son of the late Algernon Cuffe Dennant, Esq., J.P., and Irene, 2nd daur. of the Honble. Philip and Lady Lillian March Mallow; ed. Eton and Ch. Ch., Oxfordshire. *Residence*, Holm Oaks,' etc., etc. Dropping the 'Landed Gentry,' he took up a volume of the 'Arabian Nights,' which some member had left reposing on the book-rest of his chair, but instead of reading he kept looking round the room. In almost every seat, reading or snoozing, were gentlemen who, in their own estimation, might have married Penguins. For the first time it struck him with what majestic leisureliness they turned the pages of their books, trifled with their teacups, or lightly snored. Yet no two were alike—a tall man with dark moustache, thick hair, and red, smooth cheeks; another bald, with stooping shoulders; a tremendous old buck, with a grey, pointed beard and large white waistcoat; a clean-shaven dapper man past middle age, whose face was like a bird's; a long, sallow, misanthrope; and a sanguine creature fast asleep.

Asleep or awake, reading or snoring, fat or thin, hairy or bald, the insulation of their red or pale faces was complete. They were all the creatures of good form. Staring at them or reading the 'Arabian Nights' Shelton spent the time before his dinner.

He had not been long seated in the dining-room when a distant connection strolled up and took the next table.

'Ah, Shelton! Back? Somebody told me you were goin' round the world.' He scrutinised the menu through his eyeglass. 'Clear soup! . . . Read Jellaby's speech? Amusing the way he squashes all those fellows. Best man in the House; he really is.'

Shelton paused in the assimilation of asparagus; he, too, had been in the habit of admiring Jellaby, but now he wondered, why? The red and shaven face beside him above a broad, pure shirt-front was swollen by good humour; his small, very usual, and hard eyes were fixed introspectively on the successful process of his eating.

'*Success!*' thought Shelton, suddenly enlightened—'success is what we admire in Jellaby. We all want success.' . . . 'Yes,' he admitted, 'a successful beast.'

'Oh!' said his neighbour, 'I forgot. You're in the other camp?'

'Not particularly. Where did you get that idea?'

His neighbour looked round negligently.

'Oh,' said he, 'I somehow thought so'; and Shelton almost heard him adding: 'There's something not quite sound about you.'

'Why do you admire Jellaby?' he asked.

'Knows his own mind,' replied his neighbour; 'it's more than the others do. . . . This whitebait isn't fit for cats! Clever fellow, Jellaby! No nonsense about him! Have you ever heard him speak? Awful good sport to watch him sitting on the Opposition. A poor lot they are!' and he laughed, either from appreciation of Jellaby

37

sitting on a small minority, or from appreciation of the champagne bubbles in his glass.

'Minorities are always depressing,' said Shelton dryly.

'Eh? what?'

'I mean,' said Shelton, 'it's irritating to look at people who haven't a chance of success—fellows who make a mess of things, fanatics, and all that.'

His neighbour turned his eyes inquisitively.

'Er—yes, quite,' said he; 'don't you take mint sauce? It's the best part of lamb, I always think.'

The great room with its countless little tables, arranged so that every man might have the support of the gold walls to his back, began to regain its influence on Shelton. How many times had he not sat there, carefully nodding to acquaintances, happy if he got the table he was used to, a paper with the latest racing, and some one to gossip with who was not a bounder, while the sensation of having drunk enough stole over him. Happy! That is, happy as a horse is happy who never leaves his stall.

'Look at poor little Bing puffin' about,' said his neighbour, pointing to a weazened, hunchy waiter. 'His asthma's awf'ly bad; you can hear him wheezin' from the street.'

He seemed amused.

'There's no such thing as moral asthma, I suppose?' said Shelton.

His neighbour dropped his eyeglass.

'Here, take this away; it's overdone,' said he. 'Bring me some lamb.'

Shelton pushed his table back.

'Good-night!' he said; 'the Stilton's excellent!'

His neighbour raised his brows, and again bent his eyes on his plate.

In the hall Shelton went from force of habit to the weighing-scales and took his weight. 'Eleven stone!' he thought; 'gone up!' and, clipping a cigar, he sat down in the smoking-room with a novel.

After half an hour he dropped the book. There seemed something rather fatuous about this story, for though it had a thrilling plot and was full of well-connected people, it had apparently been contrived to throw no light on anything whatever. He looked at the author's name; every one was highly recommending it. He began thinking, and staring at the fire. . . .

Looking up, he saw Antonia's second brother, a young man in

the Rifles, bending over him with sunny cheeks and hazy smile, clearly just a little drunk.

'Congratulate you, old chap! I say, what made you grow that b-b-eastly beard?'

Shelton grinned.

'"Pillbottle of the Duchess!"' read young Dennant, taking up the book. 'You been reading that? Rippin', isn't it?'

'Oh, ripping!' replied Shelton.

'Ripping plot! When you get hold of a novel you don't want any rot about—what d'you call it?—psychology, you want to be amused.'

'Rather!' murmured Shelton.

'That's an awfully good bit where the President steals her dia-monds——— There's old Benjy! Hallo, Benjy!'

'Hallo, Bill, old man!'

This Benjy was a young, clean-shaven creature, whose face and voice and manner were a perfect blend of steel and geniality.

In addition to this young man who was so smooth and hard and cheery, a grey, short-bearded gentleman, with misanthropic eyes, called Stroud, came up; together with another man of Shelton's age, with a moustache and a bald patch the size of a crown-piece, who might be seen in the club any night of the year when there was no racing out of reach of London.

'You know,' began young Dennant, 'that this bounder'—he slapped the young man Benjy on the knee—'is going to be spliced to-morrow. Miss Casserol—you know the Casserols—Muncaster Gate.'

'By jove!' said Shelton, delighted to be able to say something they would understand.

'Young Champion's the best man, and I'm the second best. I tell you what, old chap, you'd better come with me and get your eye in; you won't get such another chance of practice. Benjy'll give you a card.'

'Delighted!' murmured Benjy.

'Where is it?'

'St Briabas; two-thirty. Come and see how they do the trick. I'll call for you at one; we'll have some lunch and go together.' Again he patted Benjy's knee.

Shelton nodded his assent; the piquant callousness of the affair had made him shiver, and furtively he eyed the steely Benjy, whose suavity had never wavered, and who appeared to take a greater interest in some approaching race than in his coming marriage.

But Shelton knew from his own sensations that this could not really be the case; it was merely a question of 'good form,' the conceit of a superior breeding, the duty not to give oneself away. And when in turn he marked the eyes of Stroud fixed on Benjy, under shaggy brows, and the curious greedy glances of the racing man, he felt somehow sorry for him.

'Who's that fellow with the game leg; I'm always seeing him about?' asked the racing man.

And Shelton saw a sallow man conspicuous for a want of parting in his hair and a certain restlessness of attitude.

'His name is Bayes,' said Stroud; 'spends half his time among the Chinese—must have a grudge against them! And now he's got his leg he can't go there any more.'

'Chinese? What does he do to them?'

'Bibles or guns. Don't ask me! An adventurer.'

'Looks a bit of a bounder,' said the racing man.

Shelton gazed at the twitching eyebrows of old Stroud; he saw at once how it must annoy a man who had a billet in the 'Woods and Forests,' and plenty of time for 'Bridge' and gossip at his club, to see these people with untidy lives. A minute later the man with the 'game leg' passed close behind his chair, and Shelton perceived at once how intelligible the resentment of his fellow-members was. He had eyes which, not uncommon in this country, looked like fires behind steel bars; he seemed the very kind of man to do all sorts of things that were 'bad form,' a man who might even go as far as chivalry. He looked straight at Shelton, and his uncompromising glance gave an impression of fierce loneliness; altogether, an improper person to belong to such a club. Shelton remembered the words of an old friend of his father's: 'Yes, Dick, all sorts of fellows belong here, and they come here for all sorts o' reasons, and a lot of 'em come because they've nowhere else to go, poor beggars'; and, glancing from the man with the 'game leg' to Stroud, it occurred to Shelton that even he, old Stroud, might be one of those poor beggars. One never knew! A look at Benjy, contained and cheery, restored him. Ah, the lucky devil! He would not have to come here any more! And the thought of the last evening he himself would be spending here before long flooded his mind with a sweetness that was almost pain.

'Benjy, I'll play you a hundred up!' said young Bill Dennant.

Stroud and the racing man went to watch the game; Shelton was left once more to reverie.

'Good form!' thought he; 'that fellow must be made of steel. They'll go on somewhere; stick about half the night playing poker, or some such foolery.'

He crossed over to the window. Rain had begun to fall, the streets looked wild and draughty. The cabmen were putting on their coats. Two women scurried by, huddled under one umbrella, and a thin-clothed, dogged-looking scarecrow lounged past with a surly, desperate step. Shelton, returning to his chair, threaded his way amongst his fellow-members. A procession of old school and college friends came up before his eyes. After all, what had there been in his own education, or theirs, to give them any other standard than this 'good form'? What had there been to teach them anything of life? Their imbecility was incredible when you came to think of it. They had all the air of knowing everything, and really they knew nothing—nothing of Nature, Art, or the Emotions; nothing of the bonds that bind all men together. Why, even such words were not 'good form'; nothing outside their little circle was 'good form'. They had a fixed point of view over life because they came of certain Schools, and Colleges, and Regiments! And they were those in charge of the State, of Laws, and Science, of the Army, and Religion. Well, it was their system— the system not to start too young, to form healthy fibre, and let the after-life develop it!

'Successful!' he thought, nearly stumbling over a pair of patent-leather boots belonging to a moon-faced, genial-looking member with gold nose-nippers; 'oh, it's successful!'

Somebody came and picked up from the table the very volume which had originally inspired this train of thought, and Shelton could see his solemn pleasure as he read. In the white of his eye there was a torpid and composed abstraction. There was nothing in that book to startle him or make him think.

The moon-faced member with the patent boots came up and began talking of his recent visit to the South of France. He had a scandalous anecdote or two to tell, and his broad face beamed behind his gold nose-nippers; he was a large man with such a store of easy, worldly humour that it was impossible not to appreciate his gossip, he gave so perfect an impression of enjoying life, and doing himself well. 'Well, good-night!' he murmured—'An engagement!' and the certainty he left behind that his engagement must be charming and illicit was pleasant to the soul.

And slowly taking up his glass, Shelton drank; the sense of well-being was upon him. His superiority to these his fellow-members soothed him. He saw through all the sham of this club life, the meanness of this worship of success, the shame of kid-gloved novelists, 'good form', and the terrific decency of our education. It was soothing thus to see through things, soothing thus to be superior; and from the soft recesses of his chair he puffed out smoke and stretched his limbs towards the fire; and the fire burned back at him with a discreet and venerable glow.

Chapter 8

THE WEDDING

PUNCTUAL to his word, Bill Dennant called for Shelton at one o'clock.

'I bet old Benjy's feeling a bit cheap,' said he, as they got out of their cab at the church door and passed between the crowded files of unelect, whose eyes, so curious and pitiful, devoured them from the pavement.

The ashen face of a woman, with a baby in her arms and two more by her side, looked as eager as if she had never experienced the pangs of ragged matrimony. Shelton went in inexplicably uneasy; the price of his tie was their board and lodging for a week. He followed his future brother-in-law to a pew on the bridegroom's side, for, with intuitive perception of the sexes' endless warfare, each of the opposing parties to this contract had its serried battalion, the arrows of whose suspicion kept glancing across and across the central aisle.

Bill Dennant's eyes began to twinkle.

'There's old Benjy!' he whispered; and Shelton looked at the hero of the day. A subdued pallor was traceable under the weathered uniformity of his shaven face; but the well-bred, artificial smile he bent upon the guests had its wonted steely suavity. About his dress and his neat figure was that studied ease which lifts men from the ruck of common bridegrooms. There were no holes in *his* armour through which the impertinent might pry.

'Good old Benjy!' whispered young Dennant. 'I say, they look a bit short of class, those Casserols.'

Shelton, who was acquainted with this family, smiled. The sensuous sanctity all round had begun to influence him. A perfume of flowers and dresses fought with the natural odour of the church; the rustle of whisperings and skirts struck through the native silence of the aisles. And Shelton idly fixed his eyes on a lady in the pew in front; without in the least desiring to make a speculation of this sort, he wondered whether her face was as charming as the lines of her back in their delicate, skin-tight setting of pearl grey; his glance wandered to the chancel with its stacks of flowers, to the grave, business faces of the presiding priests; till the organ began rolling out the wedding march.

'They're off!' whispered young Dennant.

Shelton was conscious of a shiver running through the audience which reminded him of a bull-fight he had seen in Spain. The bride came slowly up the aisle. 'Antonia will look like that,' he thought, 'and the church will be filled with people like this. . . . She'll be a show to them!' The bride was opposite him now, and by an instinct of common chivalry he turned away his eyes; it seemed to him a shame to look at that downcast head above the silver mystery of her perfect raiment; the modest head full, doubtless, of devotion and pure yearnings; the stately head where no such thought as, 'How am I looking, this day of all days, before all London?' had ever entered; the proud head, which no such fear as, 'How am I carrying it off?' could surely be besmirching.

He saw below the surface of this drama played before his eyes; and set his face, as a man might who found himself assisting at a sacrifice. The words fell, unrelenting, on his ears; 'For better for worse, for richer for poorer; in sickness and in health——' and opening the Prayer Book he found the Marriage Service, which he had not looked at since he was a boy, and as he read he had some very curious sensations.

All this would soon be happening to himself! He went on reading in a kind of stupor, until aroused by his companion whispering: 'No luck!' All around there rose a rustling of skirts; he saw a tall figure mount the pulpit and stand motionless. Massive and high-featured, sunken of eye, he towered, in snowy cambric and a crimson stole, above the blackness of his rostrum; it seemed he had been chosen for his beauty. Shelton was still gazing at the stitching of his gloves, when once again the organ played the Wedding March. All were smiling, and a few were weeping, craning their heads towards the bride. 'Carnival of second-hand emotions!' thought Shelton; and he, too, craned his head and brushed his hat. Then, smirking at his friends, he made his way towards the door.

In the Casserols' house he found himself at last, going round the presents with the eldest Casserol surviving, a tall girl in pale violet, who had been chief bridesmaid.

'Didn't it go off well, Mr Shelton?' she was saying.

'Oh! awfully!'

'I always think it's so awkward for the man waiting up there for the bride to come.'

'Yes,' murmured Shelton.

'Don't you think it's smart, the bridesmaids having no hats?' Shelton had not noticed this improvement, but he agreed.

'That was my idea; I think it's very chic. They've had fifteen tea-sets—so dull, isn't it?'

'By Jove!' Shelton hastened to remark.

'Oh, it's fearfully *useful* to have a lot of things you don't want; of course, you change them for those you do.'

The whole of London seemed to have disgorged its shops into this room; he looked at Miss Casserol's face, and was greatly struck by the shrewd acquisitiveness of her small eyes.

'Is that your future brother-in-law?' she asked, pointing to Bill Dennant with a little movement of her chin; 'I think he's *such* a bright boy. I want you both to come to dinner, and help to keep things jolly. It's so deadly after a wedding.'

And Shelton said they would.

They adjourned to the hall now, to wait for the bride's departure. Her face as she came down the stairs was impassive, gay, with a furtive trouble in the eyes, and once more Shelton had the odd sensation of having sinned against his manhood. Jammed close to him was her old nurse, whose puffy, yellow face was pouting with emotion, while tears rolled from her eyes. She was trying to say something, but in the hubbub her farewell was lost. There was a scamper to the carriage, a flurry of rice and flowers; the shoe was flung against the sharply drawn-up window. Then Benjy's shaven face was seen a moment, bland and steely; the footman folded his arms, and with a solemn crunch the brougham wheels rolled away. 'How splendidly it went off!' said a voice on Shelton's right, 'She looked a little pale,' said a voice on Shelton's left. He put his hand up to his forehead; behind him the old nurse sniffed.

'Dick,' said young Dennant in his ear, 'this isn't good enough; I vote we bolt!'

Shelton assenting, they walked towards the Park; nor could he tell whether the slight nausea he experienced was due to afternoon champagne or to the ceremony that had gone so well.

'What's up with you?' asked Dennant; 'you look as glum as any m-monkey.'

'Nothing,' said Shelton; 'I was only thinking what humbugs we all are!'

Bill Dennant stopped in the middle of the crossing, and clapped his future brother-in-law upon the shoulder.

'Oh,' said he, 'if you're going to talk shop, I'm off.'

Chapter 9

THE DINNER

THE dinner at the Casserols' was given to those of the bride's friends who had been conspicuous in the day's festivity. Shelton found himself between Miss Casserol and a lady undressed to much the same degree. Opposite sat a man with a single diamond stud, a white waistcoat, black moustache, and hawklike face. This was, in fact, one of those interesting houses occupied by people of the upper middle class who have imbibed a taste for smart society. Its inhabitants, by nature acquisitive and cautious, economical, tenacious, had learnt to worship the word 'smart'. The result was a kind of heavy froth, an air of thoroughly domestic vice. In addition to the conventionally fast, Shelton had met there one or two ladies, who, having been divorced, or having yet to be, still maintained their position in 'society'. Divorced ladies who did not so maintain their place were never to be found, for the Casserols had a great respect for marriage. He had also met there American ladies who were 'too amusing'—never, of course, American men, Mesopotamians of the financial or the racing type, and several of those gentlemen who had been, or were about to be, engaged in a transaction which might, or again might *not*, 'come off,' and in conduct of an order which might, or again might *not*, be spotted. The line, he knew, was always drawn at those in any category who were actually found out, for the value of these ladies and these gentlemen was not their claim to pity—nothing so sentimental—but their 'smartness', clothes, jokes, racing tips, their 'Bridge' parties, and their motors.

In sum, the house was one whose fundamental domesticity attracted and sheltered those who were too 'smart' to keep their heads for long above the water.

His host, a grey, clean-shaven City man, with a long upper lip, was trying to understand a lady the audacity of whose speech came ringing down the table. Shelton himself had given up the effort with his neighbours, and made love to his dinner, which, surviving the incoherence of the atmosphere, emerged as a work of art. It was with surprise that he found Miss Casserol addressing him.

'I always say that the great thing is to be jolly: If you can't find anything to make you laugh, pretend you do; it's so much smarter to be amusin'. Now don't you agree?'

The philosophy seemed excellent.

'We can't all be geniuses, but we can all look jolly.'

Shelton hastened to look jolly.

'I tell the governor, when he's glum, that I shall put up the shutters and leave him. What's the good of mopin' and lookin' miserable? Are you going to the Four-in-Hand Meet? We're making a party. Such fun; all the smart people!'

The splendour of her shoulders, her frizzy hair (clearly not two hours out of the barber's hands), might have made him doubtful; but the frank shrewdness in her eyes, and her carefully clipped tone of voice, were guarantees that she was part of the element at the table which was really quite respectable. He had never realised before how 'smart' she was, and with an effort abandoned himself to a sort of gaiety that would have killed a Frenchman.

And when she left him, he reflected upon the expression of her eyes, when they rested on a lady opposite, who was a true bird-of-prey. 'What is it,' their envious, inquisitive glance had seemed to say, 'that makes you so really "smart"?' And while still seeking the reason, he noticed his host pointing out the merits of his port to the hawklike man, with a deferential air quite pitiful to see, for the hawklike man was clearly a 'bad hat'. What in the name of goodness did these staid bourgeois mean by making up to vice? Was it a craving to be thought distinguished, a dread of being dull, or merely an effect of overfeeding? Again he looked at his host, who had not yet enumerated all the virtues of his port, and again felt sorry for him.

'So you're goin' to marry Antonia Dennant?' said a voice on his right, with the easy coarseness which is a mark of caste. 'Pretty girl! They've a nice place, the Dennants. D'ye know, you're a lucky feller!'

The speaker was an old baronet, with small eyes, a dusky, ruddy face, and peculiar hail-fellow-well-met expression, at once morose and sly. He was always hard up, but being a man of enterprise knew all the best people, as well as all the worst, so that he dined out every night.

'You're a lucky feller,' he repeated; 'he's got some deuced good shootin', Dennant! They come too high for me, though; never touched a feather last time I shot there. She's a pretty girl. You're a lucky feller!'

'I know that,' said Shelton humbly.

'Wish I were in your shoes. Who was that sittin' the other side of you? I'm so dashed short-sighted. Mrs Carruther? Oh ay!' An expression which if he had not been a baronet, would have been a leer, came on his lips.

Shelton felt that he was referring to the leaf in his mental pocket-book covered with the anecdotes, figures, and facts about that lady. 'The old ogre means,' thought he, 'that I'm lucky because his leaf is blank about Antonia.' But the old baronet had turned, with his smile, and his sardonic, well-bred air, to listen to a bit of scandal on the other side.

The two men on Shelton's left were talking.

'What! You don't collect anything? How's that? Everybody collects something. I should be lost without my pictures.'

'No, I don't collect anything. Given it up; I was too awfully had over my Walkers.'

Shelton had expected a more lofty reason; he applied himself to the Madeira in his glass. That had been 'collected' by his host, and its price was going up! You couldn't get it every day; worth two guineas a bottle! How precious the idea that other people couldn't get it, made it seem! Liquid delight; the price was going up! Soon there would be none left; immense! Absolutely no one, then, could drink it!

'Wish I had some of this,' said the old baronet, 'but I've drunk all mine.'

'Poor old chap!' thought Shelton; 'after all, he's not a bad old boy. I wish I had his pluck. His liver must be splendid.'

The drawing-room was full of people playing a game concerned with horses ridden by jockeys with the latest seat. And Shelton was compelled to help in carrying on this sport till early in the morning. At last he left, exhausted by his animation.

He thought of the wedding; he thought over his dinner and the wine that he had drunk. His mood of satisfaction fizzled out. These people were incapable of being real, even the smartest, even the most respectable; they seemed to weigh their pleasures

47

in the scales and to get the most that could be extracted from their money.

Between the dark, safe houses stretching for miles and miles, his thoughts were of Antonia; and as he reached his rooms he was overtaken by the moment when the town is born again. The first new air had stolen down; the sky was living, but not yet alight; the trees were quivering faintly; no living creature stirred, and nothing spoke except his heart. Suddenly the city seemed to breathe, and Shelton saw that he was not alone; an unconsidered trifle with inferior boots was asleep upon his doorstep.

Chapter 10

AN ALIEN

THE individual on the doorstep had fallen into slumber over his own knees. No greater air of prosperity clung about him than is conveyed by a rusty overcoat and wisps of cloth in place of socks. Shelton endeavoured to pass unseen, but the sleeper woke.

'Ah, it's you, monsieur!' he said. 'I received your letter this evening, and have lost no time.' He looked down at himself and tittered, as though to say: 'But what a state I'm in!'

The young foreigner's condition was indeed much more desperate than on the occasion of their first meeting, and Shelton invited him upstairs.

'You can well understand,' stammered Ferrand, following his host, 'that I didn't want to miss you this time. When one is like this——' and a spasm gripped his face.

'I'm very glad you came,' said Shelton doubtfully.

His visitor's face had a week's growth of reddish beard; the deep tan of his cheeks gave him a robust appearance at variance with the fit of trembling which had seized on him as soon as he had entered.

'Sit down—sit down,' said Shelton; 'you're feeling ill!'

Ferrand smiled.

'It's nothing,' said he; 'bad nourishment——'

Shelton left him seated on the edge of an armchair, and brought him in some whisky.

'Clothes,' said Ferrand, when he had drunk, 'are what I want. These are really not good enough.'

The statement was correct, and Shelton, placing some garments in the bath-room, invited his visitor to make himself at home. While the latter, then, was doing this, Shelton enjoyed the luxuries of self-denial, hunting up things he did not want, and laying them in an old portmanteau. This done, he waited for his visitor's return.

The young foreigner at length emerged, unshaved indeed, and innocent of boots, but having in other respects an air of gratifying affluence.

'This is a little different,' he said. 'The boots I fear'—and, pulling down his, or rather Shelton's, socks, he exhibited sores the size of half a crown. 'One doesn't sow without reaping some harvest or another. My stomach has shrunk.' he added simply. 'To see things one must suffer. *Voyager, c'est plus fort que moi!*'

Shelton failed to perceive that this was one way of disguising the human animal's natural dislike of work—there was a touch of pathos, a suggestion of God-knows-what-might-have-been, about this fellow.

'I have eaten my illusions,' said the young foreigner, smoking a cigarette. 'When you've starved a few times, your eyes are opened. *Savoir, c'est mon métier; mais remarquez ceci, monsieur:* It's not always the intellectuals who succeed.'

'When you get a job,' said Shelton, 'you throw it away, I suppose.'

'You accuse me of restlessness? Shall I explain what I think about that? I'm restless because of ambition; I want to reconquer an independent position. I put all my soul into my trials, but as soon as I see there's no future for me in that line, I give it up and go elsewhere. *Je ne veux pas être "rond de cuir,"* breaking my back to economise sixpence a day, and save enough after forty years to drag out the remains of an exhausted existence. That's not in my character.' This ingenious paraphrase of the words 'I soon get tired of things', he pronounced with an air of letting Shelton into a precious secret.

'Yes; it must be hard,' agreed the latter.

Ferrand shrugged his shoulders.

'It's not all butter,' he replied; 'one is obliged to do things that are not too delicate. There's nothing I pride myself on but frankness.'

Like a good chemist, however, he administered what Shelton could stand in a judicious way. 'Yes, yes,' he seemed to say, 'you'd like me to think that you have a perfect knowledge of life: no

49

morality, no prejudices, no illusions; you'd like me to think that you feel yourself on an equality with me, one human animal talking to another, without any barriers of position, money, clothes, or the rest—*ca, c'est un peu trop fort!* You're as good an imitation as I've come across in your class, notwithstanding your unfortunate education, and I'm grateful to you, but to tell you everything as it passes through my mind would damage my prospects. You can hardly expect that.'

In one of Shelton's old frock-coats he was impressive, with his air of natural, almost sensitive refinement. The room looked as if it were accustomed to him, and more amazing still was the sense of familiarity that he inspired, as though he were a part of Shelton's soul. It came as a shock to realise that this young foreign vagabond had taken such a place within his thoughts. The pose of his limbs and head, irregular but not ungraceful; his disillusioned lips; the rings of smoke that issued from them—all signified rebellion, and the overthrow of law and order. His thin, lop-sided nose, the rapid glances of his goggling, prominent eyes, were subtlety itself; he stood for discontent with the accepted.

'How do I live when I'm on the tramp?' he said. 'Well, there are the Consuls. The system is not delicate, but when it's a question of starving, much is permissible; besides, these gentlemen were created for the purpose. There's a coterie of German Jews in Paris living entirely upon Consuls.' He hesitated for the fraction of a second, and resumed: 'Yes, monsieur; if you have papers that fit you, you must try six or seven Consuls in a single town. You must know a language or two; but most of these gentlemen are not too well up in the tongues of the country they represent. Obtaining money under false pretences? Well, it is. But what's the difference at bottom between all this honourable crowd of directors, fashionable physicians, employers of labour, jerry-builders, military men, country priests, and Consuls themselves perhaps, who take money and give no value for it, and poor devils who do the same at far greater risk? Necessity makes the law. If those gentlemen were in my position, do you think that they would hesitate?'

Shelton's face remaining doubtful, Ferrand went on instantly: 'You're right; they *would*, from fear, not principle. One must be hard pressed before committing these indelicacies. Look deep enough, and you will see that indelicate things are daily done by the respectable for not half so good a reason as the want of meals.'

Shelton also took a cigarette—his own income was derived

from property for which he gave no value in labour.

'I can give you an instance,' said Ferrand, 'of what can be done by resolution. One day in a German town, *étant dans la misère*, I decided to try the French Consul. Well, as you know, I am a Fleming, but something had to be screwed out somewhere. He refused to see me; I sat down to wait. After about two hours a voice bellowed:

'"Hasn't the brute gone?" and my Consul appears. "I've nothing for fellows like you," says he, "clear out!"

'"Monsieur," I answered, "I am skin and bone; I really must have assistance."

'"Clear out," he says, "or the police shall throw you out!"

'I don't budge. Another hour passes, and back he comes again.

'"Still here!" says he. "Fetch a sergeant."

'The sergeant comes.

'"Sergeant," says the Consul, "turn this creature out."

'"Sergeant," I say, "this house is France!" Naturally, I had calculated upon that. In Germany they're not too fond of those who undertake the business of the French.

'"He is right," says the sergeant; "I can do nothing."

'"You refuse?"

'"Absolutely." And he went away.

'"What do you think you'll get by staying?" says my Consul.

'"I have nothing to eat or drink, and nowhere to sleep," say I.

'"What will you go for?"

'"Ten marks."

'"Here, then, get out!" I can tell you, monsieur, one mustn't have a thin skin if one wants to exploit Consuls.'

His yellow fingers slowly rolled the stump of his cigarette, his ironical lips flickered. Shelton thought of his own ignorance of life. He could not recollect ever having gone without a meal.

'I suppose,' he said feebly, 'you've often starved.' For, having always been so well fed, the idea of starvation was attractive.

Ferrand smiled.

'Four days is the longest,' said he. 'You won't believe that story. . . . It was in Paris, and I had lost my money on the racecourse. There was some due from home which didn't come. Four days and nights I lived on water. My clothes were excellent, and I had jewellery; but I never even thought of pawning them. I suffered most from the notion that people might guess my state. You don't recognise me now?'

'How old were you then?' said Shelton.

'Seventeen; it's curious what one's like at that age.'

By a flash of insight Shelton saw the well-dressed boy, with sensitive, smooth face, always on the move about the streets of Paris, for fear that people should observe the condition of his stomach. The story was a valuable commentary. His thoughts were brusquely interrupted; looking in Ferrand's face, he saw to his dismay tears rolling down his cheeks.

'I've suffered too much,' he stammered; 'what do I care now what becomes of me?'

Shelton was disconcerted; he wished to say something sympathetic, but, being an Englishman, could only turn away his eyes.

'Your turn's coming,' he said at last.

'Ah! when you've lived my life,' broke out his visitor, 'nothing's any good. My heart's in rags. Find me anything worth keeping, in this menagerie.'

Moved though he was, Shelton wriggled in his chair, a prey to racial instinct, to an ingrained overtenderness, perhaps, of soul that forbade him from exposing his emotions, and recoiled from the revelation of other people's. He could stand it on the stage, he could stand it in a book, but in real life he could not stand it. When Ferrand had gone off with the portmanteau, he sat down and told Antonia:

'. . . The poor chap broke down and sat crying like a child; and instead of making me feel sorry it turned me into stone. The more sympathetic I wanted to be, the gruffer I grew. Is it fear of ridicule, independence, or consideration for others that prevents one from showing one's feelings?'

He went on to tell her of Ferrand's starving four days sooner than face a pawnbroker, and reading the letter over before addressing it, the faces of the three ladies round their snowy cloth arose before him—Antonia's face, so fair and calm and wind-fresh; her mother's face, a little creased by time and weather; the maiden aunt's, somewhat too thin—and they seemed to lean at him, alert and decorous, and the words, 'That's rather nice!' rang in his ears. He went out to post the letter, and buying a five-shilling order, enclosed it to the little barber, Carolan, as a reward for delivering his note to Ferrand. He omitted to send his address with this donation, but whether from delicacy or from caution he could not have said. Beyond doubt, however, on receiving through Ferrand the following reply, he felt ashamed and pleased:

'From every well-born soul humanity is owing. A thousand thanks. I received this morning your postal order; your heart henceforth for me will be placed beyond all praise.

'J. CAROLAN.'

Chapter 11

THE VISION

A FEW days later he received a letter from Antonia which filled him with excitement:

'. . . Aunt Charlotte is ever so much better, so mother thinks we can go home—hurrah! But she says that you and I must keep to our arrangement not to see each other till July. There will be something fine in being so near and having the strength to keep apart. . . . All the English are gone. I feel it so empty out here; these people are so funny—all foreign and shallow. Oh, Dick! how splendid to have an ideal to look up to! Write at once to Brewer's Hotel and tell me you think the same. . . . We arrive at Charing Cross on Sunday at half-past seven, stay at Brewer's for a couple of nights, and go down on Tuesday to Holm Oaks. . . .

'Always your
'ANTONIA.'

'To-morrow!' he thought; 'she's coming to-morrow!' and leaving his neglected breakfast, he started out to walk off his emotion. His square ran into one of those slums that still rub shoulders with the most distinguished situations, and in it he came upon a little crowd assembled round a dog-fight. One of the dogs was being mauled, but the day was muddy, and Shelton, like any well-bred Englishman, had a horror of making himself conspicuous even in a decent cause; he looked for a policeman. One was standing by, to see fair play, and Shelton made appeal to him. The official suggested that he should not have brought out a fighting dog, and advised him to throw cold water over them.

'It isn't my dog,' said Shelton.

'Then I should let 'em be,' remarked the policeman, with evident surprise.

53

Shelton appealed indefinitely to the lower orders. The lower orders, however, were afraid of being bitten.

'I wouldn't meddle with that there job if I was you,' said one. 'Nasty breed o' dawg is that.'

He was therefore obliged to cast away respectability, spoil his trousers and his gloves, break his umbrella, drop his hat in the mud, and separate the dogs. At the conclusion of the 'job' the lower orders said to him in a rather shamefaced manner :

'Well, I never thought you'd have managed that, sir'; but, like all men of inaction, Shelton after action was more dangerous.

'D——n it!' he said, 'one can't let a dog be killed'; and he marched off, towing the injured dog with his pocket-handkerchief, and looking scornfully at harmless passers-by. Having satisfied for once the smouldering fires within him, he felt entitled to hold a low opinion of these men in the street. 'The brutes,' he thought, 'won't stir a finger to save a poor dumb creature, and as for policemen——' But growing cooler, he began to see that people weighted down by 'honest toil' could not afford to tear their trousers or get a bitten hand, and that even the policeman, though he had looked so like a demi-god, was absolutely made of flesh and blood. He took the dog home, and, sending for a vet., had him sewn up.

He was already tortured by the doubt whether or no he might venture to meet Antonia at the station and after sending his servant with the dog to the address marked on its collar, he formed the resolve to go and see his mother, with some vague notion that she might help him to decide. She lived in Kensington, and, crossing the Brompton Road, he was soon amongst that maze of houses into the fibre of whose structure architects have wrought the motto : 'Keep what you have—wives, money, a good address, and all the blessings of a moral state !'

Shelton pondered as he passed house after house of such intense respectability that even dogs were known to bark at them. His blood was still too hot; it is amazing what incidents will promote the loftiest philosophy. He had been reading in his favourite review an article eulogising the freedom and expansion which had made the upper middle class so fine a body; and with eyes wandering from side to side, he nodded his head ironically. 'Expansion and freedom,' ran his thoughts: 'Freedom and expansion !'

Each house-front was cold and formal, the shell of an owner with from three to five thousand pounds a year, and each one

54

was armoured against the opinion of its neighbours by a sort of daring regularity. 'Conscious of my rectitude, and by the strict observance of exactly what is necessary and no more, I am enabled to hold my head up in the world. The person who lives in me has four thousand two hundred and fifty-five pounds each year, after allowing for the income tax.' Such seemed the legend of these houses.

Shelton passed ladies in ones and two and threes going out shopping, or to classes of drawing, cooking, ambulance. Hardly any men were seen, and they were mostly policemen; but a few disillusioned children were being wheeled towards the Park by fresh-cheeked nurses, accompanied by a great army of hairy or of hairless dogs.

There was something of her brother's large liberality about Mrs Shelton—a tiny lady with affectionate eyes, warm cheeks, and chilly feet; fond as a cat of a chair by the fire, and full of the sympathy that has no insight. She kissed her son at once with rapture, and, as usual, began to talk of his engagement. For the first time a tremor of doubt ran through her son; his mother's view of it grated on him like the sight of a blue-pink dress; it was too rosy. Her splendid optimism damped him; it had too little traffic with the reasoning powers.

'What right,' he asked himself, 'has she to be so certain? It seems to me a kind of blasphemy.'

'The *dear*!' she cooed. 'And is she coming back to-morrow? Hurrah! how I long to see her!'

'But you know, mother, we've agreed not to meet again until July.'

Mrs Shelton rocked her foot, and, holding her head on one side like a little bird, looked at her son with shining eyes.

'Dear old Dick!' she said, 'how happy you must be!'

Half a century of sympathy with weddings of all sorts—good, bad, indifferent—beamed from her.

'I suppose,' said Shelton gloomily, 'I ought not to go and meet her at the station.'

'Cheer up!' replied his mother, and her son felt dreadfully depressed.

That 'Cheer up!'—the panacea which had carried her blind and bright through every evil—was as void of meaning to him as wine without a flavour.

'And how is your sciatica?' he asked.

'Oh, pretty bad,' returned his mother; 'I expect it's all right,

55

really. Cheer up!' She stretched her little figure, canting her head still more.

'Wonderful woman!' Shelton thought. She had, in fact, like many of her fellow-countrymen, mislaid the darker side of things, and, enjoying the benefits of orthodoxy with an easy conscience, had kept as young in her heart as any girl of thirty.

Shelton left her house as doubtful whether he might meet Antonia as when he entered it. He spent a restless afternoon.

The next day—that of her arrival—was a Sunday. He had made Ferrand a promise to go with him to hear a sermon in the slums, and, catching at any diversion which might allay excitement, he fulfilled it. The preacher in question—an amateur—so Ferrand told him, had an original method of distributing the funds that he obtained. To male sheep he gave nothing, to ugly female sheep a very little, to pretty female sheep the rest. Ferrand hazarded an inference, but he was a foreigner. The Englishman preferred to look upon the preacher as guided by a purely abstract love of beauty. His eloquence, at any rate, was unquestionable, and Shelton came out feeling sick.

It was not yet seven o'clock, so, entering an Italian restaurant to kill the half-hour before Antonia's arrival, he ordered a bottle of wine for his companion, a cup of coffee for himself, and, lighting a cigarette, compressed his lips. There was a strange, sweet sinking in his heart. His companion, ignorant of this emotion, drank his wine, crumbled his roll, and blew smoke through his nostrils, glancing caustically at the rows of little tables, the cheap mirrors, the hot, red velvet, the chandeliers. His juicy lips seemed to be murmuring: 'Ah! if you only knew the dirt behind these feathers!' Shelton watched him with disgust. Though his clothes were now so nice, his nails were not quite clean, and his finger tips seemed yellow to the bone. An anæmic waiter in a shirt some four days old, with grease-spots on his garments and a crumpled napkin on his arm, stood leaning an elbow amongst doubtful fruits, and reading an Italian journal. Resting his tired feet in turn, he looked like overwork personified, and when he moved, each limb accused the sordid smartness of the walls. In the far corner sat a lady eating, and, mirrored opposite, her feathered hat, her short, round face, its coat of powder and dark eyes, gave Shelton a shiver of disgust. His companion's gaze rested long and subtly on her.

'Excuse me, monsieur,' he said at length. 'I think I know that lady!' And leaving his host, he crossed the room, bowed, accosted

56

her, and sat down. With Pharisaic delicacy, Shelton refrained from looking. But presently Ferrand came back; the lady rose and left the restaurant; she had been crying. The young foreigner was flushed, his face contorted; he did not touch his wine.

'I was right,' he said; 'she is the wife of an old friend. I used to know her well.'

He was suffering from emotion, but some one less absorbed than Shelton might have noticed a kind of relish in his voice, as though he were savouring life's dishes, and glad to have something new, and spiced with tragic sauce, to set before his patron.

'You can find her story by the hundred in your streets, but nothing hinders these paragons of virtue'—he nodded at the stream of carriages—'from turning up their eyes when they see ladies of her sort pass. She came to London just three years ago. After a year one of her little boys took fever—the shop was avoided—her husband caught it and died. There she was, left with two children and everything gone to pay the debts. She tried to get work; no one helped her. There was no money to pay anyone to stay with the children; all the work she could get in the house was not enough to keep them alive. She's not a strong woman. Well, she put the children out to nurse, and went to the streets. The first week was frightful, but now she's used to it—one gets used to anything.'

'Can nothing be done?' asked Shelton, startled.

'No,' returned his companion. 'I know that sort; if they once take to it, all's over. They get used to luxury. One doesn't part with luxury after tasting destitution. She tells me she does very nicely; the children are happy; she's able to pay well and see them sometimes. She was a girl of good family, too, who loved her husband, and gave up much for him. What would you have? Three-quarters of your virtuous ladies placed in her position would do the same if they had the necessary looks.'

It was evident that he felt the shock of this discovery, and Shelton understood that personal acquaintance makes a difference, even in a vagabond.

'This is her beat,' said the young foreigner, as they passed the illuminated crescent, where nightly the shadows of hypocrites and women fall; and Shelton went from these comments on Christianity to the station of Charing Cross. There, while he stood waiting in the shadow, his heart was in his mouth; and it struck him as odd that he should have come to this meeting fresh from a vagabond's society.

57

Presently, amongst the stream of travellers, he saw Antonia. She was close to her mother, who was parleying with a footman; behind them were a maid carrying a bandbox and a porter with the travelling-bags. Antonia's figure, with its throat settled in the collar of her cape, slender, tall, severe, looked impatient and remote amongst the bustle. Her eyes, shadowed by the journey, glanced eagerly about, welcoming all she saw; a wisp of hair was loose above her ear, her cheeks glowed cold and rosy. She caught sight of Shelton, and bending her neck, stag-like, stood looking at him; a brilliant smile parted her lips, and Shelton trembled. Here was the embodiment of all he had desired for weeks. He could not tell what was behind that smile of hers—passionate aching or only some ideal, some chaste and glacial intangibility. It seemed to be shining past him into the gloomy station. There was no trembling and uncertainty, no rage of possession in that brilliant smile; it had the gleam of fixedness, like the smiling of a star. What did it matter? She was there, beautiful as a young day, and smiling at him; and she was only divided from him by a space of time. He took a step; her eyes fell at once, her face regained aloofness; he saw her, encircled by mother, footman, maid, and porter, take her seat and drive away.

It was over; she had seen him, she had smiled, but alongside his delight lurked another feeling, and, by a bitter freak, not *her* face came up before him, but the face of that lady in the restaurant —short, round, and powdered, with black-circled eyes. What right had one to scorn them? Had *they* mothers, footmen, porters, maids? He shivered, but this time with physical disgust; the powdered face with dark-fringed eyes had vanished; the fair, remote figure of the railway-station came back again.

He sat long over dinner, drinking, dreaming; he sat long after, smoking, dreaming, and when at length he drove away, wine and dreams fumed in his brain. The dance of lamps, the cream-cheese moon, the rays of clean wet light on his horse's harness, the jingling of the cab bell, the whirring wheels, the night air and the branches—it was all so good! He threw back the hansom doors to feel the touch of the warm breeze. The crowds on the pavement gave him strange delight; they were like shadows in some great illusion, happy shadows, thronging, wheeling round the single figure of his world.

Chapter 12

ROTTEN ROW

WITH a headache and a sense of restlessness, hopeful and un-happy, Shelton mounted his hack next morning for a gallop in the Park.

In the sky was mingled all the languor and the violence of the spring. The trees and flowers wore an awakened look in the gleams of light that came stealing down from behind the purple of the clouds. The air was rain-washed, and the passers-by seemed to wear an air of tranquil carelessness, as if anxiety were paralysed by the irresponsibility of the firmament.

Thronged by riders, the Row was all astir.

Near to Hyde Park Corner a figure by the rails caught Shelton's eye. Straight and thin, one shoulder humped a little, as if its owner were reflecting, clothed in a frock-coat and a brown felt hat pinched up in lawless fashion, this figure was so detached from its surround-ings that it would have been noticeable anywhere. It belonged to Ferrand, obviously waiting till it was time to breakfast with his patron. Shelton found pleasure in thus observing him unseen, and sat quietly on his horse, hidden behind a tree.

It was just at that spot where riders, unable to get further, are for ever wheeling their horses for another turn; and there Ferrand, the bird of passage, with his head a little to one side, watched them cantering, trotting, wheeling up and down.

Three men walking along the rails were snatching off their hats before a horsewoman at exactly the same angle and with precisely the same air, as though in the modish performance of this ancient rite they were satisfying some instinct very dear to them.

Shelton noted the curl of Ferrand's lip as he watched this sight. 'Many thanks, gentlemen,' it seemed to say; 'in that charming little action you have shown me all your souls.'

What a singular gift the fellow had of divesting things and people of their garments, of tearing away their veil of shams, and their phylacteries! Shelton turned and cantered on; his thoughts were with Antonia, and he did not want the glamour stripped away.

He was glancing at the sky which every moment threatened to discharge a violent shower of rain, when suddenly he heard his name called from behind, and who should ride up to him on either side but Bill Dennant and—Antonia herself!

They had been galloping; and she was flushed—flushed as when she stood on the old tower at Hyères, but with a joyful radiance different from the calm and conquering radiance of that other moment. To Shelton's delight they fell into line with him, and all three went galloping along the strip between the trees and rails. The look she gave him seemed to say: 'I don't care if it is forbidden!' but she did not speak. He could not take his eyes off her. How lovely she looked, with the resolute curve of her figure, the glimpse of gold under her hat, the glorious colour in her cheeks, as if she had been kissed.

'It's so splendid to be at home! Let's go faster!' she cried out.

'Take a pull. We shall get run in,' grumbled her brother, with a chuckle.

They reined in round the bend, and jogged more soberly down on the far side; still not a word from her to Shelton, and Shelton in his turn spoke only to Bill Dennant. He was afraid to speak to her, for he knew that her mind was dwelling on this chance forbidden meeting in a way quite different from his own.

Approaching Hyde Park Corner, where Ferrand was still standing against the rails, Shelton, who had forgotten his existence, suffered a shock when his eyes fell suddenly on that impassive figure. He was about to raise his hand, when he saw that the young foreigner, noting his instinctive feeling, had at once adapted himself to it. They passed again without a greeting, unless that swift inquisition, followed by unconsciousness in Ferrand's eyes, could so be called. But the feeling of idiotic happiness left Shelton; he grew irritated at this silence. It tantalised him more and more, for Bill Dennant had lagged behind to chatter to a friend, Shelton and Antonia were alone, walking their horses, without a word, not even looking at each other. At one moment he thought of galloping ahead and leaving her, then of breaking the vow of muteness she seemed to be imposing on him, and he kept thinking: 'I ought to be either one thing or the other. I can't stand this.' Her calmness was getting on his nerves; she seemed to have determined just how far she meant to go, to have fixed cold-bloodedly a limit. In her happy young beauty and radiant coolness she summed up that sane consistent something existing in nine out of ten of the people Shelton knew. 'I can't stand it long,' he thought, and all of a sudden spoke; but as he did so, she frowned and cantered on. When he caught her she was smiling, lifting her face to catch the raindrops which were falling fast. She gave him just a nod, and waved her hand as a sign for him to go, and when he would not, she frowned. He saw Bill Dennant posting after them, and, seized by a sense of the ridiculous, lifted his hat, and galloped off.

The rain was coming down in torrents now, and every one was scurrying for shelter. He looked back from the bend, and could still make out Antonia riding leisurely, her face upturned, and revelling in the shower. Why hadn't she either cut him altogether or taken the sweets the gods had sent? It seemed wicked to have wasted such a chance, and ploughing back to Hyde Park Corner, he turned his head to see if by any chance she had relented.

His irritation was soon gone, but his longing stayed. Was ever anything so beautiful as she had looked with her face turned to the rain? She seemed to love the rain. It suited her—suited her ever so much better than the sunshine of the South. Yes, she was very English! Puzzling and fretting, he reached his rooms. Ferrand had not arrived, in fact, did not turn up that day. His non-appearance afforded Shelton another proof of the delicacy that went hand in hand with the young vagrant's cynicism. In the afternoon he received a note:

'. . . You see, Dick' (he read), 'I ought to have cut you; but I felt too crazy—everything seems so jolly at home, even this stuffy old London. Of course, I wanted to talk to you badly—there are heaps of things one can't say by letter—but I should have been sorry afterwards. I told mother. She said I was quite right, but I don't think she took it in. Don't you feel that the only thing that really matters is to have an ideal, and to keep it so safe that you can always look forward and feel that you have been—— I can't exactly express my meaning.'

Shelton lit a cigarette and frowned. It seemed to him queer that she should set more store by an 'ideal' than by the fact that they had met for the first and only time in many weeks.

'I suppose she's right,' he thought—'I suppose she's right. I ought not to have tried to speak to her!' As a matter of fact, he did not at all feel that she was right.

Chapter 13

AN 'AT HOME'

ON Tuesday morning he wandered off to Paddington, hoping for a chance view of her on her way down to Holm Oaks; but the sense of the ridiculous, on which he had been nurtured, was strong enough to keep him from actually entering the station and lurking about until she came. With a pang of disappointment he retraced his steps from Praed Street to the Park, and once there tried no further to waylay her. He paid a round of calls in the afternoon, mostly on her relations; and, seeking out Aunt Charlotte, he dolorously related his encounter in the Row. But she found it 'rather nice,' and on his pressing her with his views, she murmured that it was 'quite romantic, don't you know.'

'Still, it's very hard,' said Shelton; and he went away disconsolate.

As he was dressing for dinner his eye fell on a card announcing the 'at home' of one of his own cousins. Her husband was a composer, and he had a vague idea that he would find at the house of a composer some quite unusually free kind of atmosphere. After dining at the club, therefore, he set out for Chelsea. The party was held in a large room on the ground-floor, which was already crowded with people when Shelton entered. They stood or sat about in groups with smiles fixed on their lips, and the light from balloon-like lamps fell in patches on their heads and hands and shoulders. Someone had just finished rendering on the piano a composition of his own. An expert could at once have picked out from amongst the applauding company those who were musicians by profession, for their eyes sparkled, and a certain acidity pervaded their enthusiasm. This freemasonry of professional intolerance flew from one to the other like a breath of unanimity, and the faint shrugging of shoulders and the exclamations of approval were as harmonious as though one of the high windows had been opened suddenly, admitting a draught of chill May air.

Shelton made his way up to his cousin—a fragile, grey-haired woman in black velvet and Venetian lace, whose starry eyes beamed at him, until her duties, after the custom of these social

62

gatherings, obliged her to break off conversation just as it began to interest him. He was passed on to another lady who was already talking to two gentlemen, and their volubility being greater than his own, he fell into the position of observer. Instead of the profound questions he had somehow expected to hear raised, everybody seemed gossiping, or searching the heart of such topics as where to go this summer, or how to get new servants. Trifling with coffee-cups, they dissected their fellow-artists in the same way as his Society friends of the other night had dissected the fellow 'smart'; and the varnish on the floor, the pictures, and the piano was reflected on all the faces round. Shelton moved from group to group disconsolate.

A tall, imposing person stood under a Japanese print holding the palm of one hand outspread; his unwieldy trunk and thin legs wobbled in concert to his ingratiating voice.

'War,' he was saying, 'is not necessary. War is not necessary. I hope I make myself clear. War is not necessary; it depends on nationality, but nationality is not necessary.' He inclined his head to one side. 'Why do we have nationality? Let us do away with boundaries—let us have the warfare of commerce. If I see France looking at Brighton'—he laid his head upon one side, and beamed at Shelton—'what do I do? Do I say: "Hands off"? No. "Take it," I say—"take it!"' He archly smiled. 'But do you think they would?'

And the softness of his contours fascinated Shelton.

'The soldier,' the person underneath the print resumed, 'is necessarily on a lower plane—intellectually—oh, intellectually—than the philanthropist. His sufferings are less acute; he enjoys the compensations of advertisement—you admit that?' he breathed persuasively. 'For instance—I am quite impersonal—I suffer; but do I talk about it?' But, someone gazing at his well-filled waistcoat, he put his thesis in another form. 'I have one acre and one cow, my brother has one acre and one cow; do I seek to take them away from him?'

Shelton hazarded: 'Perhaps you're weaker than your brother.'

'Come, come! Take the case of women: now, I consider our marriage laws are barbarous.'

For the first time Shelton conceived respect for them; he made a comprehensive gesture, and edged himself into the conversation of another group, for fear of having all his prejudices overturned. Here an Irish sculptor, standing in a curve, was saying furiously: 'Bees are not bhumpkins, d——n their sowls!' A Scotch painter, who listened with a curly smile, seemed trying to compromise this proposition, which appeared to have relation to the middle classes; and though agreeing with the Irishman, Shelton felt nervous over his discharge of electricity. Next to them two American ladies, assembled under the tent of hair belonging to a writer of songs, were discussing the emotions aroused in them by Wagner's operas.

'They projuice a strange condition of affairs in me,' said the thinner one.

'They're divine,' said the fatter.

'I don't just know if you can call the fleshly lusts divine,' replied the thinner, looking into the eyes of the writer of the songs.

Amidst all the hum of voices and the fumes of smoke, a sense of formality was haunting Shelton. Sandwiched between a Dutchman and a Prussian poet, he could understand neither of his neighbours; so, assuming an intelligent expression, he fell to thinking that an assemblage of free spirits is as much bound by the convention of exchanging their ideas as commonplace people are by the convention of having no ideas to traffic in. He could not help wondering whether, in the bulk, they were not just as dependent on each other as the inhabitants of Kensington; whether, like locomotives, they could run at all without these opportunities for blowing off the steam, and what would be left when the steam had all escaped. Somebody ceased playing the violin, and close to him a group began discussing ethics.

Aspirations were in the air all round, like a lot of hungry ghosts. He realised that, if tongue be given to them, the flavour vanishes from ideas which haunt the soul.

Again the violinist played.

'Cock gracious!' said the Prussian poet, falling into English as the fiddle ceased : '*Colossal! Aber, wie er ist grossartig!*'

'Have you read that thing of Besom's?' asked a shrill voice behind.

'Oh, my dear fellow! too horrid for words; he ought to be hanged!'

'The man's dreadful,' pursued the voice, shriller than ever; 'nothing but a volcanic eruption would cure *him*.'

Shelton turned in alarm to look at the authors of these statements. They were two men of letters talking of a third.

'*C'est un grand naïf, vous savez*,' said the second speaker.

'These fellows don't exist,' resumed the first; his small eyes gleamed with a green light, his whole face had a look as if he

64

gnawed himself. Though not a man of letters, Shelton could not help recognising from those eyes what joy it was to say those words: 'These fellows don't exist!'

'Poor Besom! You know what Moulter said. . . .'

Shelton turned away, as if he had been too close to one whose hair smelt of cantharides; and, looking round the room, he frowned. With the exception of his cousin, he seemed the only person there of English blood. Americans, Mesopotamians, Irish, Italians, Germans, Scotch, and Russians. He was not contemptuous of them for being foreigners; it was simply that God and the climate had made him different by a skin or so.

But at this point his conclusions were denied (as will sometimes happen) by his introduction to an Englishman—a Major Somebody, who, with smooth hair and blond moustache, neat eyes and neater clothes, seemed a little anxious at his own presence there. Shelton took a liking to him, partly from a fellow-feeling, and partly because of the gentle smile with which he was looking at his wife. Almost before he had said 'How do you do?' he was plunged into a discussion on Imperialism.

'Admitting all that,' said Shelton, 'what I hate is the humbug with which we pride ourselves on benefiting the whole world by our so-called civilising methods.'

The soldier turned his reasonable eyes.

'But *is* it humbug?'

Shelton saw his argument in peril. If we really thought it, was it humbug?

He replied, however:

'Why should *we*, a small portion of the world's population, assume that our standards are the proper ones for every kind of race? If it's not humbug, it's sheer stupidity.'

The soldier, without taking his hands out of his pockets, but by a forward movement of his face showing that he was both sincere and just, replied:

'Well, it must be a good sort of stupidity; it makes us the nation that we are.'

Shelton felt dazed. The conversation buzzed around him; he heard the smiling prophet saying, 'Altruism, altruism,' and in his voice a something seemed to murmur: 'Oh, I do so hope I make a good impression!'

He looked at the soldier's clear-cut head with its well-opened eyes, the tiny crow's-feet at their corners, the conventional moustache; he envied the certainty of the convictions lying under that well-parted hair.

'I would rather we were men first and then Englishmen,' he muttered; 'I think it's all a sort of national illusion, and I can't stand illusions.'

'If you come to that,' said the soldier, 'the world lives by illusions. I mean, if you look at history, you'll see that the creation of illusions has always been her business, don't you know.'

This Shelton was unable to deny.

'So,' continued the soldier (who was evidently a highly cultivated man), 'if you admit that movement, labour, progress, and all that, have been properly given to building up these illusions, that—er—in fact, they're what you might call—er—the outcome of the world's crescendo'—he rushed his voice over this phrase as if ashamed of it—'why do you want to destroy them?'

Shelton thought a moment, then, squeezing his body with his folded arms, replied:

'The past has made us what we are, of course, and cannot be destroyed; but how about the future? It's surely time to let in air. Cathedrals are very fine, and everybody likes the smell of incense; but when they've been for centuries without ventilation you know what the atmosphere gets like.'

The soldier smiled.

'By your own admission,' he said, 'you'll only be creating a fresh set of illusions.'

'Yes,' answered Shelton, 'but at all events they'll be the honest necessities of the present.'

The pupils of the soldier's eyes contracted; he evidently felt the conversation slipping into generalities; he answered:

'I can't see how thinking small beer of ourselves is going to do us any good!'

Shelton felt in danger of being thought unpractical in giving vent to the remark:

'One must trust one's reason; I never can persuade myself that I believe in what I don't.'

A minute later, with a cordial handshake, the soldier left, and Shelton watched his courteous figure shepherding his wife away.

'Dick, may I introduce you to Mr Wilfred Curly?' said his cousin's voice behind, and he found his hand being diffidently shaken by a fresh-cheeked youth with a dome-like forehead, who was saying nervously:

'How do you do? Yes, I am very well, thank you!'

He now remembered that when he had first come in he had

66

watched this youth, who had been standing in a corner indulging himself in private smiles. He had an uncommon look, as though he were in love with life—as though he regarded it as a creature to whom one could put questions to the very end—interesting, humorous, earnest questions. He looked diffident, and amiable, and independent, and he, too, was evidently English.

'Are you good at argument?' said Shelton, at a loss for a remark.

The youth smiled, blushed, and, putting back his hair, replied:

'Yes—no—I don't know; I think my brain doesn't work fast enough for argument. You know how many motions of the brain-cells go to each remark. It's awfully interesting;' and bending from the waist in a mathematical position, he extended the palm of one hand, and started to explain.

Shelton stared at the youth's hand, at his frowns and the taps he gave his forehead while he found the expression of his meaning; he was intensely interested. The youth broke off, looked at his watch, and, blushing brightly, said:

'I'm afraid I have to go; I have to be at the "Den" before eleven.'

'I must be off, too,' said Shelton. Making their adieux together, they sought their hats and coats.

Chapter 14

THE NIGHT CLUB

'MAY I ask,' said Shelton, as he and the youth came out into the chilly street, 'what it is you call the "Den"?'

His companion, smiling, answered:

'Oh, the night club. We take it in turns. Thursday is my night. Would you like to come? You see a lot of types. It's only round the corner.'

Shelton digested a momentary doubt, and answered:

'Yes, immensely.'

They reached the corner house in an angle of a dismal street, through the open door of which two men had just gone in. Following, they ascended some wooden, fresh-washed stairs, and entered a large boarded room smelling of saw-dust, gas, stale coffee, and old clothes. It was furnished with a bagatelle board, two or three wooden tables, some wooden forms, and a wooden book-case. Seated on these wooden chairs, or standing up, were youths, and older men of the working class, who seemed to Shelton to be peculiarly dejected. One was reading, one against the wall was drinking coffee with a disillusioned air, two were playing chess, and a group of four made a ceaseless clatter with the bagatelle.

A little man in a dark suit, with a pale face, thin lips, and deep-set, black-encircled eyes, who was obviously in charge, came up with an anæmic smile.

'You're rather late,' he said to Curly, and, looking ascetically at Shelton, asked, without waiting for an introduction: 'Do you play chess? There's young Smith wants a game.'

A youth with a wooden face, already seated before a fly-blown chess-board, asked him drearily if he would have black or white. Shelton took white; he was oppressed by the virtuous odour of this room.

The little man with the deep eyes came up, stood in an uneasy attitude, and watched.

'Your play's improving, young Smith,' he said. 'I should think you'd be able to give Banks a knight.' His eyes rested on Shelton, fanatical and dreary; his monotonous voice was suffering and nasal; he was continually sucking in his lips, as though determined to subdue the flesh. 'You should come here often,' he said to Shelton, as the latter received checkmate; 'you'd get some good practice. We've several very fair players. You're not as good as Jones or Bartholomew,' he added to Shelton's opponent, as though he felt it a duty to put the latter in his place. 'You ought to come here often,' he repeated to Shelton; 'we have a lot of very good young fellows;' and, with a touch of complacency, he glanced around the dismal room. 'There are not so many here to-night as usual. Where are Toombs and Body?'

Shelton, too, looked anxiously around. He could not help feeling sympathy with Toombs and Body.

'They're getting slack, I'm afraid,' said the little deep-eyed man. 'Our principle is to amuse every one. Excuse me a minute; I see that Carpenter is doing nothing.' He crossed over to the man who had been drinking coffee, but Shelton had barely time to glance at his opponent and try to think of a remark, before the little man was back. 'Do you know anything about astronomy?' he asked of Shelton. 'We have several very interested in astronomy; if you could talk to them a little it would help.'

Shelton made a motion of alarm.

'Please—no,' said he; 'I——'

'I wish you'd come sometimes on Wednesdays; we have most interesting talks, and a service afterwards. We're always anxious to get new blood;' and his eyes searched Shelton's brown, rather tough-looking face, as though trying to see how much blood there was in it. 'Young Curly says you've just been round the world; you could describe your travels.'

'May I ask,' said Shelton, 'how your club is made up?'

Again a look of complacency, and blessed assuagement, visited the little man.

'Oh,' he said, 'we take anybody, unless there's anything against them. The Day Society sees to that. Of course, we shouldn't take anyone if they were to report against them. You ought to come to our committee meetings; they're on Mondays at seven. The women's side, too——'

'Thank you,' said Shelton; 'you're very kind——'

'We should be pleased,' said the little man; and his face seemed to suffer more than ever. 'They're mostly young fellows here to-night, but we have married men, too. Of course, we're very careful about that,' he added hastily, as though he might have injured Shelton's prejudices—'that, and drink, and anything criminal, you know.'

'And do you give pecuniary assistance, too?'

'Oh yes,' replied the little man; 'if you were to come to our committee meetings you would see for yourself. Everything is most carefully gone into; we endeavour to sift the wheat from the chaff.'

'I suppose,' said Shelton, 'you find a great deal of chaff?'

The little man smiled a suffering smile. The twang of his toneless voice sounded a trifle shriller.

'I was obliged to refuse a man to-day—a man and a woman, quite young people, with three small children. He was ill and out of work; but on inquiry we found they were not man and wife.'

There was a slight pause; the little man's eyes were fastened on his nails, and, with an appearance of enjoyment, he began to bite them. Shelton's face had grown a trifle red.

'And what becomes of the woman and the children in a case like that?' he said.

The little man's eyes began to smoulder.

'We make a point of not encouraging sin, of course. Excuse me a minute; I see they've finished bagatelle.'

He hurried off, and in a moment the clack of bagatelle began again. He himself was playing with a cold and spurious energy, running after the balls and exhorting the other players, upon whom a wooden acquiescence seemed to fall.

Shelton crossed the room, and went up to young Curly. He was sitting on a bench, smiling to himself his private smiles.

'Are you staying here much longer?' Shelton asked.

Young Curly rose with nervous haste.

'I'm afraid,' he said, 'there's nobody very interesting here to-night.'

'Oh, not at all!' said Shelton; 'on the contrary. Only I've had a rather tiring day, and somehow I don't feel up to the standard here.'

His new acquaintance smiled.

'Oh, really! do you think—that is——'

But he had not time to finish before the clack of bagatelle balls ceased, and the voice of the little deep-eyed man was heard saying: 'Anybody who wants a book will put his name down. There will be the usual prayer-meeting on Wednesday next. Will you all go quietly? I am going to turn the lights out.'

One gas-jet vanished, and the remaining jet flared suddenly. By its harder glare the wooden room looked harder too, and disenchanting. The figures of its occupants began filing through the door. The little man was left in the centre of the room, his deep eyes smouldering upon the backs of the retreating members, his thumb and finger raised to the turncock of the metre.

'Do you know this part?' asked young Curly as they emerged into the street. 'It's really jolly; one of the darkest bits in London —it is really. If you care, I can take you through an awfully dangerous place where the police never go.' He seemed so anxious for the honour that Shelton was loath to disappoint him. 'I come here pretty often,' he went on, as they ascended a sort of alley rambling darkly between a wall and row of houses.

'Why?' asked Shelton; 'it doesn't smell too nice.'

The young man threw up his nose and sniffed, as if eager to add any new scent that might be about to his knowledge of life.

'No, that's one of the reasons, you know,' he said; 'one must find out. The darkness is jolly, too; anything might happen here. Last week there was a murder; there's always the chance of one.'

Shelton stared; but the charge of morbidness would not lie against this fresh-cheeked stripling.

'There's a splendid drain just here,' his guide resumed; 'the people are dying like flies of typhoid in those three houses;' and, under the first light, he turned his grave, cherubic face to indicate the houses. 'If we were in the East End, I could show you other places quite as good. There's a coffee-stall keeper in one that knows all the thieves in London; he's a splendid type, but,' he added, looking a little anxiously at Shelton, 'it mightn't be safe for you. With me it's different; they're beginning to know me. I've nothing to take, you see.'

'I'm afraid it can't be to-night,' said Shelton; 'I must get back.'

'Do you mind if I walk with you? It's so jolly now the stars are out.'

'Delighted,' said Shelton; 'do you often go to that club?'

His companion raised his hat, and ran his fingers through his hair.

'They're rather too high-class for me,' he said. 'I like to go where you can see people eat—school treats, or somewhere in the country. It does one good to see them eat. They don't get enough you see, as a rule, to make bone; it's all used up for brain and muscle. There are some places in the winter where they give them bread and cocoa; I like to go to those.'

'I went once,' said Shelton, 'but I felt ashamed for putting my nose in.'

'Oh, they don't mind; most of them are half-dead with cold, you know. You see splendid types; lots of dipsomaniacs . . . It's useful to me,' he went on as they passed a police-station, 'to walk about at night; one can take so much more notice. I had a jolly night last week in Hyde Park; a chance to study human nature there.'

'And do you find it interesting?' asked Shelton.

His companion smiled.

'Awfully,' he replied; 'I saw a fellow pick three pockets.'

'What did you do?'

'I had a jolly talk with him.'

Shelton thought of the little deep-eyed man, who made a point of not encouraging sin.

'He was one of the professionals from Notting Hill, you know; told me his life. Never had a chance, of course. The most interesting part was telling him I'd seen him pick three pockets—like creeping into a cave, when you can't tell what's inside.'

'Well?'

'He showed me what he'd got—only fivepence-halfpenny.'

'And what became of your friend?' asked Shelton.

71

'Oh, went off; he had a splendidly low forehead.'

They had reached Shelton's rooms.

'Will you come in,' said the latter, 'and have a drink?'

The youth smiled, blushed, and shook his head.

'No, thank you,' he said; 'I have to walk to Whitechapel. I'm living on porridge now; splendid stuff for making bone. I generally live on porridge for a week at the end of every month. It's the best diet if you're hard up;' once more blushing and smiling, he was gone.

Shelton went upstairs and sat down on his bed. He felt a little miserable. Sitting there, slowly pulling out the ends of his white tie, disconsolate, he had a vision of Antonia with her gaze fixed wonderingly on him. And this wonder of hers came as a revelation —just as that morning when, looking from his window, he had seen a passer-by stop suddenly and scratch his leg; and it had come upon him in a flash that that man had thoughts and feelings of his own. He would never know what Antonia really felt and thought. 'Till I saw her at the station, I didn't know how much I loved her, or how little I knew her;' and sighing deeply, he hurried into bed.

Chapter 15

POLE TO POLE

THE waiting in London for July to come was daily more unbearable to Shelton, and if it had not been for Ferrand, who still came to breakfast, he would have deserted the metropolis. On June 1 the latter presented himself rather later than his custom, and announced that, through a friend, he had heard of a position as interpreter to an hotel at Folkestone.

'If I had money to face the first necessities,' he said, swiftly turning over a collection of smeared papers with his yellow fingers, as if searching for his own identity, 'I'd leave to-day. This London blackens my spirit.'

'Are you certain to get this place?' asked Shelton.

'I think so,' the young foreigner replied; 'I have some good recommendations.'

Shelton could not help a dubious glance at the papers in his hand. A hurt look passed on to Ferrand's curly lips beneath his

72

nascent red moustache.

'You mean that to have false papers is as bad as theft. No, no; I shall never be a thief—I've had too many opportunities,' said he, with pride and bitterness. 'That's not in my character. I never do harm to anyone. This'—he touched the papers—'is not delicate, but it does harm to no one. If you have no money you must have papers; they stand between you and starvation. Society has an excellent eye for the helpless; it never treads on people unless they're really down.' He looked at Shelton.

'You've made me what I am amongst you,' he seemed to say; 'now put up with me.' . . .

'But there are always the workhouses,' Shelton remarked at last.

'Workhouses!' returned Ferrand; 'certainly there are—regular palaces. I will tell you one thing; I've never been in places so discouraging as your workhouses; they take one's very heart out.'

'I always understood,' said Shelton coldly, 'that our system was better than that of other countries.'

Ferrand leaned over in his chair, an elbow on his knee, his favourite attitude when particularly certain of his point.

'Well,' he replied. 'it's always permissible to think well of your own country. But, frankly, I've come out of those places here with little strength and no heart at all, and I can tell you why.' His lips lost their bitterness, and he became an artist expressing the result of his experience. 'You spend your money freely, you have fine buildings, self-respecting officers, but—you lack the spirit of hospitality. The reason is plain; you have a horror of the needy. You invite us, and when we come you treat us justly enough, but as if we were numbers, criminals, beneath contempt —as if we had inflicted a personal injury on you; and when we get out again, we are naturally degraded.'

Shelton bit his lips.

'How much money will you want for your ticket, and to make a start?' he asked.

The nervous gesture escaping Ferrand at this juncture betrayed how far the most independent thinkers are dependent when they have no money in their pockets. He took the note that Shelton proffered him.

'A thousand thanks,' said he. 'I shall never forget what you have done for me;' and Shelton could not help feeling that there was true emotion behind his titter of farewell.

He stood at the window watching Ferrand start into the world

73

again; then looked back at his own comfortable room, with the number of things that had accumulated somehow—the photographs of countless friends, the old arm-chairs, the stock of coloured pipes. Into him restlessness had passed with the farewell clasp of the foreigner's damp hand. To wait about in London was unbearable.

He took his hat, and, heedless of direction, walked towards the river. It was a clear, bright day, with a bleak wind driving showers before it. During one of such Shelton found himself in Little Blank Street.

'I wonder how the little Frenchman that I saw is getting on!' he thought. On a fine day he would probably have passed by on the other side; he now entered and tapped upon the wicket.

No 3, Little Blank Street had abated nothing of its stone-flagged dreariness; the same blowsy woman answered his inquiry. Yes, Carolan was always in; you could never catch him out—seemed afraid to go into the street! To her call the little Frenchman made his appearance as punctually as if he had been the rabbit of a conjuror. His face was as yellow as a guinea.

'Ah! it's you, monsieur!' he said.

'Yes,' said Shelton; 'and how are you?'

'It's five days since I came out of hospital,' muttered the little Frenchman, tapping on his chest; 'a crisis of this bad atmosphere. I live here, shut up in a box; it does me harm, being from the South. If there's anything I can do for you, monsieur, it will give me pleasure.'

'Nothing,' replied Shelton. 'I was just passing, and thought I should like to hear how you were getting on.'

'Come into the kitchen, monsieur; there is nobody in there. *Brrr! Il fait un froid étonnant!*'

'What sort of customers have you just now?' asked Shelton, as they passed into the kitchen.

'Always the same clientèle,' replied the little man, 'not so numerous, of course, it being summer.'

'Couldn't you find anything better than this to do?'

The barber's crow-feet radiated irony.

'When I first came to London,' said he, 'I secured an engagement at one of your public Institutions. I thought my fortune made. Imagine, monsieur, in that sacred place I was obliged to shave at the rate of ten a penny! Here, it's true, they don't pay me half the time; but when I'm paid, I'm paid. In this climate, and being *poitrinaire*, one doesn't make experiments. I shall finish my

74

days here. Have you seen that young man who interested you? There's another! He has spirit, as I had once—*il fait de la philosophie*, as I do—and you will see, monsieur, it will finish him. In this world what you want is to have no spirit. Spirit ruins you.'

Shelton looked sideways at the little man with his sardonic, yellow, half-dead face, and the incongruity of the word 'spirit' in his mouth struck him so sharply that he smiled a smile with more pity in it than any burst of tears.

'Shall we sit down?' he said, offering a cigarette.

'*Merci, monsieur*, it is always a pleasure to smoke a good cigarette. You remember that old actor who gave you a Jeremiad? Well, he's dead. I was the only one at his bedside; a funny fellow. He was another who had spirit. And you will see, monsieur, that young man in whom you take an interest, he'll die in a hospital, or in some hole or other, or even on the highroad, having closed his eyes once too often some cold night; and all because he has something in him which will not accept things as they are, believing always that they should be better. *Il n'y a rien de plus tragique!*'

'According to you, then,' said Shelton, and the conversation seemed to him of a sudden to have taken too personal a turn, 'rebellion of any sort is fatal.'

'Ah!' replied the little man, with the eagerness of one whose ideal it is to sit under the awning of a café and talk life upside down, 'you pose me a great problem there! If one makes rebellion, it is always probable that one will do no good to anyone and harm one's self. The law of the majority arranges that. But I would draw your attention to this'—and he paused, as if it were a real discovery, to blow smoke through his nose—'if you rebel, it is in all likelihood because you are forced by your nature to rebel; this is one of the most certain things in life. In any case, it is necessary to avoid falling between two stools—which is unpardonable,' he ended, with complacence.

Shelton thought he had never seen a man who looked more completely as if he had fallen between two stools, and he had inspiration enough to feel that the little barber's intellectual rebellion and the action logically required by it had no more than a bowing acquaintanceship.

'By nature,' went on the little man, 'I am an optimist; it is in consequence of this that I now make pessimism. I have always had ideals. Seeing myself cut off from them for ever, I must complain. To complain, monsieur, is very sweet!'

Shelton wondered what these ideals had been, but had no answer ready; so he nodded, and again held out his cigarettes, for, like a true Southerner, the little man had thrown the first away, half smoked.

'The greatest pleasure in life,' continued the Frenchman, with a bow, 'is to talk a little to a being who is capable of understanding you. At present we have no one here now that that old actor's dead. Ah! *there* was a man who was rebellion incarnate! He made rebellion as other men make money, *c'était son métier*; when he was no longer capable of active revolution, he made it getting drunk. At the last this was his only way of protesting against Society. An interesting personality, *je le regrette beaucoup*. But, as you see, he died in great distress, without a soul to wave him farewell, because as you can well understand, monsieur, I don't count myself. He died drunk. *C'était un homme!*'

Shelton had continued staring kindly at the little man; the barber added hastily:

'It's difficult to make an end like that—one has moments of weakness.'

'Yes,' assented Shelton, 'one has indeed.'

The little barber looked at him with cynical discretion.

'Oh!' he said, 'it is to the destitute that such things are important. When one has money, all these matters——'

He shrugged his shoulders. A smile had lodged amongst his crow's-feet; he waved his hand as though to end the subject.

A sense of having been exposed came over Shelton.

'You think, then,' said he, 'that discontent is peculiar to the destitute?'

'Monsieur,' replied the little barber, 'a plutocrat knows too well that if he mixes in that *galère* there's not a dog in the streets more lost than he.'

Shelton rose.

'The rain is over. I hope you'll soon be better; perhaps you'll accept this in memory of that old actor,' and he slipped a sovereign into the little Frenchman's hand.

The latter bowed.

'Whenever you are passing, monsieur,' he said eagerly, 'I shall be charmed to see you.'

And Shelton walked away. '"Not a dog in the streets more lost,"' thought he; 'now what did he mean by that?'

Something of that 'lost dog' feeling had gripped his spirit. Another month of waiting would kill all the savour of anticipation, might even kill his love. In the excitement of his senses and his nerves, caused by this strain of waiting, everything seemed too vivid; all was beyond life size; like Art—whose truths, too strong for daily use, are thus unpopular with healthy people. As the bones will in a worn face, the spirit underlying things had reached the surface; the meanness and intolerable measure of hard facts were too apparent. Some craving for help, some instinct, drove him into Kensington, for he found himself before his mother's house. Providence seemed bent on flinging him from pole to pole.

Mrs Shelton was in town, and though it was the first of June, sat warming her feet before a fire; her face, with its pleasant colour, was crow's-footed like the little barber's, but from optimism, not rebellion. She smiled when she saw her son, and the wrinkles round her eyes twinkled with vitality.

'Well, my dear boy!' she said, 'it's lovely to see you. And how is that sweet girl?'

'Very well, thank you,' replied Shelton.

'She must be *such* a dear!'

'Mother,' stammered Shelton, 'I must give it up.'

'Give it up? My dear Dick, give what up? You look quite worried. Come and sit down, and have a cosy chat. Cheer up!' and Mrs Shelton, with her head askew, gazed at her son quite irrepressibly.

'Mother,' said Shelton, who, confronted by her optimism, had never, since his time of trial began, felt so wretchedly dejected, 'I can't go on waiting about like this.'

'My dear boy, what *is* the matter?'

'Everything is wrong!'

'Wrong?' cried Mrs Shelton. 'Come, tell me all about it!'

But Shelton shook his head.

'You surely haven't had a quarrel——'

Mrs Shelton stopped; the question seemed so vulgar—one might have asked it of a groom.

'No,' said Shelton, and his answer sounded like a groan.

'You know, my dear old Dick,' murmured his mother, 'it seems a little mad.'

'I know it seems mad.'

'Come!' said Mrs Shelton, taking his hand between her own; 'you never used to be like this.'

'No,' said Shelton, with a laugh; 'I never used to be like this.'

Mrs Shelton snuggled in her Chudda shawl.

77

'Oh,' she said, with cheery sympathy, 'I know exactly how you feel!'

Shelton, holding his head, stared at the fire, which played and bubbled like his mother's face.

'But you're so fond of each other,' she began again. 'Such a sweet girl!'

'You don't understand,' muttered Shelton gloomily; 'it's not she —it's nothing—it's—myself!'

Mrs Shelton again seized his hand, and this time pressed it to her soft, warm cheek, which had lost the elasticity of youth.

'Oh!' she cried again; 'I understand. I know exactly what you're feeling.' But Shelton saw from the fixed beam in her eyes that she had not an inkling. To do him justice, he was not so foolish as to try to give her one. Mrs Shelton sighed. 'It would be so lovely if you could wake up to-morrow and think differently. If I were you, my dear, I would have a good long walk, and then a Turkish bath; and then I would just write to her, and tell her all about it, and you'll see how beautifully it'll all come straight;' and in the enthusiasm of advice Mrs Shelton rose, and, with a faint stretch of her tiny figure, still so young, clasped her hands together. 'Now *do*, that's a dear old Dick! You'll just see how lovely it'll be!' Shelton smiled; he had not the heart to chase away this vision. 'And give her my warmest love, and tell her I'm longing for the wedding. Come, now, my dear boy, promise me that's what you'll do.'

And Shelton said: 'I'll think about it.'

Mrs Shelton had taken up her stand with one foot on the fender, in spite of her sciatica.

'Cheer up!' she cried; her eyes beamed as if intoxicated by her sympathy.

Wonderful woman! The uncomplicated optimism which carried her through good and ill had not descended to her son.

From pole to pole he had been thrown that day, from the French barber, whose intellect accepted nothing without carping, and whose little fingers worked all day to save himself from dying out, to his own mother, whose intellect accepted anything presented with sufficient glow, but who, until she died, would never stir a finger. When Shelton reached his rooms, he wrote to Antonia:

'I can't wait about in London any longer; I am going down to Bideford to start a walking tour. I shall work my way to Oxford,

78

and stay there till I may come to Holm Oaks. I shall send you my address; *do* write as usual.'

He collected all the photographs he had of her—amateur groups, taken by Mrs Dennant—and packed them in the pocket of his shooting-jacket. There was one where she was standing just below her little brother, who was perched upon a wall. In her half-closed eyes, round throat, and softly tilted chin, there was something cool and watchful, protecting the ragamuffin up above her head. This he kept apart to be looked at daily, as a man says his prayers.

Part Two

THE COUNTRY

Chapter 16

THE INDIAN CIVILIAN

ONE morning, then, a week later, Shelton found himself looking at the walls of Princetown Prison.

He had seen this lugubrious stone cage before. But the magic of his morning walk across the moor, the sight of the pagan tors, the songs of the last cuckoo, had unprepared him for that dreary building. He left the street, and, entering the fosse, began a circuit, scanning the walls with morbid fascination.

This, then, was the system by which men enforced the will of the majority, and it was suddenly borne in on him that all the ideas and maxims which his Christian countrymen believed themselves to be fulfilling daily were stultified in every cellule of the social honeycomb. Such teachings as 'He that is without sin amongst you,' had been pronounced unpractical by peers and judges, bishops, statesmen, merchants, husbands—in fact, by every truly Christian person in the country.

'Yes,' thought Shelton, as if he had found out something new, 'the more Christian the nation, the less it has to do with the Christian spirit.'

Society was a charitable organisation, giving nothing for nothing, little for sixpence; and it was only fear which forced it to give at all!

He took a seat on a wall, and began to watch a warder who was slowly paring a last year's apple. The expression of his face, the way he stood with his solid legs apart, his head poked forward, and his lower jaw thrust out, all made him a perfect pillar of Society. He was undisturbed by Shelton's scrutiny, watching the rind coil down the apple, until in a springing spiral it fell on the path and collapsed like a toy snake. He took a bite; his teeth were jagged, and his mouth immense. It was obvious that he considered himself a most superior man. Shelton frowned, got down slowly from the wall, and proceeded on his way.

A little further down the hill he stopped again to watch a group of convicts in a field. They seemed to be dancing in a slow and sad cotillon, while behind the hedge on every side were warders armed with guns. Just such a sight, substituting spears, could have been seen in Roman times.

While he thus stood looking, a man, walking rapidly, stopped beside him, and asked how many miles it was to Exeter. His round visage, and long, brown eyes, sliding about beneath their brows, his cropped hair and short neck, seemed familiar.

'Your name is Crocker, isn't it?'

'Why, it's the Bird!' exclaimed the traveller, putting out his hand. 'Haven't seen you since we both went down.'

Shelton returned his hand-grip. Crocker had lived above his head at college, and often kept him sleepless half the night by playing on the hautboy.

'Where have you sprung from?'

'India. Got my long leave. I say, are you going this way? Let's go together.'

They went, and very fast; faster and faster every minute.

'Where are you going at this pace?' asked Shelton.

'London.'

'Oh! only as far as London?'

'I've set myself to do it in a week.'

'Are you in training?'

'No.'

'You'll kill yourself.'

Crocker answered with a chuckle.

Shelton noted with alarm the expression of his eye; there was a sort of stubborn aspiration in it. 'Still an idealist!' he thought; 'poor fellow!' 'Well,' he inquired, 'what sort of a time have you had in India?'

'Oh,' said the Indian civilian absently, 'I've had the plague.'

'Good God!'

Crocker smiled, and added:

'Caught it on famine duty.'

'I see,' said Shelton; 'plague and famine! I suppose you fellows really think you're doing good out there?'

His companion looked at him surprised, then answered modestly:

'We get very good screws.'

'That's the great thing,' responded Shelton.

After a moment's silence, Crocker, looking straight before him, asked:

'Don't you think we *are* doing good?'

'I'm not an authority; but, as a matter of fact, I don't.'

Crocker seemed disconcerted.

'Why?'

Shelton was not anxious to explain his views, and he did not reply.

His friend repeated:

'Why don't you think we're doing good in India?'

'Well,' said Shelton gruffly, 'how can progress be imposed on nations from outside?'

The Indian civilian, glancing at Shelton in an affectionate and doubtful way, replied:

'You haven't changed a bit, old chap.'

'No, no,' said Shelton; 'you're not going to get out of it that way. Give me a single example of a nation, or an individual, for that matter, who's ever done any good without having worked up to it from within.'

Crocker grunted.

Shelton went on: 'We take peoples entirely different from our own, and stop their natural development by substituting a civilisation grown for our own use. Suppose, looking at a tropical fern in a hothouse, you were to say: "This heat's unhealthy for me; therefore it must be bad for the fern. I'll take it up and plant it outside in the fresh air."'

'Do you know that means giving up India?' said the Indian civilian shrewdly.

'I don't say that; but to talk about doing *good* to India is—h'm!'

Crocker knitted his brows, trying to see the point of view his friend was showing him.

'Come, now! Should we go on administering India if it were dead loss? No. Well, to talk about administering the country for the purpose of pocketing money is cynical, and there's generally some truth in cynicism; but to talk about the administration of a country by which we profit, as if it were a great and good thing, is cant. I hit you in the wind for the benefit of myself—all right: law of Nature; but to say it does you good at the same time is beyond me.'

'But suppose it does,' returned Crocker, grave and anxious.

'Wait a bit. It's all a question of horizons; you look at it from too close. Put the horizon further back. You hit India in the wind, and say it's virtuous. Well, now let's see what happens. Either the wind never comes back, and India gasps to an untimely death, or the wind does come back, and in the pant of reaction your blow

—that's to say your labour—is lost, morally lost—labour that you might have spent where it wouldn't have been lost.'

'Aren't you an Imperialist?' asked Crocker, genuinely concerned.

'I may be, but I keep my mouth shut about the benefits we're conferring upon other people.'

'Then you can't believe in abstract right, or justice?'

'What on earth have *our* ideas of justice or right got to do with India?'

'If I thought as you do,' sighed the unhappy Crocker, 'I should be all adrift.'

'Quite so. We always think our standards best for the whole world. It's a capital belief for us. Read the speeches of our public men. Doesn't it strike you as amazing how sure they are of being in the right? It's so charming to benefit yourself and others at the same time, though, when you come to think of it, one man's meat is usually another's poison. Look at Nature. But in England we never look at Nature—there's no necessity. Our national point of view has filled our pockets, that's all that matters.'

'I say, old chap, that's awfully bitter,' said Crocker with a sort of wondering sadness.

'It's enough to make anyone bitter the way we Pharisees wax fat, and at the same time give ourselves the moral airs of a balloon. I must stick a pin in sometimes, just to hear the gas escape.' Shelton was surprised at his own heat, and for some strange reason thought of Antonia—surely she was not a Pharisee!

His companion strode along, and Shelton felt sorry for the signs of trouble on his face.

'To fill your pockets,' said Crocker, 'isn't the main thing. One has just got to do things without thinking of why we do them.'

'Do you ever see the other side of any question?' asked Shelton. 'I suppose not. You always begin to act before you stop thinking, don't you?'

Crocker grinned.

'He's a Pharisee, too,' thought Shelton, 'without a Pharisee's pride. Queer thing that!'

After walking some distance, as if thinking deeply, Crocker chuckled out:

'You're not consistent; you ought to be in favour of giving up India.'

Shelton smiled uneasily.

'Why shouldn't we fill our pockets? I only object to the humbug that we *talk*.'

The Indian civilian put his hand shyly through his arm.

'If I thought like you,' he said, 'I couldn't stay another day in India.'

And to this Shelton made no reply.

The wind had now begun to drop, and something of the morning's magic was stealing again upon the moor. They were nearing the outskirt fields of cultivation. It was past five when, dropping from the level of the tors, they came into the sunny vale of Monkland.

'They say,' said Crocker, reading from his guide book—'they say this place occupies a position of unique isolation.'

The two travellers, in tranquil solitude, took their seats under an old lime-tree on the village green. The smoke of their pipes, the sleepy air, the warmth from the baked ground, the constant hum, made Shelton drowsy.

'Do you remember,' his companion asked, 'those "jaws" you used to have with Busgate and old Halidome in my rooms on Sunday evenings? How is old Halidome?'

'Married,' replied Shelton.

Crocker sighed. 'And are *you*?' he asked.

'Not yet,' said Shelton grimly; 'I'm—engaged.'

Crocker took hold of his arm above the elbow, and, squeezing it, he grunted. Shelton had not received congratulations that pleased him more; there was the spice of envy in them.

'I should like to get married while I'm home,' said the Indian civilian after a long pause. His legs were stretched apart, throwing shadows on the green, his hands deep thrust into his pockets, his head a little to one side. An absent-minded smile played round his mouth.

The sun had sunk behind a tor, but the warmth kept rising from the ground, and the sweet-briar on a cottage bathed them with its spicy perfume. From the converging lanes figures passed now and then, lounged by, staring at the strangers, gossiping amongst themselves, and vanished into the cottages that headed the incline. A clock struck seven, and round the shady lime tree a chafer or some heavy insect commenced its booming rushes. All was marvellously sane and slumbrous. The soft air, the drawling voices, the shapes, and murmurs, the rising smell of woodsmoke from fresh kindled fires—were full of the spirit of security and of home. The outside world was far indeed. Typical of some island nation was this nest of refuge—where men grew quietly tall, fattened and without fuss dropped off their perches; where contentment flourished, as sunflowers flourish in the sun.

Crocker's cap slipped off; he was nodding, and Shelton looked at him. From a manor house in some such village he had issued; to one of a thousand such homes he would find his way at last, untouched by the struggles with famines or with plagues, uninfected in his fibre, his prejudices, and his principles, unchanged by contact with strange peoples, new conditions, odd feelings, or queer points of view!

The chafer buzzed against his shoulder, gathered flight again, and boomed away. Crocker roused himself, and, turning his amiable face, jogged Shelton's arm.

'What are you thinking about, Bird?' he asked.

Chapter 17

A PARSON

SHELTON continued to travel with his college friend and on Wednesday night, four days after joining company, they reached the village of Dowdenhame. All day long the road had lain through pastureland, with thick green hedges and heavily feathered elms. Once or twice they had broken the monotony by a stretch along the towing-path of a canal, which, choked with water-lily plants and shining weeds, brooded sluggishly beside the fields. Nature, in one of her ironic moods, had cast a grey and iron-hard cloak over all the country's bland luxuriance. From dawn till darkness fell there had been no movement in the steely distant sky; a cold wind ruffled in the hedge-tops, and sent shivers through the branches of the elms. The cattle, dappled, pied, or bay, or white, continued grazing with an air of grumbling at their birthright. In a meadow close to the canal Shelton saw five magpies, and about five o'clock the rain began, a steady, cold-sneering rain, which Crocker, looking at the sky, declared was going to be over in a minute. But it was *not* over in a minute; they were soon drenched. Shelton was tired, and it annoyed him very much that his companion, who was also tired, should grow more cheerful. His thoughts kept harping upon Ferrand: 'This must be something like what he described to me, tramping on and on when you're dead-beat, until you can cadge up supper and a bed.' And sulkily he kept on ploughing through the mud with glances at the exasperating Crocker, who had skinned one heel and was limping horribly. It suddenly came home to him that life for three-quarters of the world meant physical exhaustion every day, without a possibility of alternative, and that as soon as for some cause beyond control, they failed thus to exhaust themselves, they were reduced to beg or starve. 'And then we, who don't know the meaning of the word exhaustion, call them "idle scamps,"' he said aloud.

It was past nine and dark when they reached Dowdenhame. The street yielded no accommodation, and while debating where to go they passed the church, with a square tower, and next to it a house which was certainly the parsonage.

'Suppose,' said Crocker, leaning his arms upon the gate, 'we ask him where to go;' and without waiting for Shelton's answer, he rang the bell.

The door was opened by the parson, a bloodless and clean-shaven man, whose hollow cheeks and bony hands suggested a perpetual struggle. Ascetically benevolent were his grey eyes; a pale and ghostly smile played on the curves of his thin lips.

'What can I do for you?' he asked. 'Inn? Yes, there's the Blue Chequers, but I'm afraid you'll find it shut. They're early people, I'm glad to say;' and his eyes seemed to muse over the proper fold for these damp sheep. 'Are you Oxford men, by any chance?' he asked, as if that might throw some light upon the matter. 'Of Mary's? Really! I'm of Paul's myself. Ladyman—Billington Ladyman; you might remember my youngest brother. I could give you a room here if you could manage without sheets. My house-keeper has two days' holiday; she's foolishly taken the keys.'

Shelton accepted gladly, feeling that the intonation in the parson's voice was necessary unto his calling, and that he did not want to patronise.

'You're hungry, I expect, after your tramp. I'm very much afraid there's—er—nothing in the house but bread. I could boil you water; hot lemonade is better than nothing.'

Conducting them into the kitchen, he made a fire, and put a kettle on to boil; then, after leaving them to shed their soaking clothes, returned with ancient, greenish coats, some carpet slippers, and some blankets. Wrapped in these, and carrying their glasses, the travellers followed to the study, where, by doubtful lamplight, he seemed, from the books upon the table, to have been working at his sermon.

'We're giving you a lot of trouble,' said Shelton; 'it's really very good of you.'

89

'Not at all,' the parson answered; 'I'm only grieved the house is empty.'

It was a truly dismal contrast to the fatness of the land they had been passing through, and the parson's voice issuing from bloodless lips, although complacent, was pathetic. It was peculiar, that voice of his, seeming to indicate an intimate acquaintance-ship with what was fat and fine, to convey contempt for the vulgar need of money, while all the time his eyes—those watery, ascetic eyes—as plain as speech they said:

'Oh, to know what it must be like to have a pound or two to spare just once a year, or so!'

Everything in the room had been bought for cheapness; no luxuries were there, and necessaries not enough. It was bleak and bare; the ceiling cracked, the wall-paper discoloured, and those books—prim, shining books, fat-backed, with arms stamped on them——glared in the surrounding barrenness.

'My predecessor,' said the parson, 'played rather havoc with the house. The poor fellow had a dreadful struggle, I was told. You can, unfortunately, expect nothing else these days, when livings have come down so terribly in value! He was a married man—large family!'

Crocker, who had drunk his steaming lemonade, was smiling and already nodding in his chair; with his black garment buttoned closely round his throat, his long legs rolled up in a blanket, and stretched towards the feeble flame of the newly-lighted fire, he had a rather patchy air. Shelton, on the other hand, had lost his feeling of fatigue; the strangeness of the place was stimulating to his brain; he kept stealing glances at the scantiness around; the room, the parson, the furniture, the very fire, all gave him the feeling caused by seeing legs that have outgrown their trousers. But there was something underlying that leanness of the landscape, some-thing superior and academic, which defied all sympathy. It was pure nervousness which made him say:

'Ah! why *do* they have such families?'

A faint red mounted to the parson's cheeks, its appearance there was startling, and Crocker chuckled, as a sleepy man will chuckle who feels bound to show that he is not asleep.

'It's very unfortunate,' murmured the parson, 'certainly, in many cases.'

Shelton would now have changed the subject, but at this moment the unhappy Crocker snored. Being a man of action, he had gone to sleep.

'It seems to me,' said Shelton hurriedly as he saw the parson's eyebrows rising at the sound, 'almost what you might call wrong.'

'Dear me! but how can it be wrong?'

Shelton now felt that he must justify his saying somehow.

'I don't know,' he said, 'only one hears of such a lot of cases—clergymen's families; I've two uncles of my own, who——'

A new expression gathered on the parson's face; his mouth had tightened, and his chin receded slightly. 'Why, he's like a mule!' thought Shelton. His eyes, too, had grown harder, greyer, and more parroty. Shelton no longer liked his face.

'Perhaps you and I,' the parson said, 'would not understand each other on such matters.'

And Shelton felt ashamed.

'I should like to ask you a question in turn, however,' the parson said, as if desirous of meeting Shelton on his low ground : 'How do you justify marriage if it is not to follow the laws of nature?'

'I can only tell you what I personally feel.'

'My dear sir, you forget that a woman's chief delight is in her motherhood.'

'I should have thought it a pleasure likely to pall with too much repetition. Motherhood is motherhood, whether of one or of a dozen.'

'I'm afraid,' replied the parson, with impatience, though still keeping on his guest's low ground, 'your theories are not calculated to populate the world.'

'Have you ever lived in London?' Shelton asked. 'It always makes me feel a doubt whether we have any right to have children at all.'

'Surely,' said the parson with wonderful restraint, and the joints of his fingers cracked with the grip he had upon his chair, 'you are leaving out duty towards the country; national growth is paramount!'

'There are two ways of looking at that. It depends on what you want your country to become.'

'I didn't know,' said the parson—fanaticism now had crept into his smile—'there could be any doubt on such a subject.'

The more Shelton felt that commands were being given him, the more controversial he naturally became—apart from the merits of this subject, to which he had hardly ever given thought.

'I dare say I'm wrong,' he said, fastening his eyes on the blanket in which his legs were wrapped; 'but it seems to me at least an open question whether it's better for the country to be so well populated as to be quite incapable of supporting itself.'

'Surely,' said the parson, whose face regained its pallor, 'you're not a little Englander?'

On Shelton this phrase had a mysterious effect. Resisting an impulse to discover what he really was, he answered hastily:

'Of course I'm not!'

The parson followed up his triumph, and shifting the ground of the discussion from Shelton's to his own, he gravely said:

'Surely you must see that your theory is founded in immorality. It is, if I may say so, extravagant, even wicked.'

But Shelton, suffering from irritation at his own dishonesty, replied with heat:

'Why not say at once, sir, "hysterical, unhealthy"? Any opinion which goes contrary to that of the majority is always called so, I believe.'

'Well,' returned the parson, whose eyes seemed trying to bind Shelton to his will, 'I must say your ideas *do* seem to me both extravagant and unhealthy. The propagation of children is enjoined of marriage.'

Shelton bowed above his blanket, but the parson did not smile.

'We live in very dangerous times,' he said, 'and it grieves me when a man of your standing panders to these notions.'

'Those,' said Shelton, 'whom the shoe doesn't pinch make this rule of morality, and thrust it on to such as the shoe does pinch.'

'The rule was never *made*,' said the parson; 'it was given us.'

'Oh!' said Shelton, 'I beg your pardon.' He was in danger of forgetting the delicate position he was in. 'He wants to ram his notions down my throat,' he thought; and it seemed to him that the parson's face had grown more like a mule's, his accent more superior, his eyes more dictatorial. To be right in this argument seemed now of great importance, whereas, in truth, it was of no importance whatsoever. That which, however, was important was the fact that in nothing could they ever have agreed.

But Crocker suddenly had ceased to snore; his head had fallen so that a peculiar whistling arose instead. Both Shelton and the parson looked at him, and the sight sobered them.

'Your friend seems very tired,' said the parson.

Shelton forgot all his annoyance, for his host seemed suddenly pathetic, with those baggy garments, hollow cheeks and the slightly reddened nose that comes from not imbibing quite enough.

A kind fellow, after all!

The kind fellow rose, and putting his hands behind his back, placed himself before the blackening fire. Whole centuries of authority stood behind him. It was an accident that the mantelpiece was chipped and rusty, the fire-irons bent and worn, his linen frayed about the cuffs.

'I don't wish to dictate,' said he, 'but where it seems to me that you are wholly wrong is, that your ideas foster in women those lax views of family life that are so prevalent in Society nowadays.'

Thoughts of Antonia with her candid eyes, the touch of freckling on her pink-white skin, the fair hair gathered back, sprang up in Shelton, and that word 'lax' seemed ridiculous. And the women he was wont to see dragging about the streets of London with two or three small children, women bent beneath the weight of babies that they could not leave, women going to work with babies still unborn, anæmic-looking women, impecunious mothers in his own class, with twelve or fourteen children, all the victims of the sanctity of marriage, and again the word 'lax' seemed to be ridiculous.

'We are not put into the world to exercise our——'

'Wits?' muttered Shelton.

'Our wanton wills,' the parson said severely.

'That may have been all right for the last generation, sir; the country is more crowded now. I can't see why we shouldn't decide it for ourselves.'

'Such a view of morality,' said the parson, looking down at Crocker with a ghostly smile, 'to me is unintelligible.'

Crocker's whistling grew in tone and in variety.

'What I hate,' said Shelton, 'is the way we men decide what women are to bear, and then call them immoral, decadent, or what you will, if they don't fall in with our views.'

'Mr Shelton,' said the parson, 'I think we may safely leave it in the hands of God.'

Shelton was silent.

'The questions of morality,' said the parson promptly, 'have always lain through God in the hands of men, not women. We are the reasonable sex.'

Shelton stubbornly replied:

'We're certainly the greater humbugs, if that's the same.'

'This is too bad,' exclaimed the parson with some heat.

'I'm sorry, sir; but how can you expect women nowadays to have the same views as our grandmothers? We men, by our

93

commercial enterprise, have brought about a different state of things; yet, for the sake of our own comfort, we try to keep women where they were. It's always those men who are most keen about their comfort'—and in his heat the sarcasm of using the word 'comfort' in that room was lost on him—'who are so ready to accuse women of deserting the old morality.'

The parson quivered with impatient irony.

'Old morality! new morality!' he said. 'These are strange words.'

'Forgive me,' explained Shelton; 'we're talking of working morality, I imagine. There's not a man in a million fit to talk of true morality.'

The eyes of his host contracted.

'I think,' he said—and his voice sounded as if he had pinched it in the endeavour to impress his listener—'that any well-educated man who honestly tries to serve his God has the right humbly—I say humbly—to claim morality.'

Shelton was on the point of saying something bitter, but checked himself. 'Here am I,' thought he, 'trying to get the last word, like an old woman.'

At this moment there was heard a piteous mewing; the parson went towards the door.

'Excuse me a moment; I'm afraid that's one of my cats out in the wet.' He returned a minute later with a wet cat in his arms. 'They will get out,' he said to Shelton, with a smile on his thin face, suffused by stooping. And absently he stroked the dripping cat, while a drop of wet ran off his nose. 'Poor pussy, poor pussy!' The sound of that 'Poor pussy!' like nothing human in its cracked superiority, the softness of that smile, like the smile of gentleness itself, haunted Shelton till he fell asleep.

Chapter 18

ACADEMIC

THE last sunlight was playing on the roofs when the travellers entered that High Street grave and holy to all Oxford men. The spirit hovering above the spires was as different from its concretions in their caps and gowns as ever the spirit of Christ was from Church dogmas.

'Shall we go into Grinnings'?' asked Shelton, as they were passing the club.

But each looked at his clothes, for two elegant young men in flannel suits were coming out.

'You go,' said Crocker, with a smirk.

Shelton shook his head. Never before had he felt such love for this old city. It was gone now from out his life, but everything about it seemed so good and fine; even its exclusive air was not ignoble. Clothed in the calm of history, the golden web of glorious tradition, radiant with the alchemy of memories, it bewitched him like the perfume of a woman's dress. At the entrance of a college they glanced in at the cool grey patch of stone beyond, and the scarlet of a window flower-box—secluded, mysteriously calm—a narrow vision of the sacred past. Pale and trencher-capped, a youth with pimply face and random nose, grabbing at his sloven gown, was gazing at the notice-board. The college porter—large man, fresh-faced, small-mouthed—stood at his lodge door in a frank and deferential attitude. An image of routine, he looked like one engaged to give a decorous air to multitudes of peccadilloes. His blue eyes rested on the travellers. 'I don't know you, sirs, but if you want to speak I shall be glad to hear the observations you may have to make,' they seemed to say.

Against the wall reposed a bicycle with tennis-racquet buckled to its handle. A bull-dog bitch, working her snout from side to side, was snuffling horribly; the great iron-studded door to which her chain was fastened stayed immovable. Through this narrow mouth, human metal had been poured for centuries—poured, moulded, given back.

'Come along,' said Shelton.

They now entered the Bishop's Head, and had their dinner in the room where Shelton had given his Derby dinner to four-and-twenty well-bred youths; here was the picture of the racehorse that the wineglass, thrown by one of them, had missed when it hit the waiter; and there, serving Crocker with anchovy sauce, was the very waiter. When they had finished, Shelton felt the old desire to rise with difficulty from the table; the old longing to patrol the streets with arm hooked in some other arm; the old eagerness to dare and do something heroic and unlawful; the old sense that he was of the finest set, in the finest college, of the finest country in the finest world. The streets, all grave and mellow in the sunset, seemed to applaud this after-dinner stroll; the entrance quad of his old college—spaciously majestic, monastically modern, for years the heart of his universe, the focus of what had gone before it in his life, casting the shadow of its grey walls over all that had come after—brought him a sense of rest from conflict, and trust in his own important safety. The garden-gate, whose lofty spikes he had so often crowned with empty soda-water bottles, failed to rouse him. Nor when they passed the staircase where he had flung a leg of lamb at some indelicate disturbing tutor, did he feel remorse. High on that staircase were the rooms in which he had crammed for his degree, upon the system by which the scholar simmers on the fire of cramming, boils over at the moment of examination, and is extinct for ever after . . . His coach's face recurred to him, a man with thrusting eyes, who reeled off knowledge all the week, and disappeared to town on Sundays.

They passed their tutor's staircase.

'I wonder if little Turl would remember us?' said Crocker; 'I should like to see him. Shall we go and look him up?'

'Little Turl?' said Shelton dreamily.

Mounting, they knocked upon a solid door.

'Come in,' said the voice of Sleep itself.

A little man, with a pink face and large red ears, was sitting in a fat pink chair, as if he had been grown there.

'What do you want?' he asked them, blinking.

'Don't you know me, sir?'

'God bless me! Crocker, isn't it? I didn't recognise you with a beard.'

Crocker, who had not been shaved since starting on his travels, chuckled feebly.

'You remember Shelton, sir?' he said.

'Shelton? Oh yes! How do you do, Shelton? Sit down; take a cigar;' and, crossing his fat little legs, the little gentleman looked them up and down with drowsy interest, as who should say: 'Now, after all you know, why come and wake me up like this?'

Shelton and Crocker took two other chairs; they, too, seemed thinking: 'Yes, why *did* we come and wake him up like this?' And Shelton, who could not tell the reason why, took refuge in the smoke of his cigar. The panelled walls were hung with prints of celebrated Greek remains; the soft, thick carpet was grateful to his tired feet; the backs of many books gleamed richly in the light of the oil lamps; the culture and tobacco smoke stole on his senses; he but vaguely comprehended Crocker's amiable talk, vaguely the answers of his little host whose face, blinking behind

96

the bowl of his huge meerschaum pipe, had such a queer resemblance to a moon. The door was opened, and a tall creature, whose eyes were large and brown, whose face was rosy and ironical, entered with a manly stride.

'Oh!' he said, looking round him with his chin a little in the air, 'am I intruding, Turl?'

The little host, blinking more than ever, murmured:

'Not at all, Berryman—take a pew!'

The visitor called Berryman sat down, and gazed up at the wall with his fine eyes.

Shelton had a faint remembrance of this don, and bowed; but the newcomer sat smiling, and did not notice the salute.

'Trimmer and Washer are coming round,' he said, and as he spoke the door opened to admit these gentlemen. Of the same height, but different appearance, their manner was faintly jocular, faintly supercilious, as if they tolerated everything. The one whose name was Trimmer had patches of red on his large cheekbones, and on his cheeks a bluish tint. His lips were rather full, so that he had a likeness to a spider. Washer, who was thin and pale, wore an intellectual smile.

The little host moved the hand that held the meerschaum.

'Crocker, Shelton,' he said.

An awkward silence followed. Shelton tried to rouse the cultured portion of his wits; but the sense that nothing would be treated seriously paralysed his faculties; he stayed silent, staring at the glowing tip of his cigar. It seemed to him unfair to have intruded on these gentlemen without its having been made quite clear to them beforehand who and what he was; he rose to take his leave, but Washer had begun to speak.

'"Madame Bovary"!' he said quizzically, reading the title of the book on the little fat man's book-rest; and, holding it closer to his boiled-looking eyes, he repeated, as though it were a joke: '"Madame Bovary"!'

'Do you mean to say, Turl, that you can stand that stuff?' said Berryman. As might have been expected, this celebrated novel's name had galvanised him into life; he strolled over to the book-case, took down a book, opened it, and began to read, wandering, in a desultory way, about the room.

'Ha! Berryman,' said a conciliatory voice behind—it came from Trimmer, who had set his back against the hearth, and grasped with either hand a fist-full of his gown—'the book's a classic!'

'Classic!' exclaimed Berryman, transfixing Shelton with his eyes; 'the fellow ought to have been horse-whipped for writing such putridity!'

A feeling of hostility instantly sprang up in Shelton; he looked at his little host, who, however, merely blinked.

'Berryman only means,' explained Washer, a certain malice in his smile, 'that the author isn't one of his particular pets.'

'For God's sake, you know, don't get Berryman on his horse!' growled the little fat man suddenly.

Berryman returned his volume to the shelf and took another down. There was something almost godlike in his sarcastic absent-mindedness.

'Imagine a man writing that stuff,' he said, 'if he'd ever been at Eton! What do we want to know about that sort of thing? A writer should be a sportsman and a gentleman;' and again he looked down over his chin at Shelton, as though expecting him to controvert the sentiment.

'Don't you——' began the latter.

But Berryman's attention had wandered to the wall.

'I really don't care,' said he, 'to know what a woman feels when she is going to the dogs; it doesn't interest me.'

The voice of Trimmer made things pleasant:

'Question of moral standards, that, and nothing more.'

He had stretched his legs like compasses, and the way he grasped his gown-wings seemed to turn him to a pair of scales. His lowering smile embraced the room, deprecating strong expressions. 'After all,' he seemed to say, 'we are men of the world; we know there's not very much in anything. This is the modern spirit; why not give it a look in?'

'Do I understand you to say, Berryman, that you don't enjoy a spicy book?' asked Washer with his smile; and at this question the little fat man sniggered, blinking tempestuously, as if to say: 'Nothing pleasanter, don't you know, before a hot fire in cold weather.'

Berryman paid no attention to the impertinent inquiry, continuing to dip into his volume and walk up and down.

'I've nothing to say,' he remarked, stopping before Shelton, and looking down, as if at last aware of him, 'to those who talk of being justified through Art. I call a spade a spade.'

Shelton did not answer, because he could not tell whether Berryman was addressing him or society at large. And Berryman went on:

'Do we want to know about the feelings of a middle-class woman with a taste for vice? Tell me the point of it. No man who was in the habit of taking baths would choose such a subject.'

'You come to the question of—ah—subjects,' the voice of Trimmer genially buzzed—he had gathered his garments tight across his back—'my dear fellow, Art, properly applied, justifies all subjects.'

'For Art,' squeaked Berryman, putting back his second volume and taking down a third, 'you have Homer, Cervantes, Shakespeare, Ossian; for garbage, a number of unwashed gentlemen.'

There was a laugh; Shelton glanced round at all in turn. With the exception of Crocker, who was half asleep and smiling idiotically, they wore, one and all, a look as if by no chance could they consider any subject fit to move their hearts; as if, one and all, they were so profoundly anchored on the sea of life that waves could only seem impertinent. It may have been some glimmer in this glance of Shelton's that brought Trimmer once more to the rescue with his compromising air.

'The French,' said he, 'have quite a different standard from ourselves in literature, just as they have a different standard in regard to honour. All this is purely artificial.'

What he meant, however, Shelton found it difficult to tell.

'Honour,' said Washer, '*l'honneur*, *die Ehre*, duelling, unfaithful wives——'

He was clearly going to add to this, but it was lost; for the little fat man, taking the meerschaum with trembling fingers, and holding it within two inches of his chin, murmured:

'You fellows, Berryman's awf'ly strong on honour.'

He blinked twice, and put the meerschaum back between his lips.

Without returning the third volume to its shelf Berryman took down a fourth; with chest expanded, he appeared about to use the books as dumb-bells.

'Quite so,' said Trimmer; 'the change from duelling to law courts is profoundly——'

Whether he were going to say significant' or 'insignificant,' in Shelton's estimate he did not know himself. Fortunately Berryman broke in:

'Law courts or not, when a man runs away with a wife of mine, I shall punch his head!'

'Come, come!' said Trimmer, spasmodically grasping his two wings.

Shelton had a gleam of inspiration. 'If *your* wife deceived you,' he thought, looking at Trimmer's eyes, '*you'd* keep it quiet, and hold it over her.'

Washer passed his hand over his pale chaps; his smile had never wavered; he looked like one for ever lost in the making of an epigram.

The punching theorist stretched his body, holding the books level with his shoulders, as though to stone his hearers with his point of view. His face grew paler, his fine eyes finer, his lips ironical. Almost painful was this combination of the 'strong' man and the student who was bound to go to pieces if you hit him a smart blow.

'As for forgiving faithless wives,' he said, 'and all that sort of thing, I don't believe in sentiment.'

The words were high-pitched and sarcastic. Shelton looked hastily around. All their faces were complacent. He grew red, and suddenly remarked, in a soft, clear voice:

'I see!'

He was conscious that he had never before made an impression of this sort, and that he never would again. The cold hostility flashing out all round was most enlightening; it instantly gave way to the polite, satirical indulgence peculiar to highly-cultivated men. Crocker rose nervously; he seemed scared, and was obviously relieved when Shelton, following his example, grasped the little fat man's hand, who said good-night in a voice shaken by tobacco.

'Who *are* your unshaven friends?' he heard as the door was closed behind them.

Chapter 19

AN INCIDENT

'ELEVEN o'clock,' said Crocker, as they went out of college. 'I don't feel sleepy; shall we stroll along the "High" a bit?'

Shelton assented; he was too busy thinking of his encounter with the dons to heed the soreness of his feet. This, too, was the last day of his travels, for he had not altered his intention of waiting at Oxford till July.

'We call this place the heart of knowledge,' he said, passing a great building that presided, white and silent, over darkness; 'it seems to me as little that, as Society is the heart of true gentility.'

Crocker's answer was a grunt; he was looking at the stars, calculating possibly in how long he could walk to heaven.

'No,' proceeded Shelton: 'we've too much common-sense up here to strain our minds. We know when it's time to stop. We pile up news of Papias and all the verbs in $\mu\iota$, but as for news of life or of oneself! Real seekers after knowledge are a different sort. They fight in the dark—no quarter given. We don't grow that sort up here.'

'How jolly the limes smell!' said Crocker.

He had halted opposite a garden, and taken hold of Shelton by a button of his coat. His eyes, like a dog's, stared wistfully. It seemed as though he wished to speak, but feared to give offence.

'They tell you,' pursued Shelton, 'that we learn to be gentlemen up here. We learn that better through one incident that stirs our hearts than we learn it here in all the time we're up.'

'Hum!' muttered Crocker, twisting at the button; 'those fellows who seemed the best sorts up here have turned out the best sorts afterwards.'

'I hope not,' said Shelton gloomily; 'I was a snob when I was up here. I believed all I was told, anything that made things pleasant; my "set" were nothing but——'

Crocker smiled in the darkness; he had been too 'cranky' to belong to Shelton's 'set'.

'You never were much like your "set", old chap,' he said.

Shelton turned away, sniffing the perfume of the limes. Images were thronging through his mind. The faces of his old friends strangely mixed with those of people he had lately met—the girl in the train, Ferrand, the lady with the short, round, powdered face, the little barber; others, too, and floating, mysterious—connected with them all—Antonia's face. The scent of the lime-trees drifted at him with its magic sweetness. From the street behind, the footsteps of the passers-by sounded muffled, yet exact, and on the breeze was borne the strain: 'For he's a jolly good fellow! For he's a jolly good fellow! For he's a jolly good fe-ellow! And so say all of us!'

'Ah!' he said, 'they were good chaps.'

'I used to think,' said Crocker dreamily, 'that some of them had too much side.'

And Shelton laughed.

'The thing sickens me,' said he—'the whole snobbish, selfish business. The place sickens me, lined with cotton-wool—made so beastly comfortable.'

Crocker shook his head.

'It's a splendid old place,' he said, his eyes fastening at last on Shelton's boots. 'You know, old chap,' he stammered, 'I think you —you ought to take care!'

'Take care? What of?'

Crocker pressed his arm convulsively.

'Don't be waxy, old boy,' he said; 'I mean that you seem some-how—to be—to be losing yourself.'

'Losing myself! Finding myself, you mean!'

Crocker did not answer; his face was disappointed. Of what exactly was he thinking? In Shelton's heart there was a bitter pleasure in knowing that his friend was uncomfortable on his account, a sort of contempt, a sort of aching. Crocker broke the silence.

'I think I shall do a bit more walking to-night,' he said, 'I feel very fit. Don't you really mean to come any further with me, Bird?'

And there was anxiety in his voice, as though Shelton were in danger of missing something good. The latter's feet had instantly begun to ache and burn.

'No!' he said; 'you know what I'm staying here for.'

Crocker nodded.

'She lives near here. Well, then, I'll say good-bye. I should like to do another ten miles to-night.'

'My dear fellow, you're tired and lame.'

Crocker chuckled.

'No,' he said; 'I want to get on. See you in London. Good-bye!' and gripping Shelton's hand, he turned and limped away.

Shelton called after him: 'Don't be an idiot! You'll only knock yourself up.'

But the sole answer was the pale moon of Crocker's face screwed round towards him in the darkness, and the waving of his stick.

Shelton strolled slowly on; leaning over the bridge, he watched the oily gleam of lamps on the dark water underneath the trees. He felt relieved yet sorry. His thoughts were random, curious, half mutinous, half sweet. That afternoon five years ago, when he had walked back from the river with Antonia across the Christchurch meadows, was vivid to his mind; the scent of that afternoon had never died away from him—the aroma of his love. Soon she would be his wife—his wife! The faces of the dons sprang up before him. They had wives, perhaps—fat, lean, satirical, and compromising! What was it that through diversity they had in common? Cultured intolerance! . . . Honour! A queer subject to discuss. Honour! The honour that made a fuss, and claimed its rights! And Shelton smiled. 'As if man's *honour* suffered when he's injured!' And slowly he walked along the echoing, empty street to his room at the Bishop's Head. Next morning he received the following wire:

'Thirty miles left eighteen hours heel bad but going strong CROCKER' . . .

He passed a fortnight at the Bishop's Head, waiting for the end of his probation, and the end seemed long in coming. To be so near Antonia, and as far as if he lived upon another planet, was worse than ever. Each day he took a sculling skiff, and pulled down to near Holm Oaks, on the chance of her being on the river; but the house was two miles off, and the chance but slender. She never came. After spending the afternoon like this he would return, pulling hard against the stream, with a queer feeling of relief, dine heartily, and fall a-dreaming over his cigar. Each morning he awoke in an excited mood, devoured his letter, if he had one, and sat down to write to her. These letters of his were the most amazing portion of that fortnight. They were remarkable for failing to express any single one of his real thoughts, but they were full of sentiments which were not what he was truly feeling; and when he set himself to analyse, he had such moments of delirium that he was scared, and shocked, and quite unable to write anything. He made the discovery that no two human beings ever tell each other what they really feel, except, perhaps, in situations with which he could not connect Antonia's ice-blue eyes and brilliant smile. All the world was too engaged in planning decency.

Absorbed by longing, he but vaguely realised the turmoil of Commemoration, which had gathered its hundreds for their annual cure of salmon mayonnaise and cheap champagne. In preparation for his visit to Holm Oaks he shaved his beard and had some clothes sent down from London. With them was forwarded a letter from Ferrand, which ran as follows:

'MY DEAR SIR,

'Forgive me for not having written to you before, but I have been so bothered that I have felt no taste for writing; when I have the time, I have some curious stories to tell you. Once again I have encountered that demon of misfortune which dogs my footsteps. Being occupied all day and nearly all night upon business which brings me a heap of worries and next to no profit, I have no chance to look after my things. Thieves have entered my room, stolen everything, and left me an empty box. I am once again almost without clothes, and know not where to turn to make that figure necessary for the fulfilment of my duties. You see, I am not lucky. Since coming to your country, the sole piece of fortune I have had was to tumble on a man like you. Excuse me for not writing more at this moment. Hoping that you are in good health, and in affectionately pressing your hand,

'I am,

'Always your devoted
'LOUIS FERRAND.'

Upon reading this letter Shelton had once more a sense of being exploited, of which he was ashamed; he sat down immediately and wrote the following reply:

'BISHOP'S HEAD HOTEL,
'OXFORD.
'My DEAR FERRAND, 'June 25.

'I am grieved to hear of your misfortunes. I was much hoping that you had made a better start. I enclose you Post Office Orders for four pounds. Always glad to hear from you.

'Yours sincerely,
'RICHARD SHELTON.'

He posted it with the satisfaction that a man feels who nobly shakes off his responsibilities.

Three days before July he met with one of those disturbing incidents which befall no persons who attend quietly to their property and reputation.

The night was unbearably hot, and he had wandered out with his cigar; a woman came sidling up and spoke to him. He perceived her to be one of those made by men into mediums for their pleasure, to feel sympathy with whom was sentimental. Her face was flushed, her whisper hoarse; she had no attractions but the curves of a tawdry figure. Shelton was repelled by her proprietary tone, by her blowzy face, and by the scent of patchouli. Her touch on his arm startled him, sending a shiver through his marrow; he almost leaped aside, and walked the faster. But her breathing as she followed sounded laboured; it suddenly seemed pitiful that a woman should be panting after him like that.

'The least I can do,' he thought, 'is to speak to her.' He stopped and, with a mixture of hardness and compassion, said: 'It's impossible.'

In spite of her smile, he saw by her disappointed eyes that she accepted the impossibility.

'I'm sorry,' he said.

She muttered something.

Shelton shook his head.

'I'm sorry,' he said once more. 'Good-night!'

The woman bit her lower lip.

'Good-night,' she answered dully.

At the corner of the street he turned his head. The woman was hurrying uneasily; a policeman coming from behind had caught her by the arm.

His heart began to beat. 'Heavens!' he thought, 'what shall I do now?' His first impulse was to walk away, and think no more about it—to act, indeed, like any averagely decent man who did not care to be concerned in such affairs.

He retraced his steps, however, and halted half a dozen paces from their figures.

'Ask the gentleman! He spoke to me,' she was saying in her brassy voice, through the emphasis of which Shelton could detect her fear.

'That's all right,' returned the policeman; 'we know all about that.'

'You——police!' cried the woman tearfully. 'I've got to get my living, haven't I, the same as you?'

Shelton hesitated, then, catching the expression in her frightened face, stepped forward. The policeman turned, and at the sight of his pale, heavy jowl, cut by the cheek-strap, and the bullying eyes, he felt both hate and fear, as if brought face to face with all that he despised and loathed, yet strangely dreaded. The cold certainty of law and order upholding the strong, treading underfoot the weak, the smug front of meanness that only the purest spirits may attack, seemed to be facing him. And the odd thing was, this man was only carrying out his duty. Shelton moistened his lips.

'You're not going to charge her?'

'Aren't I?' returned the policeman.

'Look here, constable, you're making a mistake.'

The policeman took out his note-book.

'Oh, I'm making a mistake? I'll take your name and address, please; we have to report these things.'

'By all means,' said Shelton, angrily giving it. 'I spoke to her first.'

'Perhaps you'll come up to the court to-morrow morning, and repeat that,' replied the policeman, with incivility.

Shelton looked at him with all the force at his command.

'You had better be careful, constable,' he said; but in the act of uttering these words he thought how pitiable they sounded.

'We're not to be trifled with,' returned the policeman in a threatening voice.

Shelton could think of nothing but to repeat:

'You had better be careful, constable.'

'You're a gentleman,' replied the policeman. 'I'm only a policeman. You've got the riches; I've got the power.'

Grasping the woman's arm, he began to move along with her. Shelton turned and walked away.

He went to Grinnings' Club, and flung himself down upon a sofa. His feeling was not one of pity for the woman, nor of peculiar anger with the policeman, but rather of dissatisfaction with himself.

'What ought I to have done?' he thought. 'The beggar was within his rights.'

He stared at the pictures on the wall, and a tide of disgust surged up in him.

'One or other of us,' he reflected, 'we make these women what they are. And when we've made them, we can't do without them, we don't want to; but we give them no proper homes, and then— we run them in. Ha! that's good—that's excellent! We run them in! And here we sit and carp. But what do we *do*? Nothing! Our system is the most highly moral known. We get the benefit without soiling even the hem of our phylacteries—the women are the only ones that suffer. And why shouldn't they—inferior things?'

He lit a cigarette, and ordered the waiter to bring a drink.

'I'll go to the court,' he thought; but suddenly it occurred to him that the case would get into the local papers. The press would never miss so nice a little bit of scandal—'Gentleman v. Policeman!' And he had a vision of Antonia's father, a neighbouring and conscientious magistrate, solemnly reading this. Someone, at all events, was bound to see his name and make a point of mentioning it;—too good to be missed!—and suddenly he saw with horror that to help the woman he would have to assert again that he had spoken to her first.

'I *must* go to the court!' he kept thinking, as if to assure himself that he was not a coward.

He lay awake half the night worrying over his dilemma.

'But I *didn't* speak to her first,' he told himself; 'I shall only be telling a lie, and they'll make me swear it too!'

He tried to persuade himself that this was against his principles, but at the bottom of his heart he knew that he would not object to telling such a lie if only guaranteed immune from consequences; it appeared to him, indeed, but obvious humanity.

'But why should I suffer?' he thought. '*I've* done nothing. It's neither reasonable nor just.'

He hated the unhappy woman who was causing him these horrors of uncertainty. Whenever he decided one way or other, the policeman's face, with its tyrannical and muddy eyes, rose before him like a nightmare, and forced him to an opposite conviction. He fell asleep at last with the full determination to go and see what happened.

He woke with a sense of odd disturbance. 'I can do no good by going,' he thought, remembering, and lying very still; 'they're certain to believe the policeman; I shall only blacken myself for nothing;' and the combat began again within him, but with far less fury. It was not what other people thought, not even the risk of perjury that mattered (all this he made quite clear)—it was Antonia. It was not fair to her to put himself in such a false position; in fact, not decent.

He breakfasted. In the room were some Americans, and the face of one younger girl reminded him a little of Antonia. Fainter and fainter grew the incident; it seemed to have its right proportions.

Two hours later, looking at the clock, he found that it was lunch-time. He had not gone, had not committed perjury; but he wrote to a daily paper, pointing out the danger run by the community from the power which a belief in their infallibility places in the hands of the police—how, since they are the sworn bettors of right and justice, their word is almost necessarily taken to be gospel; how one and all they hang together, from mingled interest and *esprit de corps*! Was it not, he said, reasonable to suppose that amongst thousands of human beings invested with such opportunities there would be found bullies who would take advantage of them, and rise to distinction in the service upon the helplessness of the unfortunate and the cowardice of people with anything to lose? Those who had in their hands the sacred duties of selecting a practically irresponsible body of men were bound, for the sake of freedom and humanity, to exercise those duties with the utmost care and thoroughness. . . .

However true, none of this helped him to think any better of himself at heart, and he was haunted by the feeling that a stout and honest bit of perjury was worth more than a letter to a daily paper.

He never saw his letter printed, containing, as it did, the germs of an unpalatable truth.

In the afternoon he hired a horse, and galloped on Port Meadow. The strain of his indecision over, he felt like a man recovering from an illness, and he carefully abstained from looking at the local papers. There was that within him, however, which resented the worsting of his chivalry.

Chapter 20

HOLM OAKS

HOLM OAKS stood back but little from the road—an old manorhouse, not set upon display, but dwelling close to its barns, stables, and walled gardens, like a good mother; long, flat-roofed, red, it had Queen Anne windows, on whose white-framed diamond panes the sunbeams glinted.

In front of it a fringe of elms, of all trees the tree of most established principle, bordered the stretch of turf between the gravel drive and road; and these elms were the homes of rooks—of all birds the most conventional. A huge aspen—impressionable creature—shivered and shook beyond, apologising for appearance among such imperturbable surroundings. It was frequented by a cuckoo, who came once a year to hoot at rules of life, but seldom made long stay; for boys threw stones at it, exasperated by the absence of its morals.

The village which clustered in the dip had not yet lost its dread of motor-cars. About this group of flat-faced cottages with gabled roofs the scent of hay, manure, and roses clung continually; just now the odour of the limes troubled its servile sturdiness. Beyond the dip again, a square-towered church kept within grey walls the record of the village flock, births, deaths, and marriages—even the births of bastards, even the deaths of suicides—and seemed to stretch a hand invisible above the heads of common folk to grasp the fingers of the manor-house. Decent and discreet the two roofs caught the eye to the exclusion of all meaner dwellings, seeming to have joined in a conspiracy to keep them out of sight.

The July sun had burned his face all the way from Oxford, yet pale was Shelton when he walked up the drive and rang the bell.

'Mrs Dennant at home, Dobson?' he asked of the grave butler, who, old servant that he was, still wore coloured trousers (for it was not yet twelve o'clock, and he regarded coloured trousers up to noon as a sacred distinction between the footman and himself).

'Mrs Dennant,' replied this personage, raising his round and hairless face, while on his mouth appeared that apologetic pout which comes of living with good families—'Mrs Dennant has gone into the village, sir; but Miss Antonia is in the morning-room.'

Shelton crossed the panelled, low-roofed hall, through whose far side the lawn was visible, a vision of serenity. He mounted six wide, shallow steps, and stopped. From behind a closed door there came the sound of scales, and he stood, a prey to his emotions, the notes mingling in his ears with the beating of his heart. He softly turned the handle, a fixed smile on his lips.

Antonia was at the piano; her head was bobbing to the movements of her fingers, and pressing down the pedals were her slim, monotonously moving feet. She had been playing tennis, for a racquet and her tam-o'-shanter were flung down, and she was dressed in a blue skirt and creamy blouse, fitting collarless about her throat. Her face was flushed, and wore a little frown; and as her fingers raced along the keys her neck swayed, and the silk clung and shivered on her arms.

Shelton's eyes were fastened on the silent, counting lips, on the fair hair about her forehead, the darker eyebrows slanting down towards the nose, the undimpled cheeks with the faint finger-marks beneath the ice-blue eyes, the softly-pointed and undimpled chin, the whole remote, sweet, suntouched, glacial face.

She turned her head, and, springing up, cried:

'Dick! What fun!' She gave him both her hands, but her

smiling face said very plainly, 'Oh, don't let us be sentimental!'

'Aren't you glad to see me?' muttered Shelton.

'Glad to see you! You *are* funny, Dick!—as if you didn't know! Why, you've shaved your beard! Mother and Sybil have gone into the village to see old Mrs Hopkins. Shall we go out? Thea and the boys are playing tennis. It's so jolly that you've come!' She caught up the tam-o'-shanter, and pinned it to her hair. Almost as tall as Shelton, she looked taller, with arms raised and loose sleeves quivering like wings to the movements of her fingers. 'We might have a game before lunch; you can have my other racquet.'

'I've got no things,' said Shelton blankly.

Her calm glance ran over him.

'You can have some of old Bernard's; he's got any amount. I'll wait for you.' She swung her racquet, looked at Shelton, cried: 'Be quick!' and vanished.

Shelton ran upstairs and dressed in the undecided way of men assuming other people's clothes. She was in the hall when he descended, humming a tune and prodding at her shoe; her smile showed all her pearly upper teeth. He caught hold of her sleeve and whispered:

'Antonia!'

The colour rushed into her cheeks; she looked back across her shoulder.

'Come along, old Dick!' she cried; and, flinging open the glass-door, ran into the garden.

Shelton followed.

The tennis-ground was divided by tall netting from a paddock. A holm-oak tree shaded one corner, and its thick dark foliage gave an unexpected depth to the green smoothness of the scene. As Shelton and Antonia came up, Bernard Dennant stopped and cordially grasped Shelton's hand. From the far side of the net Thea, in a shortish skirt, tossed back her straight fair hair, and warding off the sun, came strolling up to them. The umpire, a small boy of twelve, was lying on his stomach, squealing and tickling a collie. Shelton bent and pulled his hair.

'Hallo, Toddles! you young ruffian!'

One and all they stood round Shelton, and there was a frank and pitiless inquiry in their eyes, in the angle of their noses something chaffing and distrustful, as though about him were some subtle poignant scent exciting curiosity and disapproval.

When the setts were over, and the girls resting in the double hammock underneath the holm-oak, Shelton went with Bernard to the paddock to hunt for the lost balls.

'I say, old chap,' said his old schoolfellow, smiling drily, 'you're in for a wigging from the Mater.'

'A wigging?' murmured Shelton.

'I don't know much about it, but from something she let drop it seems you've been saying some queer things in your letters to Antonia;' and again he looked at Shelton with his dry smile.

'Queer things?' said the latter angrily. 'What d'you mean?'

'Oh, don't ask me. The Mater thinks she's in a bad way—unsettled, or what d'you call it. You've been telling her that things are not what they seem. That's bad, you know;' and still smiling, he shook his head.

Shelton dropped his eyes.

'Well, they aren't!' he said.

'Oh, that's all right! But don't bring your philosophy down here, old chap.'

'Philosophy!' said Shelton, puzzled.

'Leave us a sacred prejudice or two.'

'Sacred! Nothing's sacred, except——' But Shelton did not finish his remark. 'I don't understand,' he said.

'Ideals, that sort of thing! You've been diving down below the line of "practical politics," that's about the size of it, my boy;' and, stooping suddenly, he picked up the last ball. 'There *is* the Mater!' Shelton saw Mrs Dennant coming down the lawn with her second daughter, Sybil.

By the time they had reached the holm-oak the three girls had departed towards the house, walking arm in arm, and Mrs Dennant was standing there alone, in a grey dress, talking to an under-gardener. Her hands, cased in tan gauntlets, held a basket which warded off the bearded gardener from the severe but ample lines of her useful-looking skirt. The collie, erect upon its haunches, looked at their two faces, pricking his ears in his endeavour to appreciate how one of these two bipeds differed from the other.

'Thank you; that'll do, Bunyan. Ah, Dick! Charmin' to see you here, at last!'

In his intercourse with Mrs Dennant, Shelton never failed to mark the typical nature of her personality. It always seemed to him that he had met so many other ladies like her. He felt that her undoubtable quality had a non-individual flavour, as if standing for her class. She thought that standing for herself was not the thing; yet she was full of character. Tall, with nose a trifle beaked, long, sloping chin, and an assured benevolent mouth, showing, perhaps, too many teeth—though thin, she was not unsubstantial. Her accent in speaking showed her heritage; it was a kind of drawl which disregarded vulgar merits such as tone, leaned on some syllables, and despised the final *g*—one of the peculiar accents, in fact, of aristocracy, adding its deliberate joys to life.

Shelton knew that she had many interests; she was never really idle, from the time (7 a.m.) when her maid brought her a little china pot of tea with a single biscuit and her pet dog, Tops, till eleven o'clock at night, when she lighted a wax candle in a silver candlestick, and with this in one hand, and in the other a new novel, or, better still, one of those charming volumes written by great people about the still greater people they have met, she said good-night to her children and her guests.

No! What with photography, the presidency of a local league, visiting the rich, superintending the poor, gardening, reading, keeping all her ideas so tidy that no foreign notions might stay in, she was never idle. The information she collected from these sources was both vast and varied, but she never let it flavour her opinions, which lacked sauce, and were drawn from some sort of dish into which, with all her class, she dipped her fingers.

He liked her. No one could help liking her. She was kind, and of such good quality, with a suggestion about her of thin, excellent, and useful china; and she was scented, too—not with verbena, violets, or those essences which women love, but with nothing, as if she had taken stand against all meretricity. In her intercourse with persons not 'quite the thing' (she excepted the vicar from this category, though his father had dealt in haberdashery), her refinement gently, unobtrusively, and with great practical good sense, seemed continually to murmur : 'I am, and you—well, *are* you, don't you know?' But there was no self-consciousness about this attitude, for she was really not a common woman. She simply could not help it; all her people had done this. Their nurses breathed above them in the cradles something that, inhaled into their systems, ever afterwards prevented them from taking good, clear breaths. And her manner! Ah! her manner—it concealed the inner woman so as to leave doubt of her existence!

Shelton listened to the kindly briskness with which she dwelt upon the under-gardener.

'Poor Bunyan! he lost his wife six months ago, and was quite cheerful just at first, but now he's really too distressin'. I've done all I can to rouse him; it's so melancholy to see him mopin'. And, my dear Dick, the way he mangles the new rose-trees! I'm afraid he's goin' mad; I shall have to send him away, poor fellow!'

It was clear that she sympathised with Bunyan, or, rather, believed him entitled to a modicum of wholesome grief, the loss of wives being a canonised and legal source of sorrow. But excesses! Oh! dear no!

'I've told him I shall raise his wages,' she sighed. 'He used to be such a splendid gardener! That reminds me, my dear Dick; I want to have a talk with you. Shall we go in to lunch?'

Consulting the memorandum-book in which she had been noting the case of Mrs Hopkins, she slightly preceded Shelton to the house.

It was somewhat late that afternoon when Shelton had his 'wigging'; nor did it seem to him, hypnotised by the momentary absence of Antonia, such a very serious affair.

'Now, Dick,' the Honourable Mrs Dennant said in her decisive drawl, 'I don't think it's right to put ideas into Antonia's head.'

'Ideas!' murmured Shelton in confusion.

'We all know,' continued Mrs Dennant, 'that things are not always what they ought to be.'

Shelton looked at her; she was seated at her writing-table, addressing in her large, free writing a dinner invitation to a Bishop. There was not the faintest trace of awkwardness about her, yet Shelton could not help a certain sense of shock. If she—she—did not think things were what they ought to be—in a bad way things must be indeed!

'Things?' he muttered.

Mrs Dennant looked at him firmly but kindly, with the eyes that would remind him of a hare's

'She showed me some of your letters, you know. Well, it's not a bit of use denyin', my dear Dick, that you've been thinkin' too much lately.'

Shelton perceived that he had done her an injustice; she handled 'things' as she handled under-gardeners—put them away when they showed signs of running to extremes.

'I can't help that, I'm afraid,' he answered.

'My dear boy! you'll never get on that way. Now, I want you to promise me you won't talk to Antonia about those sort of things.'

Shelton raised his eyebrows.

'Oh, you know what I mean!'

He saw that to press Mrs Dennant to say what she meant by

'things' would really hurt her sense of form; it would be cruel to force her thus below the surface!

He therefore said: 'Quite so!'

To his extreme surprise, flushing the peculiar and pathetic flush of women past their prime, she drawled out:

'About the poor—and criminals—and marriages—there was that wedding, don't you know?'

Shelton bowed his head. Motherhood had been too strong for her; in her maternal flutter she had committed the solecism of touching in so many words on 'things'.

'Doesn't she really see the fun,' he thought, 'in one man dining out of gold and another dining in the gutter; or in two married people living on together in perfect discord—*pour encourager les autres*—or in worshipping Jesus Christ and claiming all her rights at the same time; or in despising foreigners because they *are* foreigners; or in war; or in anything that *is* funny?' But he did her a certain amount of justice by recognising that this was natural, since her whole life had been passed in trying not to see the fun in all these things.

But Antonia stood smiling in the doorway. Brilliant and gay she looked, yet resentful, as if she knew they had been talking of her. She sat down by Shelton's side, and began asking him about the youthful foreigner whom he had spoken of; and her eyes made him doubt whether she, too, saw the fun that lay in one human being patronising others.

'But I suppose he's really *good*,' she said—'I mean, all those things he told you about were only——'

'Good!' he answered, fidgeting. 'I don't really know what the word means.'

Her eyes clouded. 'Dick, how can you?' they seemed to say. Shelton stroked her sleeve.

'Tell us about Mr Crocker,' she said, taking no heed of this caress.

'The lunatic!' he said.

'Lunatic! Why, in your letters he was splendid.'

'So he is,' said Shelton, half ashamed; 'he's not a bit mad, really —that is, I only wish I were half as mad.'

'Who's that mad?' queried Mrs Dennant from behind the urn— 'Tom Crocker? Ah, yes! I knew his mother; she was a Springer.'

'Did he do it in the week?' said Thea, appearing in the window with a kitten.

'I don't know,' Shelton was obliged to answer.

Thea shook back her hair.

'I call it awfully slack of you not to have found out.'

Antonia frowned,

'You were very sweet to that young foreigner, Dick,' she murmured with a smile at Shelton. 'I wish that we could see him.'

But Shelton shook his head.

'It seems to me,' he muttered, 'that I did about as little for him as I could.'

Again her face grew thoughtful, as though his words had chilled her.

'I don't see what more you could have done,' she answered.

A desire to get close to her, half fear, half ache, a sense of futility and bafflement, an inner burning, made him feel as though a flame were licking at his heart.

Chapter 21

ENGLISH

JUST as Shelton was starting to walk back to Oxford he met Mr Dennant coming from a ride. Antonia's father was a spare man of medium height, with yellowish face, thin, grey moustache, ironical eyebrows, and some tiny crow's-feet. In his old, short grey coat, with a little slip up the middle of the back, his drab cord breeches, ancient mahogany leggings, and carefully blacked boots, he had a dry, threadbare quality not without distinction.

'Ah, Shelton!' he said, in his quietly festive voice; 'glad to see the pilgrim here, at last. You're not off already?' and, laying his hand on Shelton's arm, he proposed to walk a little way with him across the fields.

This was the first time they had met since the engagement; and Shelton began to nerve himself to express some sentiment, however bald, about it. He squared his shoulders, cleared his throat, and looked askance at Mr Dennant. That gentleman was walking stiffly, his cord breeches faintly squeaking. He switched a yellow, jointed cane against his leggings, and after each blow looked at his legs satirically. He himself was rather like that yellow cane —pale, and slim, and jointed, with features arching just a little, like the arching of its handle.

'They say it'll be a bad year for fruit,' Shelton said at last.

'My dear fellow, you don't know your farmer, I'm afraid. We ought to hang some farmers—do a world of good. Dear souls! I've got some perfect strawberries.'

'I suppose,' said Shelton, glad to postpone the evil moment, 'in a climate like this a man *must* grumble.'

'Quite so, quite so! Look at us poor slaves of landowners; if I couldn't abuse the farmers I should be wretched. Did you ever see anything finer than this pasture? And they want me to lower their rents!'

And Mr Dennant's glance satirically wavered, rested on Shelton, and whisked back to the ground, as though he had seen something that alarmed him. There was a pause.

'Now for it!' thought the younger man.

Mr Dennant kept his eyes fixed on his boots.

'If they'd said, now,' he remarked jocosely, 'that the frost had nipped the partridges, there'd have been some sense in it; but what can you expect? They've no consideration, dear souls!'

Shelton took a breath, and, with averted eyes, he hurriedly began :

'It's awfully hard, sir, to——'

Mr Dennant switched his cane against his shin.

'Yes,' he said, 'it's awfully hard to put up with, but what can a fellow do? One must have farmers. Why, if it wasn't for the farmers, there'd still be a hare or two about the place!'

Shelton laughed spasmodically; again he glanced askance at his future father-in-law. What did the waggling of his head mean, the deepening of his crow's-feet, the odd contraction of the mouth? And his eye caught Mr Dennant's eye; its expression was queer above the fine, dry nose (one of the sort that reddens in a wind).

'I've never had much to do with farmers,' he said at last.

'Haven't you? Lucky fellow! The most—yes, *quite* the most trying portion of the human species—next to daughters.'

'Well, sir, you can hardly expect *me*——' began Shelton.

'I don't—oh, I don't! D'you know, I really believe we're in for a ducking.'

A large black cloud had covered up the sun, and some drops were spattering on Mr Dennant's hard felt hat.

Shelton welcomed the shower; it appeared to him an intervention on the part of Providence. He would *have* to say something, but not now, later.

'I'll go on,' he said; 'I don't mind the rain. But you'd better get back, sir.'

'Dear me! I've a tenant in this cottage,' said Mr Dennant in his leisurely, dry manner, 'and a beggar he is to poach, too. Least we can do's to ask for a little shelter; what do you think?' and smiling sarcastically, as though deprecating his intention to keep dry, he rapped on the door of a prosperous-looking cottage.

It was opened by a girl of Antonia's age and height.

'Ah, Phœbe! Your father in?'

'No,' replied the girl, fluttering; 'father's out, Mr Dennant.'

'So sorry! Will you let us bide a bit out of the rain?'

The sweet-looking Phœbe dusted them two chairs, and, curtseying, left them in the parlour.

'What a pretty girl!' said Shelton.

'Yes, she's a pretty girl; half the young fellows are after her, but she won't leave her father. Oh! he's a charming rascal is that fellow!'

This remark suddenly brought home to Shelton the conviction that he was further than ever from avoiding the necessity for speaking. He walked over to the window. The rain was coming down with fury, though a golden line far down the sky promised the shower's quick end. 'For goodness' sake,' he thought 'let me say something, however idiotic, and get it over!' But he did not turn; a kind of paralysis had seized on him.

'Tremendous heavy rain!' he said at last; 'coming down in waterspouts!'

It would have been just as easy to say: 'I believe your daughter to be the sweetest thing on earth; I love her, and I'm going to make her happy!' Just as easy, just about the same amount of breath required; but—he couldn't say it! He watched the rain stream and hiss against the leaves and churn the dust in the parched road with its insistent torrent; and he noticed with precision all the details of the process going on outside—how the rain-drops darted at the leaves like spears, and how the leaves shook themselves free a hundred times a minute, while little runnels of water, ice-clear, rolled over their edges, soft and quick. He noticed too, the mournful head of a sheltering cow which was chewing at the hedge.

Mr Dennant had not replied to his remark about the rain. So disconcerting was this silence that Shelton turned. His future father-in-law, upon his wooden chair, was staring at his well-blacked boots, bending forward above his parted knees, and prodding at the carpet; a glimpse at his face disturbed Shelton's resolution. It was not forbidding, stern, discouraging—not in the least; it had merely for the moment ceased to look satirical. This was so startling that Shelton lost his chance of speaking. There seemed a heart to Mr Dennant's gravity; as though for once he were looking grave because he felt so. But glancing up at Shelton his dry jocosity reappeared at once.

'What a day for ducks!' he said; and again there was unmistakable alarm about his eye. Was it possible that he, too, dreaded something?

'I can't express——' began Shelton hurriedly.

'Yes, it's beastly to get wet,' said Mr Dennant, and he sang:

> ' "For we can wrestle and fight, my boys,
> And jump out anywhere."

You'll be with us for that dinner-party next week, eh? Capital! There's the Bishop of Blumenthal and old Sir Jack Buckwell; I must get my wife to put you between them—

> ' "For it's my delight of a starry night."

The Bishop's a great anti-divorce man, and old Buckwell's been in the court at least twice—

> ' "In the season of the year!" '

'Will you please to take some tea, gentlemen?' said the voice of Phœbe in the doorway.

'No, thank you, Phœbe. That girl ought to get married,' went on Mr Dennant, as Phœbe blushingly withdrew. A flush showed queerly on his sallow cheeks. 'A shame to keep her tied like this to her father's apron-strings—selfish fellow, that!' He looked up sharply, as if he had made a dangerous remark.

> ' "The keeper he was watching us,
> For him we didn't care!" '

Shelton suddenly felt certain that Antonia's father was just as anxious to say something expressive of his feelings, and as unable as himself. And this was comforting.

'You know, sir——' he began.

But Mr Dennant's eyebrows rose, his crow's-feet twinkled; his personality seemed to shrink together.

'By Jove!' he said, 'it's stopped! Now's our chance! Come along, my dear fellow; delays are dangerous!' and with his bantering courtesy he held the door for Shelton to pass out. 'I think we'll part here,' he said—'I almost think so. Good luck to you!'

He held out his dry yellow hand. Shelton seized it, wrung it hard, and muttered the word:

'Grateful!'

Again Mr Dennant's eyebrows quivered as if they had been tweaked; he had been found out, and he disliked it. The colour in his face had died away; it was calm, wrinkled, dead-looking under the flattened, narrow brim of his grey bowler; his grey moustache drooped thinly; the crow's-feet hardened round his eyes; his nostrils were distended by the queerest smile.

'Gratitude!' he said; 'almost a vice, isn't it? Good-night!'

Shelton's face quivered; he raised his hat, and, turning as abruptly as his senior, proceeded on his way. He had been playing in a comedy that could only have been played in England. He could afford to smile now at his past discomfort, having no longer this sense of duty unfulfilled. Everything had been said that was right and proper to be said, in the way that we such things should say. No violence had been done; he could afford to smile— smile at himself, at Mr Dennant, at to-morrow; smile at the sweet aroma of the earth, the shy, unwilling sweetness that only rain brings forth.

Chapter 22

THE COUNTRY HOUSE

THE luncheon hour at Holm Oaks was, as in many well-bred country houses, out of the shooting season, be it understood, the soulful hour. The ferment of the daily doings was then at its full height, and the clamour of its conversation on the weather and the dogs, the horses, neighbours, cricket, golf, was mingled with a literary murmur; for the Dennants were superior, and it was quite usual to hear remarks like these: 'Have you read that charming thing of Poser's?' or, 'Yes, I've got the new edition of old "Babling-ton"; delightfully bound—so light.' And it was in July that Holm Oaks, as a gathering-place of the elect, was at its best. For in July it had become customary to welcome there many of those poor souls from London who arrived exhausted by the season, and than whom no seamstress in a two-pair back could better have earned her holiday. The Dennants themselves never went to London for the season. It was their good pleasure not to. A week or fortnight of it satisfied them. They had a radical weakness for fresh air, and, Antonia, even after her presentation two seasons back, had insisted on returning home stigmatising London balls as 'stuffy things'.

When Shelton arrived the stream had only just begun, but every day brought fresh, or rather jaded, people to occupy the old, dark, sweet-smelling bedrooms. Individually he liked his fellow-guests, but he found himself observing them. He knew that, if a man judged people singly, almost all were better than himself; only when judged in bulk were they worthy of the sweeping criticisms he felt inclined to pass on them. He knew this just as he knew that the conventions, having been invented to prevent man from following his natural desires, were merely the disapproving sums of innumerable individual approvals.

It was in the bulk, then, that he found himself observing. But with his amiability and dread of notoriety he remained to all appearance a well-bred, docile creature, and he kept his judgments to himself.

In the matter of intellect he made a rough division of the guests —those who accepted things without a murmur, those who accepted them with carping jocularity; in the matter of morals he found they all accepted things without the semblance of a kick. To show sign of private moral judgment was to have lost your soul, and, worse, to be a bit of an outsider. He gathered this by intuition rather than from conversation; for conversation naturally tabooed such questions, and was carried on in the loud and cheerful tones peculiar to people of good breeding. Shelton had never been able to acquire this tone, and he could not help feeling that the inability made him more or less an object of suspicion. The atmosphere struck him as it never had before, causing him to feel a doubt of his gentility. Could a man suffer from passion, heart-searchings, or misgivings, and remain a gentleman? It seemed improbable. One of his fellow-guests, a man called Edgbaston, small-eyed and semi-bald, with a dark moustache and a distinguished air of meanness, disconcerted him one day by remarking of an unknown person, 'A half-bred-lookin' chap; didn't seem to know his mind.'

Shelton was harassed by a horrid doubt.

Everything seemed divided into classes, carefully docketed and valued. For instance, a Briton was of more value than a man, and wives than women. Those things or phases of life with which people had no personal acquaintance were regarded with a faint amusement and a certain disapproval. The principles of the upper class, in fact, were strictly followed.

He was in that hypersensitive and nervous state favourable for recording currents foreign to itself. Things he had never before noticed now had profound effect on him, such as the tone in which men spoke of women—not precisely with hostility, nor exactly with contempt—best, perhaps, described as a cultured jeering; never, of course, when men spoke of their own wives, mothers, sisters, or immediate friends, but merely when they spoke of any other women. He reflected upon this, and came to the conclusion that, among the upper classes, each man's own property was holy, while other women were created to supply him with gossip, jests, and spice. Another thing that struck him was the way in which the war, then going on, was made into an affair of class. In their view it was a baddish business, because poor Jack Blank and Peter Blank-Blank had lost their lives, and poor Teddy Blank had now one arm instead of two. Humanity in general was omitted, but not the upper classes, nor, incidentally, the country which belonged to them. For there they were, all seated in a row, with eyes fixed on the horizon of their lawns.

Late one evening, billiards and music being over and the ladies gone, Shelton returned from changing to his smoking-suit, and dropped into one of the great armchairs that even in summer made a semicircle round the fendered hearth. Fresh from his good-night parting with Antonia, he sat perhaps ten minutes before he began to take in all the figures in their parti-coloured smoking-jackets, cross-legged, with glasses in their hands and cigars between their teeth.

The man in the next chair roused him by putting down his tumbler with a tap, and seating himself upon the cushioned fender. Through the mist of smoke, with shoulders hunched, elbows and knees crooked out, cigar protruding, beak-ways, below his nose, and the crimson collar of his smoking-jacket buttoned close as plumage on his breast, he looked a little like a gorgeous bird.

'They do you awfully well,' he said.

A voice from the chair on Shelton's right replied:

'They do you better at Verado's.'

'The Veau d'Or's the best place; they give you Turkish baths for nothing!' drawled a fat man with a tiny mouth.

The suavity of this pronouncement enfolded all as with a blessing. And at once, as if by magic, in the old, oak-panelled room, the world fell naturally into its three departments: that, where they do you well; that, where they do you better; and that, where they give you Turkish baths for nothing.

'If you want Turkish baths,' said a tall youth with a clean red face, who had come into the room, and stood, with his mouth a little open, and long feet jutting with sweet helplessness in front of him, 'you should go, you know, to Buda Pesth; most awfully rippin' there.'

Shelton saw an indescribable appreciation rise on every face, as though they had been offered truffles or something equally delicious.

'Oh no, Poodles,' said the man perched on the fender; 'a Johnny I know tells me they're nothing to Sofia.' His face was transfigured by the subtle gloating of a man enjoying vice by proxy.

'Ah!' drawled the small-mouthed man, 'but there's nothing fit to hold a candle to Baghda-ad.'

Once again his utterance enfolded all as with a blessing, and once again the world fell into its three departments: that, where they do you well; that, where they do you better; and—Baghdad.

Shelton thought to himself: 'Why don't I know a place that's better than Baghdad?'

He felt so insignificant. It seemed that he knew none of these delightful spots; that he was of no use to any of his fellow-men; though privately he was convinced that all these speakers were as ignorant as himself, and merely found it warming to recall such things as they had heard, with that peculiar gloating look. Alas! his anecdotes would never earn for him that prize of persons in society, the label of a 'good chap' and 'sportsman'.

'Have you ever been in Baghdad?' he feebly asked.

The fat man did not answer; he had begun an anecdote, and in his broad expanse of face his tiny mouth writhed like a caterpillar. The anecdote was humorous.

With the exception of Antonia, Shelton saw but little of the ladies, for, following the well-known custom of the country house, men and women avoided each other as much as might be. They met at meals, and occasionally joined in tennis and in croquet; otherwise it seemed—almost Orientally—agreed that they were better kept apart.

Chancing one day to enter the withdrawing-room, while searching for Antonia, he found that he had lighted on a feminine discussion. He would have beaten a retreat, of course, but it seemed too obvious that he was merely looking for his fiancèe; so, sitting down, he listened.

The Honourable Charlotte Penguin, still knitting a silk tie—the sixth since that she had been knitting at Hyères—sat on the low window-seat close to a hydrangea, the petals of whose round flowers almost kissed her sanguine cheek. Her eyes were fixed with languid aspiration on the lady who was speaking. This was a square woman of medium height, with grey hair brushed from her low forehead, the expression of whose face was brisk and rather cross. She was standing with a book, as if delivering a sermon. Had she been a man she might have been described as a bright young man of business; for, though grey, she never could be old, nor ever lose the power of forming quick decisions. Her features and her eyes were prompt and slightly hard, tinged with faith fanatical in the justice of her judgments, and she had that fussy simpleness of dress which indicates the right to meddle. Not red, not white, neither yellow nor quite blue, her complexion was suffused with a certain mixture of these colours, adapted to the climate; and her smile had a strange, sour sweetness, like nothing but the flavour of an apple on the turn.

'I don't care what they tell you,' she was saying—not offensively, though her voice seemed to imply that she had no time to waste in pleasing; 'in all my dealings with them I've found it best to treat them quite like children.'

A lady, behind *The Times*, smiled; her mouth—indeed, her whole hard, handsome face—was reminiscent of dappled rocking-horses found in the Soho Bazaar. She crossed her feet, and some rich and silk stuff rustled. Her whole personality seemed to creak as, without looking, she answered in harsh tones :

'*I* find the poor are most delightful persons.'

Sybil Dennant, seated on the sofa, with a feathery laugh, shot a barking terrier dog at Shelton.

'Here's Dick,' she said. 'Well, Dick, what's *your* opinion?'

Shelton looked around him, scared. The elder ladies who had spoken had fixed their eyes on him, and in their gaze he read his utter insignificance.

'Oh, that young man!' they seemed to say. 'Expect a practical remark from him? Now, come!'

'Opinion,' he stammered, 'of the poor? I haven't any.'

The person on her feet, whose name was Mrs Mattock, directing her peculiar sweet-sour smile at the distinguished lady with *The Times*, said:

'Perhaps you've not had experience of them in London, Lady Bonington?'

Lady Bonington, in answer, rustled.

'Oh, do tell us about the slums, Mrs Mattock!' cried Sybil. 'Slumming must be splendid! It's so deadly here—nothing but flannel petticoats.'

'The poor, my dear,' began Mrs Mattock, 'are not the least bit what you think them——'

'Oh, d'you think, I know they're *rather* nice!' broke in Aunt Charlotte close to the hydrangea.

'You think so!' said Mrs Mattock sharply. '*I* find they do nothing but grumble.'

'They don't grumble at *me*; they are delightful persons;' and Lady Bonington gave Shelton a grim smile.

He could not help thinking that to grumble in the presence of that rich, despotic personality would require a superhuman courage.

'They're the most ungrateful people in the world,' said Mrs Mattock. 'Why then,' thought Shelton 'do you go amongst them?' But she was continuing: 'One *must* do them good, one *must* do one's duty, but as to getting thanks——'

Lady Bonington sardonically said:

'Poor things! they have a lot to bear.'

'The little children!' murmured Aunt Charlotte, with a flushing cheek and shining eyes; 'it's *rather* pathetic.'

'Children indeed!' said Mrs Mattock. 'It puts me out of all patience to see the way they neglect them. People are so sentimental about the poor.'

Lady Bonington creaked again. Her splendid shoulders were wedged into her chair; her fine dark hair, gleaming with silver, sprang back upon her brow; a ruby bracelet glowed on the powerful wrist that held the journal; she rocked her copper-slippered foot. She did not appear to be too sentimental.

'I know they often have a very easy time,' said Mrs Mattock, as if someone had injured her severely. And Shelton saw, not without pity, that Fate had scored her kind and squashed-up face with wrinkles, whose tiny furrows were eloquent of good intentions frustrated by the unpractical and discontented poor. 'Do what you will, they are never satisfied; they only resent one's help, or else they take the help and never thank you for it!'

'Oh!' murmured Aunt Charlotte, 'that's *rather* hard.'

Shelton had been growing more uneasy. He said abruptly:

'I should do the same if I were they.'

Mrs Mattock's brown eyes flew at him; Lady Bonington spoke to *The Times*; her ruby bracelet and a bangle jingled.

'We ought to put ourselves in their places.'

Shelton could not help a smile; Lady Bonington in the places of the poor!

'Oh!' exclaimed Mrs Mattock, 'I put myself entirely in their place. I quite understand their feelings. But ingratitude is a repulsive quality.'

'They seem unable to put themselves in *your* place,' murmured Shelton; and in a fit of courage he took the room in with a sweeping glance.

Yes, that room was wonderfully consistent, with its air of perfect second-handedness, as if each picture, and each piece of furniture, each book, each lady present, had been made from patterns. They were all widely different, yet all (like works of art seen in some exhibitions) had the look of being *after* the designs of some original spirit. The whole room was chaste, restrained, derived, practical, and comfortable; neither in virtue, nor in work, neither in manner, speech, appearance, nor in theory, could it give itself away.

Chapter 23

THE STAINED-GLASS MAN

STILL looking for Antonia, Shelton went up to the morning-room. Thea Dennant and another girl were seated in the window, talking. From the looks they gave him he saw that he had better never have been born; he hastily withdrew. Descending to the hall, he came on Mr Dennant crossing to his study, with a handful of official-looking papers.

'Ah, Shelton!' said he, 'you look a little lost. Is the shrine invisible?'

Shelton grinned, said 'Yes,' and went on looking. He was not fortunate. In the dining-room sat Mrs Dennant, making up her list of books.

'Do give me your opinion, Dick,' she said. 'Everybody's readin' this thing of Katherine Asterick's. I believe it's simply because she's got a title.'

'One must read a book for some reason or other,' answered Shelton.

'Well,' returned Mrs Dennant, 'I hate doin' things just because other people do them, and I shan't get it.'

'Good!'

Mrs Dennant marked the catalogue.

'Here's Linseed's last, of course; though I must say I don't care for him, but I suppose we ought to have it in the house. And there's Quality's "The Splendid Diatribes"; *that's* sure to be good, he's always so refined. But what am I to do about this of Arthur Baal's? They say that he's a charlatan, but everybody reads him, don't you know;' and over the catalogue Shelton caught the gleam of hare-like eyes.

Decision had vanished from her face, with its arched nose and slightly sloping chin, as though some one had suddenly appealed to her to trust her instincts. It was quite pathetic. Still, there was always the book's circulation to form her judgment by.

'I think I'd better mark it,' she said, 'don't you? Were you lookin' for Antonia? If you come across Bunyan in the garden, Dick, do say I want to see him; he's gettin' to be a perfect nuisance. I can understand his feelin's, but really he's carryin' it too far.'

Primed with his message to the under-gardener, Shelton went. He took a despairing look into the billiard-room. Antonia was not there. Instead, a tall and fat-cheeked gentleman with a neat moustache, called Mabbey, was practising the spot-stroke. He paused as Shelton entered, and, pouting like a baby, asked in a sleepy voice :

'Play me a hundred up?'

Shelton shook his head, stammered out his sorrow, and was about to go.

The gentleman called Mabbey, plaintively feeling the places where his moustaches joined his pink and glossy cheeks, asked with an air of some surprise :

'What's your general game, then?'

'I really don't know,' said Shelton.

The gentleman called Mabbey chalked his cue, and, moving his round, knock-kneed legs in their tight trousers, took up his position for the stroke.

'What price that?' he said, as he regained the perpendicular; and his well-fed eyes followed Shelton with sleepy inquisition.

'Curious dark horse, Shelton,' they seemed to say.

Shelton hurried out, and was about to run down to the lower lawn, when he was accosted by another person walking in the sunshine—a slight-built man in a turned-down collar, with a thin and fair moustache, and a faint bluish tint on one side of his high forehead, caused by a network of thin veins. His face had something of the youthful, optimistic, stained-glass look of a certain refined English type. He walked elastically, yet with trim precision, as if he had a pleasant taste in furniture and churches, and held the *Spectator* in his hand.

'Ah, Shelton!' he said in high-tuned tones, halting his legs in such an easy attitude that it was impossible to interrupt it: 'come to take the air?'

Shelton's own brown face, nondescript nose, and amiable but dogged chin contrasted strangely with the clear-cut features of the stained-glass man.

'I hear from Halidome that you're going to stand for Parliament,' the latter said.

Shelton, recalling Halidome's autocratic manner of settling other people's business, smiled.

'Do I look like it?' he asked.

The eyebrows quivered on the stained-glass man. It had never occurred to him, perhaps, that to stand for Parliament a man must look like it; he examined Shelton with some curiosity.

'Ah, well,' he said, 'now you mention it, perhaps not.' His eyes, so carefully ironical, although they differed from the eyes of Mabbey, also seemed to ask of Shelton what sort of a dark horse he was.

'You're still in the Domestic Office, then?' asked Shelton.

The stained-glass man stooped to sniff a rosebush.

'Yes,' he said; 'it suits me very well. I get lots of time for my art work.'

'That must be very interesting,' said Shelton, whose glance was roving for Antonia; 'I never managed to begin a hobby.'

'Never had a hobby!' said the stained-glass man, brushing back his hair (he was walking with no hat); 'why, what the deuce d'you do?'

Shelton could not answer; the idea had never troubled him.

'I really don't know,' he said, embarrassed; 'there's always something going on, so far as I can see.'

The stained-glass man placed his hands within his pockets, and his bright glance swept over his companion.

'A fellow *must* have a hobby to give him an interest in life,' he said.

'An interest in life?' repeated Shelton grimly; 'life itself is good enough for me.'

'Oh!' replied the stained-glass man, as though he disapproved of regarding life itself as interesting. 'That's all very well, but you want something more than that. Why don't you take up wood-carving?'

'Why should I?'

'The moment I get fagged with office papers and that sort of thing I take up my wood-carving; good as a game of hockey.'

'I haven't the enthusiasm.'

The eyebrows of the stained-glass man twitched; he twisted his moustache.

'You'll find not having a hobby doesn't pay,' he said; 'you'll get old, then where'll you be?'

It came as a surprise that he should use the words 'it doesn't pay,' for he had a kind of partially enamelled look, like that modern jewellery which really seems unconscious of its market value.

'You've given up the Bar? Don't you get awfully bored having nothing to do?' pursued the stained-glass man, stopping before an ancient sun-dial.

Shelton felt a delicacy, as a man naturally would, in explaining that being in love was in itself enough to do. To do nothing is unworthy of a man! But he had never felt as yet the want of any occupation. His silence in no way disconcerted his acquaintance.

'That's a nice old article of virtue,' he said, pointing with his chin; and, walking round the sun-dial, he made its acquaintance from the other side. Its grey profile cast a thin and shortening shadow on the turf; tongues of moss were licking at its sides; the daisies clustered thick around its base; it had acquired a look of growing from the soil. 'I should like to get hold of that,' the stained-glass man remarked. 'I don't know when I've seen a better specimen,' and he walked round it once again.

His eyebrows were still ironically arched, but below them his eyes were almost calculating, and below them again, his mouth had opened just a little. A person with a keener eye would have said his face looked greedy, and even Shelton was surprised, as though he had read in the *Spectator* a confession of commercialism.

'You couldn't uproot a thing like that,' he said; 'it would lose all its charm.'

His companion turned impatiently, and his countenance looked wonderfully genuine.

'Couldn't I?' he said. 'By Jove! I thought so. 1690! The best period.' He ran his finger round the sun-dial's edges. Splendid line —clean as the day they made it. You don't seem to care much about that sort of thing;' and once again, though accustomed to the indifference of Vandals, his face regained its mask.

They strolled on towards the kitchen gardens, Shelton still busy searching every patch of shade. He wanted to say : 'Can't stop,' and hurry off; but there was about the stained-glass man a some-thing that, while stinging Shelton's feelings, made the showing of them quite impossible. 'Feelings!' that person seemed to say; 'all very well, but you want more than that. Why not take up wood-carving? . . . Feelings! I was born in England, and have been at Cambridge.'

'Are you staying long?' he asked of Shelton. 'I go on to Hali-dome's to-morrow; suppose I shan't see you there? Good chap, old Halidome; Collections of etchings very fine!'

'No; I'm staying on,' said Shelton.

'Ah!' said the stained-glass man, 'charming people, the Dennants!'

Shelton, reddening slowly, turned his head away; he picked a gooseberry, and muttered 'Yes.'

'The eldest girl especially; no nonsense about her. I thought she was a particularly nice girl.'

Shelton heard this praise of Antonia with an odd sensation; it gave him the reverse of pleasure, as though the words had cast new light upon her. He grunted hastily :

'I suppose you know that we're engaged?'

'Really!' said the stained-glass man, and again his bright, clear, non-committal glance swept over Shelton—'really! I didn't know. Congratulate you!'

It was as if he said : 'You're a man of taste; I should say she would go well in almost any drawing-room!'

'Thanks,' said Shelton; 'there she is. If you'll excuse me, I want to speak to her.'

Chapter 24

PARADISE

ANTONIA, in a sunny angle of the old brick wall, amid the pinks and poppies and cornflowers, was humming to herself. Shelton saw the stained-glass man pass out of sight, then, unobserved, he watched her smelling at the flowers, caressing her face with each in turn, casting away spoiled blossoms, and all the time humming that soft tune.

In two months, or three, all barriers between himself and this inscrutable young Eve would break; she would be part of him, and he a part of her; he would know all her thoughts, and she all his; together they would be as *one*; and all would think of them, and talk of them, as *one*; and this would come about by standing half an hour together in a church, by the passing of a ring, and the signing of their names.

The sun was burnishing her hair—she wore no hat—flushing her cheeks, sweetening and making sensuous her limbs; it had warmed her through and through, so that, like the flowers and bees, the sunlight and the air, she was all motion, light, and colour.

She turned and saw Shelton standing there.

'Oh, Dick!' she exclaimed, 'lend me your handkerchief to put these flowers in, there's a good boy!'

Her candid eyes, blue as the flowers in her hands, were clear and cool as ice, but in her smile was all the warm profusion of that corner; the sweetness had soaked into her, and was welling forth again. The sight of those sun-warmed cheeks, and fingers twining round the flower-stalks, her pearly teeth, and hair all fragrant, stole the reason out of Shelton. He stood before her, weak about the knees.

'Found you at last!' he cried.

Curving back her neck, she cried out: 'Catch!' and with a sweep of both her hands flung the flowers into Shelton's arms.

Under the rain of flowers, all warm and odorous, he dropped down on his knees, and put them one by one together, smelling at the pinks, to hide the violence of his feelings. Antonia went on picking flowers, and every time her hand was full she dropped them on his hat, his shoulder, or his arms, and went on plucking more; she smiled, and on her lips a little devil danced. She seemed

130

to know what he was suffering. And Shelton felt that she *did* know.

'Are you tired?' she asked; 'there are heaps more wanted. These are the bedroom flowers—fourteen lots. I can't think how people can live without flowers, can you?' and close above his head she buried her face in pinks.

He kept his eyes on the plucked flowers before him on the grass, and forced himself to answer:

'I think I can hold out.'

'Poor old Dick!' She had stepped back. The sun lit the clear-cut profile of her cheek, and poured its gold over the bosom of her blouse. 'Poor old Dick! Awfully hard luck, isn't it?' Burdened with mignonette, she came so close again that now she touched his shoulder, but Shelton did not look; breathless, with wildly beating heart, he went on sorting out the flowers. The seeds of mignonette rained on his neck, and as she let the blossoms fall, their perfume fanned his face. 'You needn't sort them out,' she said.

Was she enticing him? He stole a look; but she was gone again, swaying and sniffing at the flowers.

'I suppose I'm only hindering you,' he growled; 'I'd better go.'

She laughed.

'I like to see you on your knees, you look so funny!' and as she spoke she flung a clove carnation at him. 'Doesn't it smell good?'

'Too good! Oh, Antonia! why are you doing this?'

'Why am I doing what?'

'Don't you know what you are doing?'

'Why, picking flowers!' and once more she was back, bending and sniffing at the blossoms.

'That's enough.'

'Oh no,' she called; 'it's not—not nearly. Keep on putting them together, if you—love me.'

'You know I love you,' answered Shelton, in a smothered voice.

Antonia gazed at him across her shoulder; puzzled and inquiring was her face.

'I'm not a bit like you,' she said. 'What will you have for *your* room?'

'Choose!'

'Cornflowers and clove pinks. Poppies are too frivolous, and pinks too——'

'White,' said Shelton.

'And mignonette too hard and——'

'Sweet. Why cornflowers?'

131

Antonia stood before him with her hands against her sides; her figure was so slim and young, her face uncertain and so grave.

'Because they're dark and deep.'

'And why clove pinks?'

Antonia did not answer.

'And why clove pinks?'

'Because,' she said, and, flushing, touched a bee that had settled on her skirt, 'because of something in you I don't understand.'

'Ah! And what flowers shall I give *you*?'

She put her hands behind her.

'There are all the other flowers for me.'

Shelton snatched from the mass in front of him an Iceland poppy with straight stem and a curved neck, white pinks and sprigs of hard, sweet mignonette, and held it out to her.

'There,' he said, 'that's you.'

But Antonia did not move.

'Oh no, it isn't!' and behind her back her fingers slowly crushed the petals of a blood-red poppy. She shook her head, smiling a brilliant smile. The blossoms fell, he flung his arms around her, and kissed her on the lips.

But his hands dropped; not fear exactly, nor exactly shame, had come to him. She had not resisted, but he had kissed the smile away; had kissed a strange, cold, frightened look into her eyes.

'She didn't mean to tempt me, then,' he thought, in surprise and anger. 'What *did* she mean?' and, like a scolded dog, he kept his troubled watch upon her face.

Chapter 25

THE RIDE

'WHERE now?' Antonia asked, wheeling her chestnut mare, as they turned up High Street, Oxford City. 'I won't go back the same way, Dick!'

'We could have a gallop on Port Meadow, cross the Upper River twice, and get home that way; but you'll be tired.'

Antonia shook her head. Aslant her cheek the brim of a straw hat threw a curve of shade, her ear glowed transparent in the sun.

A difference had come in their relations since that kiss; outwardly she was the same good comrade, cool and quick. But as before a change one feels the subtle difference in the temper of the wind, so Shelton was affected by the inner change in her. He had made a blot upon her candour; he had tried to rub it out again, but there was left a mark, and it was ineffaceable. Antonia belonged to the most civilised division of the race most civilised in all the world, whose creed is: 'Let us love and hate, let us work and marry, but let us never give ourselves away; to give ourselves away is to leave a mark, and that is past forgiveness. Let our lives be like our faces, free from every kind of wrinkle, even those of laughter; in this way alone can we be really civilised.'

He felt that she was ruffled by a vague discomfort. That he should give himself away was natural, perhaps, and only made her wonder, but that he should give her the feeling that *she* had given herself away was a very different thing.

'Do you mind if I just ask at the Bishop's Head for letters?' he said, as they passed the old hotel.

A dirty and thin envelope was brought to him addressed 'Mr Richard Shelton, Esq.,' in a handwriting passionately clear, as though the writer had put his soul into securing delivery of the letter. It was dated three days back, and, as they rode away, Shelton read as follows:

'IMPERIAL PEACOCK HOTEL,
'FOLKESTONE.

'MON CHER MONSIEUR SHELTON,

'This is already the third time I have taken up pen to write to you, but, having nothing but misfortune to recount, I hesitated, awaiting better days. Indeed, I have been so profoundly discouraged that if I had not thought it my duty to let you know of my fortunes I know not even now if I should have found the necessary spirit. *Les choses vont de mal en mal.* From what I hear there has never been so bad a season here. Nothing going on. All the same, I am tormented by a mob of little matters which bring me not sufficient to support my life. I know not what to do; one thing is certain, in no case shall I return here another year. The patron of this hotel, my good employer, is one of those innumerable specimens who do not forge or steal, because they have no need, and if they had would lack the courage; who observe the marriage laws because they have been brought up to believe in them, and know that breaking them brings risk and loss of reputation; who do not gamble because they dare not; do not drink because it disagrees with them; go to church because their neighbours go, and to procure an appetite for the mid-day meal; commit no murder because, not transgressing in any other fashion, they are not obliged. What is there to respect in persons of this sort? Yet they are highly esteemed, and form three-quarters of Society. The rule with these good gentlemen is to shut their eyes, never use their thinking powers, and close the door on all the dogs of life for fear they should get bitten.'

Shelton paused, conscious of Antonia's eyes fixed on him with the enquiring look that he had come to dread. In that chilly questioning she seemed to say: 'I am waiting. I am prepared to be told things—that is, useful things—things that help one to believe without the risk of too much thinking.'

'It's from that young foreigner,' he said; and went on reading to himself.

'I have eyes, and here I am; I have a nose *pour flairer le humbug*. I see that amongst the value of things nothing is the equal of "free thought". Everything else they can take from me, *on ne peut pas m'ôter cela!* I see no future for me here, and certainly should have departed long ago if I had had the money; but, as I have already told you, all that I can do barely suffices to procure me *de quoi vivre. Je me sens écœuré.* Do not pay too much attention to my Jeremiads; you know what a pessimist I am. *Je ne perds pas courage.*

'Hoping that you are well, and in the cordial pressing of your hand, I subscribe myself,

> 'Your very devoted
> 'LOUIS FERRAND.'

He rode with the letter open in his hand, frowning at the curious turmoil which Ferrand excited in his heart. It was as though this foreign vagrant twanged within him a neglected string, which gave forth moans of mutiny.

'What does he say?' Antonia asked.

Should he show it to her? If he might not, what should he do when they were married?

'I don't quite know,' he said at last; 'it's not particularly cheering.'

'What is he like, Dick—I mean, to look at? Like a gentleman, or what?'

Shelton stifled a desire to laugh.

'He looks very well in a frock-coat,' he replied 'his father was a feather merchant.'

Antonia flicked her whip against her skirt.

'Of course,' she murmured, 'I don't want to hear if there's anything I ought not.'

But instead of soothing Shelton, these words had just the opposite effect. His conception of the ideal wife was not that of one from whom the half of life must be excluded.

'It's only,' he stammered again, 'that it's not cheerful.'

'Oh, all right!' she cried, and, touching her horse, flew off in front. 'I hate dismal things.'

Shelton bit his lips. It was not his fault that half the world was dark. He knew her words were loosed against himself, and, as always at a sign of her displeasure, was afraid. He galloped after her on the scorched turf.

'What is it?' he said. 'You're angry with me!'

'Oh no!'

'Darling, I can't help it if things aren't cheerful. We have eyes,' he added, quoting from the letter.

Antonia did not look at him; but touched her horse again.

'Well, I don't want to see the gloomy side,' she said, 'and I can't see why *you* should. It's wicked to be discontented;' and she galloped off.

It was not his fault if there were a thousand different kinds of men, a thousand different points of view, outside the fence of her experience! 'What business,' he thought, digging in his dummy spurs, 'has our class to patronise? We're the only people who haven't an idea of what life really means.' Chips of dried turf and dust came flying back, stinging his face. He gained on her, drew almost within reach, then, as though she had been playing with him, was left hopelessly behind.

She stooped under the far hedge, fanning her flushed face with dock-leaves.

'Aha, Dick! I knew you'd never catch me;' and she patted the chestnut mare, who turned her blowing muzzle with contemptuous humour towards Shelton's steed, while her flanks heaved rapturously, gradually darkening with sweat.

'We'd better take them steadily,' grunted Shelton, getting off and loosening his girths, 'if we mean to get home at all.'

'Don't be cross, Dick!'

'We oughtn't to have galloped them like this; they're not in condition. We'd better go home the way we came.'

Antonia dropped the reins, and straightened her back hair.

'There's no fun in that,' she said. 'Out and back again; I hate a dog's walk.'

'Very well,' said Shelton; he would have her longer to himself!

The road led up and up a hill, and from the top a vision of Saxonia lay disclosed in waves of wood and pasture. Their way branched down a gateless glade, and Shelton sidled closer till his knee touched the mare's off-flank.

Antonia's profile conjured up such visions. She was youth itself; her cheeks so glowing, and her brow unruffled; but in her smile and in the setting of her jaw lurked something resolute and mischievous. Shelton put his hand out to the mare's mane.

'What made you promise to marry me?' he said.

She smiled.

'Well, what made *you?*'

'I?' cried Shelton.

She slipped her hand over his hand.

'Oh, Dick!' she said.

'I want,' he stammered, 'to be everything to you. Do you think I shall?'

'Of course!'

Of course! The words seemed very much or very little.

She looked down at the river, gleaming below the glade in a curving silver line. 'Dick, there are such a lot of splendid things that we might do.'

Did she mean, amongst those splendid things, that they might understand each other; or were they fated to pretend to only, in the old time-honoured way?

They crossed the river by a ferry, and rode a long way in silence, while the twilight slowly fell behind the aspens. And all the beauty of the evening, with its restless leaves, its grave young moon, and lighted campion flowers, was but a part of her; the scents, the witchery and shadows, the quaint field noises, the yokels' whistling, and the plash of water-fowl, each seemed to him enchanted. The flighting bats, the forms of the dim hayricks, and sweet-brier perfume—she summed them all up in herself. The fingermarks had deepened underneath her eyes, a languor came upon her; it made her the more sweet and youthful. Her shoulders seemed to bear on them the very image of our land—grave and aspiring, eager yet contained—before there came upon that land the grin of greed, the folds of wealth, the simper of content. Fair, unconscious, free!

And he was silent, with a beating heart.

Chapter 26

THE BIRD OF PASSAGE

THAT night, after the ride, when Shelton was about to go to bed, his eyes fell on Ferrand's letter, and with a sleepy sense of duty he began to read it through a second time. In the dark, oak-panelled bedroom, his four-post bed, with back of crimson damask and dainty sheets, was lighted by the candle glow; the copper pitcher of hot water in the basin, the silver of his brushes, and the line of his well-polished boots, all shone, and Shelton's face alone was gloomy, staring at the yellowish paper in his hand.

'The poor chap wants money, of course,' he thought. But why go on for ever helping one who had no claim on him, a hopeless case, incurable—one whom it was his duty to let sink for the good of the community at large? Ferrand's vagabond refinement had beguiled him into charity that should have been bestowed on hospitals, or any charitable work but foreign missions. To give a helping hand, a bit of himself, a nod of fellowship to any fellow-being irrespective of a claim, merely because he happened to be down, was sentimental nonsense! The line must be drawn! But in the muttering of this conclusion he experienced a twinge of honesty. 'Humbug! You don't want to part with your money, that's all!'

So sitting down in shirt-sleeves at his writing-table, he penned the following on paper stamped with the Holm Oaks address and crest:

'MY DEAR FERRAND,

'I am sorry you are having such a bad spell. You seem to be dead out of luck. I hope by the time you get this things will have changed for the better. I should very much like to see you again and have a talk, but shall be away for some time longer, and doubt even when I get back whether I should be able to run down and look you up. Keep me *au courant* as to your movements. I enclose a cheque.

'Yours sincerely,
'RICHARD SHELTON.'

Before he had written out the cheque, a moth fluttering round the candle distracted his attention, and by the time he had caught and put it out he had forgotten that the cheque was not enclosed. The letter, removed with his clothes before he was awake, was posted in an empty state.

One morning a week later he was sitting in the smoking-room in the company of the gentleman called Mabbey, who was telling him how many grouse he had deprived of life on August 12 last year, and how many he intended to deprive of life on August 12 this year, when the door was opened, and the butler entered, carrying his head as though it held some fatal secret.

'A young man is asking for you, sir,' he said to Shelton, bending down discreetly. 'I don't know if you would wish to see him, sir.'

'A young man!' repeated Shelton. 'What sort of a young man?'

'I should say a sort of foreigner, sir,' apologetically replied the butler. 'He's wearing a frock-coat, but he looks as if he had been walking a good deal.'

Shelton rose with haste; the description sounded to him ominous.

'Where is he?'

'I put him in the young ladies' little room, sir.'

'All right,' said Shelton; 'I'll come and see him——' 'Now, what the deuce!' he thought, running down the stairs.

With a queer commingling of pleasure and vexation he entered the little chamber sacred to the birds, beasts, racquets, golf-clubs, and general young ladies' litter. Ferrand was standing underneath the cage of a canary, his hands folded on his pinched-up hat, a nervous smile on his lips. He was dressed in Shelton's old frock-coat, tightly buttoned, and would have cut a stylish figure but for his look of travel. He wore a pair of pince-nez, too, which somewhat veiled his cynical blue eyes, and clashed a little with the pagan look of him. In the midst of the strange surroundings he still preserved that air of knowing, and being master of, his fate, which was his chief attraction.

'I'm glad to see you,' said Shelton, holding out his hand.

'Forgive this liberty,' began Ferrand, 'but I thought it due to you, after all you've done for me, not to throw up my efforts to get employment in England without letting you know first. I'm entirely at the end of my resources.'

The phrase struck Shelton as one that he had heard before.

'But I wrote to you,' he said; 'didn't you get my letter?'

A flicker passed across the vagrant's face; he drew the letter from his pocket and held it out.

'Here it is, monsieur.'

Shelton stared at it.

'Surely,' said he, 'I sent a cheque?'

Ferrand did not smile; there was a look about him as though Shelton by forgetting to enclose that cheque had done him a real injury.

Shelton could not quite hide a glance of doubt.

'Of course,' he said, 'I—I—meant to enclose a cheque!'

Too subtle to say anything, Ferrand curled his lip. 'I am capable of much, but not of that,' he seemed to say; and at once Shelton felt the meaning of his doubt.

'Stupid of me,' he said.

'I had no intention of intruding here,' exclaimed Ferrand; 'I hoped to see you in the neighbourhood, but I arrived exhausted with fatigue. I've eaten nothing since yesterday at noon, and walked thirty miles,' He shrugged his shoulders. 'You see I had no time to lose before assuring myself whether you were here or not.'

'Of course——' began Shelton, but again he stopped.

'I should very much like,' the young foreigner went on, 'for one of your good legislators to find himself in these country villages with a penny in his pocket. In other countries bakers are obliged to sell you an equivalent of bread for a penny; here they won't sell you as much as a crust under twopence. You don't encourage poverty.'

'What is your idea now?' asked Shelton, trying to gain time.

'As I told you,' replied Ferrand, 'there's nothing to be done at Folkestone, though I should have stayed there if I had had the money to defray certain expenses;' and again he seemed to reproach his patron with the omission of that cheque. 'They say things will certainly be better at the end of the month. Now that I know English well, I thought perhaps I could procure a situation for teaching languages.'

'I see,' said Shelton.

As a fact, however, he was far from seeing; he literally did not know what to do. It seemed so brutal to give Ferrand money and ask him to clear out; besides, he chanced to have none in his pocket.

'It needs philosophy to support what I've gone through this week,' said Ferrand, shrugging his shoulders. 'On Wednesday last, when I received your letter, I had just eighteenpence, and at once

I made a resolution to come and see you; on that sum I've done the journey. My strength is nearly at an end.'

Shelton stroked his chin.

'Well,' he had just begun, 'we must think it over,' when by Ferrand's face he saw that someone had come in. He turned, and saw Antonia in the doorway. 'Excuse me,' he stammered, and, going to Antonia, drew her from the room.

With a smile she said at once: 'It's the young foreigner; I'm certain. Oh, what fun!'

'Yes,' answered Shelton slowly; 'he's come to see me about getting some sort of tutorship or other. Do you think your mother would mind if I took him up to have a wash? He's had a longish walk. And might he have some breakfast? He must be hungry.'

'Of course! I'll tell Dobson. Shall I speak to mother? He looks nice, Dick.'

He gave her a grateful furtive look, and went back to his guest; an impulse had made him hide from her the true condition of affairs.

Ferrand was standing where he had been left, his face still clothed in mordant impassivity.

'Come up to my room!' said Shelton; and while his guest was washing, brushing, and otherwise embellishing his person, he stood reflecting that Ferrand was by no means unpresentable, and he felt quite grateful to him.

He took an opportunity, when the young man's back was turned, of examining his counterfoils. There was no record, naturally, of a cheque drawn in Ferrand's favour—Shelton felt more mean than ever.

A message came from Mrs Dennant; so he took the traveller to the dining-room and left him there, while he himself went to the lady of the house. He met Antonia coming down.

'How many days did you say he went without food that time— you know?' she asked in passing.

'Four.'

'He doesn't look a bit common, Dick.'

Shelton gazed at her dubiously.

'They're surely not going to make a show of him!' he thought.

Mrs Dennant was writing, in a dark-blue dress starred over with white spots, whose fine lawn collar was threaded with black velvet.

'Have you seen the new hybrid Algy's brought me back from Kidstone? Isn't it charmin'?' and she bent her face towards this perfect rose. 'They say unique; I'm awfully interested to find out if that's true. I've told Algy I really must have some.'

Shelton thought of the unique hybrid breakfasting downstairs; he wished that Mrs Dennant would show in him the interest she had manifested in the rose. But this, he knew, was absurd of him, for the potent law of hobbies controlled the upper classes, forcing them to take more interest in birds, and roses, missionaries, or limited and highly-bound editions of old books (things, in a word, in treating which you knew exactly where you were), than in the manifestations of mere life which came before their eyes.

'Oh, Dick, about that young Frenchman. Antonia says he wants a tutorship; now, can you really recommend him? There's Mrs Robinson at the Gateways wants someone to teach her boys languages; and, if he were *quite* satisfactory, it's really time Toddles had a few lessons in French; he goes to Eton next half.'

Shelton stared at the rose; he had suddenly realised why it was that people take more interest in roses than in human beings—one could do it with a quiet heart.

'He's not a Frenchman, you know,' he said, to gain a little time.

'He's not a German, I hope,' Mrs Dennant answered, passing her fingers round a petal, to impress its fashion on her brain; 'I don't like Germans. Isn't he the one you wrote about—come down in the world? Such a pity with so young a fellow! His father was a merchant, I think you told us. Antonia says he's quite refined to look at.'

'Oh yes,' said Shelton, feeling on safe ground; 'he's refined enough to look at.'

Mrs Dennant took the rose and put it to her nose.

'Delicious perfume! That was a very touchin' story about his goin' without food in Paris. Old Mrs Hopkins has a room to let; I should like to do her a good turn. I'm afraid there's a hole in the ceilin', though. Or there's the room here in the left wing on the ground-floor where John the footman used to sleep. It's quite nice; perhaps he could have that.'

'You're awfully kind,' said Shelton, 'but——'

'I should like to do something to restore his self-respect,' went on Mrs Dennant, 'if, as you say, he's clever and all that. Seein' a little refined life again might make a world of difference to him. It's so sad when a young man loses self-respect.'

Shelton was much struck by the practical way in which she looked at things. Restore his self-respect! It seemed quite a splendid notion! He smiled, and said:

141

'You're too kind. I think——'

'I don't believe in doin' things by halves,' said Mrs Dennant; 'he doesn't drink, I suppose?'

'Oh no,' said Shelton. 'He's rather a tobacco maniac, of course!'

'Well, that's a mercy! You wouldn't believe the trouble I've had with drink, especially over cooks and coachmen. And now Bunyan's taken to it.'

'Oh, you'd have no trouble with Ferrand,' returned Shelton; 'you couldn't tell him from a gentleman as far as manners go.'

Mrs Dennant smiled one of her rather sweet and kindly smiles.

'My dear Dick,' she said, 'there's not much comfort in that. Look at poor Bobby Surcingle, look at Oliver Semples and Victor Medallion; you couldn't have better families. But if you're sure he doesn't drink! Algy'll laugh, of course; that doesn't matter—he laughs at everything.'

Shelton felt guilty; being quite unprepared for so rapid an adoption of his client.

'I really believe there's a lot of good in him,' he stammered; 'but, of course, I know very little, and from what he tells me he's had a very curious life. I shouldn't like——'

'Where was he educated?' inquired Mrs Dennant. 'They have public schools in France, so I've been told; but, of course, he can't help that, poor young fellow! Oh! and, Dick, there's one thing; has he relations? One has always to be so careful about that. It's one thing to help a young fellow, but quite another to help his family too. One sees so many cases of that where men marry girls without money, don't you know.'

'He has told me,' answered Shelton, 'his only relations are some cousins, and they are rich.'

Mrs Dennant took out her handkerchief, and, bending above the rose, removed a tiny insect.

'These green-fly get in everywhere,' she said. '*Very* sad story; can't *they* do anything for him?' and she made researches in the rose's heart.

'He's quarrelled with them, I believe,' said Shelton. 'I haven't liked to press him about that.'

'No, of course not,' assented Mrs Dennant absently—she had found another green-fly—'I always think it's painful when a young man seems so friendless.'

Shelton was silent; he was thinking deeply. He had never before felt so distrustful of the youthful foreigner.

'I think,' he said at last, 'the best thing would be for you to see him for yourself.'

'Very well,' said Mrs Dennant. 'I should be so glad if you would tell him to come up. I must say I do think that was a most touchin' story about Paris. I wonder whether the light's strong enough now for me to photograph this rose.'

Shelton withdrew and went downstairs. Ferrand was still at breakfast. Antonia stood at the sideboard carving beef for him, and in the window sat Thea with her Persian kitten.

Both girls were following the traveller's movements with inscrutable blue eyes. A shiver ran down Shelton's spine. To speak truth, he cursed the young man's coming, as though it affected his relations with Antonia.

Chapter 27

SUB ROSA

FROM the interview, which Shelton had the mixed delight of watching, between Ferrand and the Honourable Mrs Dennant, certain definite results accrued, the chief of which was the permission accorded the young wanderer to occupy the room which had formerly been tenanted by the footman John. Shelton was lost in admiration of Ferrand's manner in this scene. Its subtle combination of deference and dignity was almost paralysing; paralysing, too, the subterranean smile on his lips.

'Charmin' young man, Dick,' said Mrs Dennant, when Shelton lingered to say once more that he knew but very little of him : 'I shall send a note round to Mrs Robinson at once. They're very common, you know—the Robinsons. I think they'll take anyone I recommend.'

'I'm sure they will,' said Shelton; 'that's why I think you ought to know——'

But Mrs Dennant's eyes, fervent, hare-like, were fixed on something far away; turning, he saw the rose in a tall vase on a tall and spindly stool. It seemed to nod towards them in the sunshine. Mrs Dennant dived her nose towards her camera.

'The light's perfect now,' she said, in a voice muffled by the cloth. 'I feel sure that livin' with decent people will do wonders for him. Of course, he understands that his meals will be served to him apart.'

Shelton, doubly anxious, now that his efforts had lodged his client in a place of trust, fell back on hoping for the best; his instinct told him that, vagabond as Ferrand was, he had a curious self-respect, which would save him from a mean ingratitude.

In fact, as Mrs Dennant, who was by no means void of common sense, foresaw, the arrangement worked all right. Ferrand entered on his duties as French tutor to the little Robinsons. In the Dennants' household he kept himself to his own room, which, day and night, he perfumed with tobacco, emerging at noon into the garden, or, if wet, into the study, to teach young Toddles French. After a time it became customary for him to lunch with the house-party, partly through a mistake of Toddles, who seemed to think that it was natural, and partly through John Noble, one of Shelton's friends, who had come to stay, and discovered Ferrand to be a most awfully interesting person—he was always, indeed, discovering the most awfully interesting persons. In his grave and toneless voice, brushing his hair from off his brow, he descanted upon Ferrand with enthusiasm, to which was joined a kind of shocked amusement, as who should say: 'Of course, I know it's very odd, but really he's such an awfully interesting person.' For John Noble was a politician, belonging to one of those two Peculiar parties, which, thoroughly in earnest, of an honesty above suspicion, and always very busy, are constitutionally averse to anything peculiar for fear of finding they have over-stepped the limit of what is practical in politics. As such he inspired confidence, not caring for things unless he saw some immediate benefit to be had from them, having a perfect sense of decency, and a small imagination. He discussed all sorts of things with Ferrand; on one occasion Shelton overheard them arguing on Anarchism.

'No Englishman approves of murder,' Noble was saying, in the gloomy voice that contrasted with the optimistic cast of his fine head, 'but the main principle is right. Equalisation of property is bound to come. I sympathise with *them*, not with their methods.'

'Forgive me,' struck in Ferrand; 'do you know any Anarchists?'

'No,' returned Noble, 'I certainly do not.'

'You say you sympathise with them, but the first time it comes to action——'

'Well?'

'Oh, monsieur! one doesn't make Anarchism with the head.'

Shelton perceived that he had meant to add 'but with the heart, the lungs, the liver.' He drew a deeper meaning from the saying, and seemed to see, curling with the smoke from Ferrand's lips, the words: 'What do you, an English gentleman, of excellent position, and all the prejudices of your class, know about us outcasts? If you want to understand us you must be an outcast too; *we* are not playing at the game.'

This talk took place upon the lawn, at the end of one of Toddles' French lessons, and Shelton left John Noble maintaining to the youthful foreigner, with stubborn logic, that he, John Noble, and the Anarchists had much in common. He was returning to the house, when someone called his name from underneath the holm-oak. There, sitting Turkish fashion on the grass, a pipe between his teeth, he found a man who had arrived the night before, and impressed him by his friendly taciturnity. His name was Whyddon, and he had just returned from Central Africa; a brown-faced, large-jawed man, with small but good and steady eyes, and a strong, spare figure.

'Oh, Mr Shelton!' he said, 'I wondered if you could tell me what tips I ought to give the servants here; after ten years away I've forgotten all about that sort of thing.'

Shelton sat down beside him, unconsciously assuming, too, a cross-legged attitude, which caused him much discomfort.

'I was listening,' said his new acquaintance, 'to the little chap learning his French. I've forgotten mine. One feels a hopeless duffer knowing no languages.'

'I suppose you speak Arabic?' said Shelton.

'Oh, Arabic and a dialect or two; they don't count. That tutor has a curious face.'

'You think so?' said Shelton, interested. 'He's had a curious life.'

The traveller spread his hands, palms downwards, on the grass, and looked at Shelton with a smile.

'I should say he was a rolling stone,' he said. 'It's odd, I've seen white men in Central Africa with a good deal of his look about them.'

'Your diagnosis is a good one,' answered Shelton.

'I'm always sorry for those fellows. There's generally some good in them. They are their own enemies. A bad business to be unable to take pride in anything one does!' And there was a look of pity on his face.

'That's exactly it,' said Shelton. 'I've often tried to put it into words. Is it incurable?'

'I think so.'

145

'Can you tell me why?'

Whyddon pondered.

'I rather think,' he said at last, 'it must be because they have too strong a faculty of criticism. You can't teach a man to be proud of his own work; that lies in his blood.' Folding his arms across his breast, he heaved a sigh. Under the dark foliage, his eyes on the sunlight, he was the type of all those Englishmen who keep their spirits bright and wear their bodies out in the dark places of hard work. 'You can't think,' he said, showing his teeth in a smile, 'how delightful it is to be at home! You learn to love the old country when you're away from it.'

Shelton often thought, afterwards, of this diagnosis of the vagabond, for he was always stumbling on instances of that power of subtle criticism which was the young foreigner's prime claim to be 'a most awfully interesting,' and perhaps a rather shocking person.

An old schoolfellow of Shelton's and his wife were staying in the house, who offered to the eye the picture of a perfect domesticity. Passionless and smiling, it was impossible to imagine they could ever have a difference. Shelton, whose bedroom was next to theirs, could hear them in the mornings talking in exactly the tones they used at lunch, and laughing the same laughs. Their life seemed to accord them perfect satisfaction; they were supplied with their convictions by Society, just as, when at home, they were supplied with all the other necessaries of life by some Co-operative Stores. Their fairly handsome faces, with the fairly kind expressions, quickly and carefully regulated by a sense of compromise, began to worry him so much that when in the same room he would even read to avoid the need of looking at them. And yet they were kind—that is, fairly kind—and clean and quiet in the house, except when they laughed, which was often, and at things which made him want to howl, as a dog howls at music.

'Mr Shelton,' Ferrand said one day, 'I'm not an amateur of marriage—never had the chance, as you may well suppose; but, in any case, you have some people in the house who would make me mark time before I went committing it. They seem the ideal young married people—don't quarrel, have perfect health, agree with everybody, go to church, have children—but I should like to hear what is beautiful in their life.' And he grimaced. 'It seems to me so ugly that I can only gasp. I would much rather they ill-treated each other, just to show they had the corner of a soul between them. If that is marriage, *Dieu m'en garde!*'

But Shelton did not answer; he was thinking deeply.

The saying of John Noble's, 'He's really a most interesting person,' grew more and more upon his nerves; it seemed to describe the Dennant attitude towards this stranger within their gates. They treated him with a sort of wonder on the 'don't touch' system, like an object in an exhibition. The restoration, however, of his self-respect proceeded with success. For all the semblance of having grown too big for Shelton's clothes, for all his vividly burnt face, and the quick but guarded play of cynicism on his lips—he did much credit to his patrons. He had subdued his terror of a razor, and looked well in a suit of Shelton's flannels. For, after all, he had only been eight years exiled from middle-class gentility, and he had been a waiter half that time. But Shelton wished him at the devil. Not for his manners' sake—he was never tired of watching how subtly the vagabond adapted all his conduct to the conduct of his hosts, while keeping up his critical detachment—but because that critical detachment was a constant spur to his own vision, compelling him to analyse the life into which he had been born and was about to marry. This process was disturbing; and to find out when it had commenced, he had to go back to his meeting with Ferrand on the journey up from Dover.

There was kindness in a hospitality which opened to so strange a bird; admitting the kindness, Shelton fell to analysing it. To himself, to people of his class, the use of kindness was a luxury, not significant of sacrifice, but productive of a pleasant feeling in the heart, such as massage will set up in the legs. 'Everybody's kind,' he thought; 'the question is: What understanding is there, what real sympathy?' This problem gave him food for thought.

The progress, which Mrs Dennant not unfrequently remarked upon, in Ferrand's conquest of his strange position, seemed to Shelton but a sign that he was getting what he could out of his sudden visit to green pastures; under the same circumstances, Shelton thought that he himself would do the same. He felt that the young foreigner was making a convenient bow to property, but he had more respect for the sarcastic smile on the lips of Ferrand's heart.

It was not long before the inevitable change came in the spirit of the situation; more and more was Shelton conscious of a quaint uneasiness in the very breathing of the household.

'Curious fellow you've got hold of there, Shelton,' Mr Dennant said to him during a game of croquet, 'he'll never do any good for himself, I'm afraid.'

'In one sense I'm afraid not,' admitted Shelton.

'Do you know his story? I will bet you sixpence'—and Mr Dennant paused to swing his mallet with a proper accuracy—'that he's been in prison.'

'Prison!' ejaculated Shelton.

'I think,' said Mr Dennant, with bent knees carefully measuring his next shot, 'that you ought to make inquiries—ah! missed it! Awkward these hoops! One must draw the line somewhere.'

'I never could draw,' returned Shelton, nettled and uneasy; 'but I understand—I'll give him a hint to go.'

'Don't,' said Mr Dennant, moving after his second ball, which Shelton had smitten to the farther end, 'be offended, my dear Shelton, and by no means give him a hint; he interests me very much—a very clever, quiet young fellow.'

That this was not his private view Shelton inferred by studying Mr Dennant's manner in the presence of the vagabond. Underlying the well-bred banter of the tranquil voice, the guarded quizzicality of his pale brown face, it could be seen that Algernon Cuffe Dennant, Esq., J.P., accustomed to laugh at other people, suspected that he was being laughed at. What more natural than that he should grope about to see how this could be? A vagrant alien was making himself felt by an English Justice of the Peace—no small tribute, this, to Ferrand's personality. The latter would sit silent through a meal, and yet make his effect. He, the object of their kindness, education, patronage, inspired their fear. There was no longer any doubt; it was not of Ferrand that they were afraid, but of what they did not understand in him; of horrid subtleties meandering in the brain under that straight, wet-looking hair; of something bizarre popping from the curving lips below that thin, lopsided nose.

But to Shelton in this, as in all else, Antonia was what mattered. At first, anxious to show her lover that she trusted him she seemed never tired of doing things for his young protégé, as though she too had set her heart on his salvation; but, watching her eyes when they rested on the vagabond, Shelton was perpetually reminded of her saying on the first day of his visit to Holm Oaks: 'I suppose he's really *good*—I mean all those things you told me about were only. . . .'

Curiosity never left her glance, nor did that story of his four days' starving leave her mind; a sentimental picturesqueness clung about that incident more valuable by far than this mere human being with whom she had so strangely come in contact. She watched Ferrand, and Shelton watched her. If he had been told that he was watching her, he would have denied it in good faith; but he was bound to watch her, to find out with what eyes she viewed this visitor who embodied all the rebellious under-side of life, all that was absent in herself.

'Dick,' she said to him one day, 'you never talk to me of Monsieur Ferrand.'

'Do you want to talk of him?'

'Don't you think that he's improved?'

'He's fatter.'

Antonia looked grave.

'No, but really?'

'I don't know,' said Shelton; 'I can't judge him.'

Antonia turned her face away, and something in her attitude alarmed him.

'He was once a sort of gentleman,' she said; 'why shouldn't he become one again?'

Sitting on the low wall of the kitchen-garden, her head was framed by golden plums. The sun lay barred behind the foliage of the holm-oak, but a little patch filtering through a gap had rested in the plum-tree's heart. It crowned the girl. Her raiment, the dark leaves, the red wall, the golden plums, were woven by the passing glow to a block of pagan colour. And her face above it, chaste, serene, was like the scentless summer evening. A bird amongst the currant-bushes kept a little chant vibrating; and all the plum-tree's shape and colour seemed alive.

'Perhaps he doesn't want to be a gentleman,' said Shelton.

Antonia swung her foot.

'How can he help wanting to?'

'He may have a different philosophy of life.'

Antonia was slow to answer. 'I know nothing about philosophies of life,' she said at last.

Shelton answered coldly:

'No two people have the same.'

With the falling sun-glow the charm passed off the tree. Chilled and harder, yet less deep, it was no more a block of woven colour, warm and impassive, like a southern goddess; it was now a northern tree with a grey light through its leaves.

'I don't understand you in the least,' she said; 'everyone wishes to be good.'

'And safe?' asked Shelton gently.

Antonia stared.

149

'Suppose,' he said—'I don't pretend to know; I only suppose—what Ferrand really cares for is doing things differently from other people? If you were to load him with a character and give him money on condition that he acted as we all act, do you think he would accept it?'

'Why not?'

'Why aren't cats dogs; or Pagans Christians?'

Antonia slid down from the wall.

'You don't seem to think there's any use in trying,' she said, and turned away.

Shelton made a movement as if he would go after her, and then stood still, watching her figure slowly pass, her head outlined above the wall, her hands turned back across her narrow hips. She halted at the bend, looked back, then, with an impatient gesture, disappeared.

Antonia was slipping from him!

A moment's vision from without himself would have shown him that it was he who moved and she who was standing still, like the figure of one watching the passage of a stream with clear, direct, and sullen eyes.

Chapter 28

THE RIVER

ONE day towards the end of August, Shelton took Antonia on the river—the river that, like soft music, soothes the land; the river of the reeds and the poplars, the silver swan-tails, sun and moon, woods, and the white slumbrous clouds; where cuckoos, and the wind, the pigeons, and the weirs are always singing; and in the flash of naked bodies, the play of water-lily leaves, queer goblin stumps, and the twilight faces of the twisted tree-roots, Pan lives once more.

The reach which Shelton chose was innocent of launches, champagne bottles, and loud laughter; it was uncivilised, and seldom troubled by these humanising influences. He paddled slowly, silent and absorbed, watching Antonia. An unaccustomed languor clung about her; her eyes had shadows, as though she had not slept; colour glowed softly in her cheeks, her frock seemed all alight with golden radiance. She made Shelton pull into the reeds, and plucked two rounded lilies sailing like ships against the slow-moving water.

'Pull into the shade, please,' she said; 'it's too hot out here.'

The brim of her linen hat kept the sun from her face, but her head was drooping like a flower's head at noon.

Shelton saw that the heat was really harming her, as too hot a day will dim the icy freshness of a northern plant. He dipped his sculls, the ripples started out, and swam in grave diminuendo till they touched the banks.

He shot the boat into a cleft, and caught the branches of an overhanging tree. The skiff rested, balancing with mutinous vibration, like a living thing.

'I should hate to live in London,' said Antonia suddenly; 'the slums must be awful. What a pity, when there are places like this! But it's no good thinking.'

'No,' answered Shelton slowly; 'I suppose it is no good.'

'There are some bad cottages at the lower end of Cross Eaton. I went there one day with Miss Truecote. The people won't help themselves. It's so discouraging to help people who won't help themselves.'

She was leaning her elbows on her knees, and, with her chin resting on her hands, gazed up at Shelton. All around them hung a tent of soft, thick leaves, and, below, the water was deep-dyed with green refraction. Willow boughs, swaying above the boat, caressed Antonia's arms and shoulders; her face and hair alone were free.

'So discouraging,' she said again.

A silence fell. Antonia seemed thinking deeply.

'Doubts don't help you,' she said suddenly; 'how can you get any good from doubts? The thing is to win victories.'

'Victories?' said Shelton. 'I'd rather understand than conquer.'

He had risen to his feet, and grasped a stunted branch, canting the boat towards the bank.

'How can you let things slide like that, Dick? It's like Ferrand.'

'Have you such a bad opinion of him, then?' asked Shelton. He felt on the verge of some discovery.

She buried her chin deeper in her hands.

'I liked him at first,' she said; 'I thought that he was different. I thought he couldn't really be——'

'Really be what?'

Antonia did not answer.

'I don't know,' she said at last. 'I can't explain. I thought——'

Shelton still stood, holding to the branch; and the oscillation of the boat freed an infinity of tiny ripples.

'You thought—what?' he said.

He ought to have seen her face grow younger, more childish, even timid. She said in a voice smooth, round, and young:

'You know, Dick, I do think we ought to try. I know I don't try half hard enough. It doesn't do any good to think; when you think, everything seems so mixed, as if there were nothing to lay hold of. I do so hate to feel like that. It isn't as if we didn't know what's right. Sometimes I think, and think, and it's all no good, only a waste of time, and you feel at the end as if you had been doing wrong.'

Shelton frowned.

'What hasn't been through fire's no good,' he said; and, letting go the branch, sat down. Free from restraint, the boat edged out towards the current. 'But what about Ferrand?'

'I lay awake last night wondering what makes you like him so. He's so bitter; he makes me feel unhappy. He never seems content with anything. And he despises'—her face hardened—'I mean, he hates us all.'

'So should I if I were he,' said Shelton.

The boat was drifting on, and gleams of sunlight chased across their faces. Antonia spoke again.

'He seems to be always looking at dark things, or else he seems as if—as if he could—enjoy himself too much. I thought—I thought at first,' she stammered, 'that we could do him good.'

'Do him good! Ha, ha!'

A startled rat went swimming for its life against the stream; and Shelton saw that he had done a dreadful thing; he had let Antonia with a jerk into a secret not hitherto admitted even by himself—the secret that her eyes were not his eyes, her way of seeing things not his, nor ever would be. He quickly muffled up his laughter. Antonia had dropped her gaze; her face regained its languor, but the bosom of her dress was heaving. Shelton watched her, racking his brains to find excuses for that fatal laugh; none could he find. It was a little piece of truth. He paddled slowly on, close to the bank, on the long silence of the river.

The breeze had died away, not a fish was rising; save for the lost music of the larks no birds were piping; alone, a single pigeon at brief intervals cooed from the neighbouring wood.

They did not stay much longer in the boat.

On the homeward journey in the pony-cart, rounding a corner

of the road, they came on Ferrand in his pince-nez, holding a cigarette between his fingers and talking to a tramp, who was squatting on the bank. The young foreigner recognised them, and at once removed his hat.

'There he is,' said Shelton, returning the salute.

Antonia bowed.

'Oh!' she cried, when they were out of hearing, 'I wish he'd go. I can't bear to see him; it's like looking at the dark.'

Chapter 29

ON THE WING

THAT night, having gone up to his room, Shelton filled his pipe for his unpleasant duty. He had resolved to hint to Ferrand that he had better go. He was still debating whether to write or go himself to the young foreigner, when there came a knock, and Ferrand himself appeared.

'I should be sorry,' he said, breaking an awkward silence, 'if you were to think me ungrateful, but I see no future for me here. It would be better for me to go. I should never be content to pass my life in teaching languages—*ce n'est guère dans mon caractère.*'

As soon as what he had been cudgelling his brains to find a way of saying had thus been said for him, Shelton experienced a sense of disapproval.

'What do you expect to get that's better?' he said, avoiding Ferrand's eyes.

'Thanks to your kindness,' replied the latter, 'I find myself restored. I feel that I ought to make some good efforts to dominate my social position.'

'I should think it well over, if I were you,' said Shelton.

'I have, and it seems to me that I'm wasting my time. For a man with any courage languages are no career; and, though I've many defects, I still have courage.'

Shelton let his pipe go out, so pathetic seemed to him this young man's faith in his career; it was no pretended faith, but neither was it, he felt, his true motive for departure. 'He's tired,' he thought; 'that's it. Tired of one place.' And having the instinctive sense that nothing would keep Ferrand, he redoubled his advice.

'I should have thought,' he said, 'that you would have done better to have held on here and saved a little before going off to God knows what.'

'To save,' said Ferrand, 'is impossible for me, but, thanks to you and your good friends, I've enough to make front to first necessities. I'm in correspondence with a friend; it's of great importance for me to reach Paris before all the world returns. I've a chance to get a post in one of the West African companies. One makes fortunes out there—if one survives, and, as you know, I don't set too much store by life.'

'We have a proverb,' said Shelton : 'A bird in the hand is worth two birds in the bush !'

'That,' returned Ferrand, 'like all proverbs, is just half true. This is an affair of temperament. It's not in my character to dandle one when I see two waiting to be caught; *voyager, apprendre, c'est plus fort que moi.*' He paused, then, with a nervous goggle of the eyes and an ironic smile, he said; 'Besides, *mon cher monsieur*, it is better that I go. I have never been one to hug illusions, and I see pretty clearly that my presence is hardly acceptable in this house.'

'What makes you say that?' asked Shelton, feeling that the murder was now out.

'My dear sir, all the world has not your understanding and your lack of prejudice, and though your friends have been extremely kind to me, I am in a false position; I cause them embarrassment, which is not extraordinary when you reflect what I have been, and that they know my history.'

'Not through me,' said Shelton quickly, 'for I don't know it myself.'

'It's enough,' the vagrant said, 'that they feel I'm not a bird of their feather. They cannot change, neither can I. I have never wanted to remain where I'm not welcome.'

Shelton turned to the window, and stared into the darkness; he would never quite understand this vagabond, so delicate, so cynical, and he wondered if Ferrand had been swallowing down the words : 'Why, even you won't be sorry to see my back !'

'Well,' he said at last, 'if you must go, you must. When do you start?'

'I've arranged with a man to carry my things to the early train. I think it better not to say good-bye. I've written a letter instead; here it is. I left it open for you to read if you should wish.'

'Then,' said Shelton, with a curious mingling of relief, regret, goodwill, 'I shan't see you again?'

Ferrand gave his hand a stealthy rub, and held it out.

'I shall never forget what you have done for me,' he said.

'Mind you write,' said Shelton.

'Yes, yes'—the vagrant's face was oddly twisted—'you don't know what a difference it makes to have a correspondent; it gives one courage. I hope to remain a long time in correspondence with you.'

'I dare say you do,' thought Shelton grimly, with a certain queer emotion.

'You will do me the justice to remember that I have never asked you for anything,' said Ferrand. 'Thank you a thousand times. Good-bye!'

He again wrung his patron's hand in his damp grasp, and, going out, left Shelton with an odd sensation in his throat. 'You will do me the justice to remember that I have never asked you for anything.' The phrase seemed strange, and his mind flew back over all this queer acquaintanceship. It was a fact; from the beginning to the end the youth had never really asked for anything. Shelton sat down on his bed, and began to read the letter in his hand. It was in French.

'Dear Madame (it ran)

'It will be insupportable to me, after your kindness, if you take me for ungrateful. Unfortunately, a crisis has arrived which plunges me into the necessity of leaving your hospitality. In all lives, as you are well aware, there arise occasions that one cannot govern, and I know you will pardon me that I enter into no explanation on an event which gives me great chagrin, and, above all, renders me subject to an imputation of ingratitude, which, believe me, dear Madame, by no means lies in my character. I know well enough that it is a breach of politeness to leave you without in person conveying the expression of my profound reconnaissance, but if you consider how hard it is for me to be compelled to abandon all that is so distinguished in domestic life, you will forgive my weakness. People like me, who have gone through existence with their eyes open, have remarked that those who are endowed with riches have a right to look down on such as are not by wealth and breeding fitted to occupy the same position. I shall never dispute a right so natural and salutary, which makes of the well-born and the well-bred a race apart, the rest of

155

the world would have no standard by which to rule their lives, no anchor to throw into the depths of that vast sea of fortune and of misfortune on which we others drive before the wind. It is because of this, dear Madame, that I regard myself so doubly fortunate to have been able for a few minutes in this bitter pilgrimage called life to sit beneath the tree of safety. To have been able, if only for an hour, to sit and see the pilgrims pass, the pilgrims with the blistered feet and ragged clothes, and who yet, dear Madame, guard within their hearts a certain joy in life, illegal joy, like the desert air which travellers will tell you fills men as with wine—to be able thus to sit an hour, and with a smile to watch them pass, lame and blind, in all the rags of their deserved misfortunes, can you not conceive, dear Madame, how that must be for such as me a comfort? Whatever one may say, it is sweet, from a position of security, to watch the sufferings of others; it gives one a good sensation in the heart.

'In writing this, I recollect that I myself once had the chance of passing all my life in this enviable safety, and as you may suppose, dear Madame, I curse myself that I should ever have had the courage to step beyond the boundaries of this fine tranquil state. Yet, too, there have been times when I have asked myself: "Do we really differ from the wealthy—we others, birds of the fields, who have our own philosophy, grown from the pains of needing bread—we who see that the human heart is not always an affair of figures, or of those good maxims that one finds in copy-books—do we really differ?" It is with shame that I confess to have asked myself a question so heretical. But now, when for these four weeks I have had the fortune of this rest beneath your roof, I see how wrong I was to entertain such doubts. It is a great happiness to have decided once for all this point, for it is not in my character to pass through life uncertain—mistaken, perhaps—on psychological matters such as these. No, Madame; rest happily assured that there *is a great difference*, which in the future will be sacred for me. For, believe me, Madame, it would be calamity for high Society if by chance there should arise amongst them any understanding of all that side of life which—vast as the plains and bitter as the sea, black as the ashes of a corpse, and yet more free than any wings of birds who fly away—is so justly beyond the grasp of their philosophy. Yes, believe me, dear Madame, there is no danger in the world so much to be avoided by all the members of that circle, most illustrious, most respectable, called high Society.

'From what I have said you may imagine how hard it is for me to take my flight. I shall always keep for you the most distinguished sentiments. With the expression of my full regard for you and your good family, and of a gratitude as sincere as it is badly worded,

'Believe me, dear Madame,
'Your devoted
'LOUIS FERRAND.'

Shelton's first impulse was to tear the letter up, but this he reflected he had no right to do. Remembering, too, that Mrs Dennant's French was orthodox, he felt sure she would never understand the young foreigner's subtle innuendoes. He closed the envelope and went to bed, haunted still by Ferrand's parting look.

It was with no small feeling of embarrassment, however, that, having sent the letter to its destination by an early footman, he made his appearance at the breakfast-table. Behind the Austrian coffee-urn, filled with French coffee, Mrs Dennant, who had placed four eggs in a German egg-boiler, said 'Good morning,' with a kindly smile.

'Dick, an egg?' she asked him, holding up a fifth.

'No, thank you,' replied Shelton, greeting the table, and sitting down.

He was a little late; the buzz of conversation rose hilariously around.

'My dear,' continued Mr Dennant, who was talking to his youngest daughter, 'you'll have no chance whatever—not the least little bit of chance.'

'Father, what nonsense! You know we shall beat your heads off!'

'Before it's too late, then, I will eat a muffin. Shelton, pass the muffins!' But in making this request, Mr Dennant avoided looking in his face.

Antonia, too, seemed to keep her eyes away from him. She was talking to a Connoisseur on Art of supernatural appearances, and seemed in the highest spirits. Shelton rose, and, going to the sideboard, helped himself to grouse.

'Who was the young man I saw yesterday on the lawn?' he heard the Connoisseur remark. 'Struck me as having an—er—quite intelligent physiog.'

His own intelligent physiog, raised at a slight slant so that he might look the better through his nose-nippers, was the very pattern of approval. 'It's curious how one's always meeting with intelligence' it seemed to say.

Mrs Dennant paused in the act of adding cream, and Shelton scrutinised her face; it was hare-like, and superior as ever. Thank goodness she had smelt no rat! He felt strangely disappointed.

'You mean Monsieur Ferrand, teachin' Toddles French? Dobson, the Professor's cup.'

'I hope I shall see him again,' cooed the Connoisseur; 'he was quite interesting on the subject of young German working men. It seems they tramp from place to place to learn their trades. What nationality was he, may I ask?'

Mr Dennant, of whom he asked this question, lifted his brows, and said:

'Ask Shelton.'

'A Fleming.'

'Very interesting breed; I hope I shall see him again.'

'Well, you won't,' said Thea suddenly; 'he's gone.'

Shelton saw that their good breeding alone prevented all from adding: 'And thank goodness, too!'

'Gone? Dear me, it's very——'

'Yes,' said Mr Dennant, 'very sudden.'

'Now, Algy,' murmured Mrs Dennant, 'it's quite a charmin' letter. Must have taken the poor young man an hour to write.'

'Oh, Mother!' cried Antonia.

And Shelton felt his face go crimson. He had suddenly remembered that her French was better than her mother's.

'He seems to have had a singular experience,' said the Connoisseur.

'Yes,' echoed Mr Dennant; 'he's had some singular experience. If you want to know the details, ask friend Shelton; it's quite romantic. In the meantime, my dear, another cup?'

The Connoisseur, never quite devoid of absent-minded malice, spurred his curiosity to a further effort; and, turning his well-defended eyes on Shelton, murmured:

'Well, Mr Shelton, you are the historian, it seems.'

'There is no history,' said Shelton, without looking up.

'Ah, that's very dull,' remarked the Connoisseur.

'My dear Dick,' said Mrs Dennant, 'that was really a most touchin' story about his goin' without food in Paris.'

Shelton shot another look at Antonia; her face was frigid. 'I hate your d——d superiority!' he thought, staring at the Connoisseur.

'There's nothing,' said that gentleman, 'more enthralling than starvation. Come, Mr Shelton.'

'I can't tell stories,' said Shelton; 'never could.'

He cared not a straw for Ferrand, his coming, going, or his history; for, looking at Antonia, his heart was heavy.

Chapter 30

THE LADY FROM BEYOND

THE morning was sultry, brooding, steamy. Antonia was at her music, and from the room where Shelton tried to fix attention on a book he could hear her practising her scales with a cold fury that cast an added gloom upon his spirit. He did not see her until lunch, and then she again sat next the Connoisseur. Her cheeks were pale, but there was something feverish in her chatter to her neighbour; she still refused to look at Shelton. He felt very miserable. After lunch, when most of them had left the table, the rest fell to discussing country neighbours.

'Of course,' said Mrs Dennant, 'there are the Foliots; but nobody calls on them.'

'Ah!' said the Connoisseur, 'the Foliots—the Foliots—the people —er—who—quite so!'

'It's really distressin'; she looks so sweet ridin' about. Many people with worse stories get called on,' continued Mrs Dennant, with that large frankness of intrusion upon doubtful subjects which may be made by certain people in a certain way; 'but, after all, one couldn't ask them to meet anybody.'

'No,' the Connoisseur assented. 'I used to know Foliot. Thousand pities. They say she was a very pretty woman.'

'Oh, not pretty!' said Mrs Dennant—'more interestin' than pretty, I should say.'

Shelton, who knew the lady slightly, noticed that they spoke of her as in the past. He did not look towards Antonia; for though a little troubled at her presence while such a subject was discussed, he hated his conviction that her face was as unruffled as though the Foliots had been a separate species. There was, in fact, a curiosity about her eyes, a faint impatience on her lips; she was rolling little crumbs of bread. Suddenly yawning, she muttered some remark, and rose. Shelton stopped her at the door.

'Where are you going?'

'For a walk.'

'Mayn't I come?'

She shook her head.

'I'm going to take Toddles.'

Shelton held the door open, and went back to the table.

'Yes,' the Connoisseur said, sipping at his sherry, 'I'm afraid it's all over with young Foliot.'

'*Such* a pity!' murmured Mrs Dennant, and her kindly face looked quite disturbed. 'I've known him ever since he was a boy. Of course, I think he made a great mistake to bring her down here. Not even bein' able to get married makes it doubly awkward. Oh, I think he made a great mistake!'

'Ah!' said the Connoisseur, 'but d'you suppose that makes much difference? Even if What's-his-name gave her a divorce, I don't think, don't you know, that——'

'Oh, it *does*! So many people would be inclined to look over it in time. But as it is it's hopeless, quite. So very awkward for people, too, meetin' them about. The Telfords and the Butterwicks —by the way they're comin' here to dine to-night—live near them, don't you know.'

'Did you ever meet her before—er—before the flood?' the Connoisseur inquired; and his lips parting and unexpectedly revealing teeth, gave him a shadowy resemblance to a goat.

'Yes; I did meet her once at the Branksomes'. I thought her quite a charmin' person.'

'Poor fellow!' said the Connoisseur; 'they tell me he was going to take the hounds.'

'And there are his delightful coverts, too. Algy often used to shoot there, and now they say he just has his brother down to shoot with him. It's really quite too melancholy! Did you know him, Dick?'

'Foliot?' replied Shelton absently. 'No; I never met him. I've seen her once or twice at Ascot.'

Through the window he could see Antonia in her scarlet tam-o'-shanter, swinging her stick, and he got up feigning unconcern. Just then Toddles came bounding up against his sister. They went off arm in arm. She had seen him at the window, yet she gave no friendly glance; Shelton felt more miserable than ever. He stepped out upon the drive. There was a lurid, gloomy canopy above; the

160

elm-trees drooped their heavy blackish green, the wonted rustle of the aspen-tree was gone, even the rooks were silent. A store of force lay heavy on the heart of Nature. He started pacing slowly up and down, his pride forbidding him to follow her, and presently sat down on an old stone seat that faced the road. He stayed a long time staring at the elms, asking himself what he had done and what he ought to do. And somehow he was frightened. A sense of loneliness was on him, so real, so painful, that he shivered in the sweltering heat. He was there, perhaps, an hour, alone, and saw nobody pass along the road. Then came the sound of horse's hoofs, and at the same time he heard a motor-car approaching from the opposite direction. The rider made appearance first, riding a grey horse with an Arab's high-set head and tail. She was holding him with difficulty, for the whirr of the approaching car grew every moment louder. Shelton rose; the car flashed by. He saw the horse stagger in the gateway, crushing its rider up against the gate-post.

He ran, but before he reached the gate the lady was on foot, holding the plunging horse's bridle.

'Are you hurt?' cried Shelton breathlessly, and he, too, grabbed the bridle. 'Those beastly cars!'

'I don't know,' she said. 'Please don't; he won't let strangers touch him.'

Shelton let go, and watched her coax the horse. She was rather tall, dressed in a grey habit, with a grey Russian cap upon her head, and he suddenly recognised the Mrs Foliot whom they had been talking of at lunch.

'He'll be quiet now,' she said, 'if you wouldn't mind holding him a minute.'

She gave the reins to him, and leaned against the gate. She was very pale.

'I do hope he hasn't hurt you,' Shelton said. He was quite close to her, well able to see her face—a curious face, with high cheek-bones and a flattish moulding, enigmatic, yet strangely passionate for all its listless pallor. Her smiling, tightened lips were pallid; pallid, too, her grey and deep-set eyes with greenish tints; above all, pale the ashy mass of hair coiled under her grey cap.

'Th—thanks!' she said. 'I shall be all right directly. I'm sorry to have made a fuss.'

She bit her lips and smiled.

'I'm sure you're hurt; do let me go for——' stammered Shelton. 'I can easily get help.'

'Help!' she said, with a stony little laugh; 'oh no, thanks!'

She left the gate, and crossed the road to where he held the horse. Shelton, to conceal embarrassment, looked at the horse's legs, and noticed that the grey was resting one of them. He ran his hand down.

'I'm afraid,' he said, 'your horse has knocked his off knee; it's swelling.'

She smiled again. 'Then we're both cripples.'

'He'll be lame when he gets cold. Wouldn't you like to put him in the stable here? I'm sure you ought to drive home.'

'No, thanks; if I'm able to ride him he can carry me. Give me a hand up.'

Her voice sounded as though something had offended her. Rising from inspection of the horse's leg, Shelton saw Antonia and Toddles standing by. They had come through a wicket-gate leading from the fields.

The latter ran up to him at once.

'We saw it,' he whispered—'jolly smash-up. Can't I help?'

'Hold his bridle,' answered Shelton, and he looked from one lady to the other.

There are moments when the expression of a face fixes itself with painful clearness; to Shelton this was such a moment. Those two faces close together under their coverings of scarlet and of grey, showed a contrast almost cruelly vivid. Antonia was flushed, her eyes had grown deep blue; her look of startled doubt had passed and left a question in her face.

'Wouldn't you like to come in and wait? We could send you home in the brougham,' she said.

The lady called Mrs Foliot stood, one arm across the crupper of her saddle, biting her lips and smiling still her enigmatic smile, and it was her face that stayed most vividly on Shelton's mind, its ashy hair, its pallor, and fixed, scornful eyes.

'Oh no, thanks! You're very kind.'

Out of Antonia's face the timid, doubting friendliness had fled, and was replaced by enmity. With a long, cold look at both of them she turned away. Mrs Foliot gave a little laugh, and raised her foot for Shelton's help. He heard a hiss of pain as he swung her up, but when he looked at her she smiled.

'Anyway,' he said impatiently, 'let me come and see you don't break down.'

She shook her head. 'It's only two miles. I'm not made of sugar.'

'Then I shall simply have to follow.'

She shrugged her shoulders, fixing her resolute eyes on him.

'Would that boy like to come?' she asked.

Toddles left the horse's head.

'By Jove!' he cried. 'Wouldn't I just!'

'Then,' she said, 'I think that will be best. You've been so kind.'

She bowed, smiled inscrutably once more, touched the Arab with her whip, and started, Toddles trotting at her side.

Shelton was left with Antonia underneath the elms. A sudden puff of tepid air blew in their faces, like a warning message from the heavy, purple heat clouds, low rumbling thunder travelled slowly from afar.

'We're going to have a storm,' he said.

Antonia nodded. She was pale now, and her face still wore its cold look of offence.

'I've got a headache,' she said. 'I shall go in and lie down.'

Shelton tried to speak, but something kept him silent—submission to what was coming, like the mute submission of the fields and birds to the menace of the storm.

He watched her go, and went back to his seat. And the silence seemed to grow; the flowers ceased to exude their fragrance, numbed by the weighty air.

All the long house behind him seemed asleep, deserted. No noise came forth, no laughter, the echo of no music, the ringing of no bell; the heat had wrapped it round with drowsiness. And the silence added to the solitude within him. What an unlucky chance, that woman's accident! Designed by Providence to put Antonia further from him than before! Why was not the world composed of the immaculate alone? He started pacing up and down, tortured by a dreadful heartache.

'I must get rid of this,' he thought. 'I'll go for a good tramp, and chance the storm.'

Leaving the drive he ran on Toddles, returning in the highest spirits.

'I saw her home,' he crowed. 'I say, what a ripper, isn't she? She'll be as lame as a tree to-morrow; so will the gee. Jolly hot!'

This meeting showed Shelton that he had been an hour on the stone seat; he had thought it some ten minutes, and the discovery alarmed him. It seemed to bring the import of his miserable fear right home to him. He started with a swinging stride, keeping his eyes fixed on the road, the perspiration streaming down his face.

Chapter 31

THE STORM

IT was seven and more when Shelton returned from his walk; a few heat-drops had splashed the leaves, but the storm had not yet broken. In brooding silence the world seemed pent beneath the purple firmament.

By rapid walking in the heat Shelton had got rid of his despondency. He felt like one who is to see his mistress after long estrangement. He bathed, and, straightening his tie-ends, stood smiling at the glass. His fear, unhappiness, and doubts seemed like an evil dream; how much worse off would he not have been, had it all been true?

It was a dinner-party night, and when he reached the drawing-room the guests were there already chattering of the coming storm. Antonia was not yet down, and Shelton stood by the piano waiting for her entry. Red faces, spotless shirt-fronts, white arms, and freshly-twisted hair were all around him. Someone handed him a clove carnation, and, as he held it to his nose, Antonia came in, breathless, as though she had rushed downstairs. Her cheeks were pale no longer; her hand kept stealing to her throat. The flames of the coming storm seemed to have caught fire within her, to be scorching her in her white frock; she passed him close, and her fragrance whipped his senses.

She had never seemed to him so lovely.

Never again will Shelton breathe the perfume of melons and pineapples without a strange emotion. From where he sat at dinner he could not see Antonia, but amidst the chattering of voices the clink of glass and silver, the sights and sounds and scents of feasting, he thought how he would go to her and say that nothing mattered but her love. He drank the frosted, pale-gold liquid of champagne as if it had been water.

The windows stood wide open in the heat; the garden lay in thick, soft shadow, where the pitchy shapes of trees could be discerned. There was not a breath of air to fan the candle-flames above the flowers; but two large moths, fearful of the heavy dark, flew in and wheeled between the lights over the diners' heads. One fell scorched into a dish of fruit, and was removed;

the other, eluding all the swish of napkins and the efforts of the footmen, continued to make soft, fluttering rushes till Shelton rose and caught it in his hand. He took it to the window and threw it out into the darkness, and he noticed that the air was thick and tepid to his face. At a sign from Mr Dennant the muslin curtains were then drawn across the windows, and in gratitude, perhaps, for this protection, this filmy barrier between them and the muffled threats of Nature, everyone broke out in talk. It was such a night as comes in summer after perfect weather, frightening in its heat, and silence, which was broken by the distant thunder travelling low along the ground like the muttering of all dark places on the earth—such a night as seems, by very breathlessness, to smother life, and with its fateful threats to justify man's cowardice.

The ladies rose at last. The circle of the rosewood dining-table, which had no cloth, strewn with flowers and silver gilt, had a likeness to some autumn pool whose brown depths of oily water gleam under the sunset with red and yellow leaves; above it the smoke of cigarettes was clinging, like a mist to water when the sun goes down. Shelton became involved in argument with his neighbour on the English character.

'In England we've mislaid the recipe of life,' he said. 'Pleasure's a lost art. We don't get drunk, we're ashamed of love, and as to beauty, we've lost the eye for it. In exchange we have got money, but what's the good of money when we don't know how to spend it?' Excited by his neighbour's smile, he added: 'As to thought, we think so much of what our neighbours think that we never think at all. Have you ever watched a foreigner when he's listening to an Englishman? We're in the habit of despising foreigners; the scorn we have for them is nothing to the scorn they have for us. And they are right! Look at our taste! What is the good of owning riches if we don't know how to use them?'

'That's rather new to me,' his neighbour said. 'There may be something in it. . . . Did you see that case in the papers the other day of old Hornblower, who left the 1820 port that fetched a guinea a bottle? When the purchaser—poor feller!—came to drink it he found eleven bottles out of twelve completely ullaged—ha! ha! Well, there's nothing wrong with *this*;' and he drained his glass.

'No,' answered Shelton.

When they rose to join the ladies, he slipped out on the lawn. At once he was enveloped in a bath of heat. A heavy odour, sensual, sinister, was in the air, as from a sudden flowering of amorous shrubs. He stood and drank it in with greedy nostrils. Putting his hand down, he felt the grass; it was dry, and charged with electricity. Then he saw, pale and candescent in the blackness, three or four great lilies, the authors of that perfume. The blossoms seemed to be rising at him through the darkness, as though putting up their faces to be kissed. He straightened himself abruptly and went in.

The guests were leaving, when Shelton, who was watching, saw Antonia slip through the drawing-room window. He could follow the white glimmer of her frock across the lawn, but lost it in the shadow of the trees; casting a hasty look to see that he was not observed, he too slipped out. The blackness and the heat were stifling; he took great breaths of it as if it were the purest mountain air, and, treading softly on the grass, stole on towards the holm-oak. His lips were dry, his heart beat painfully. The mutter of the distant thunder had quite ceased; waves of hot air came wheeling in his face, and in their midst a sudden rush of cold. He thought: 'The storm is coming now!' and stole on towards the tree. She was lying in the hammock, her figure a white blur in the heart of the tree's shadow, rocking gently to a little creaking of the branch. Shelton held his breath; she had not heard him. He crept up close behind the trunk till he stood within touch of her. 'I mustn't startle her,' he thought. 'Antonia!'

There was a faint stir in the hammock, but no answer. He stood over her, but even then he could not see her face; he only had a sense of something breathing and alive within a yard of him—of something warm and soft. He whispered again, 'Antonia!' but again there came no answer, and a sort of fear and frenzy seized on him. He could no longer hear her breathe; the creaking of the branch had ceased. What was passing in that silent, living creature there so close? And then he heard again the sound of breathing, quick and scared, like the fluttering of a bird; in a moment he was staring in the dark at an empty hammock.

He stayed beside the empty hammock till he could bear uncertainty no longer. But as he crossed the lawn the sky was rent from end to end by jagged lightning, rain spattered him from head to foot, and with a deafening crack the thunder broke.

He sought the smoking-room, but, recoiling at the door, went to his own room, and threw himself down on the bed. The thunder groaned and sputtered in long volleys; the lightning showed him the shapes of things within the room with a weird distinctness that rent from them all likeness to the purpose they were made for, bereaved them of utility, of their matter-of-factness, presented them as skeletons, abstractions, with indecency in their appearance, like the naked nerves and sinews of a leg preserved in spirit. The sound of the rain against the house stunned his power of thinking. He rose to shut his windows; then, returning to his bed, threw himself down again. He stayed there till the storm was over, in a kind of stupor; but when the boom of the retreating thunder grew every minute less distinct, he rose. Then for the first time he saw something white close by the door.

It was a note:

'I have made a mistake. Please forgive me, and go away.— Antonia.'

Chapter 32

WILDERNESS

WHEN he had read this note, Shelton put it down beside his sleeve-links on his dressing-table, stared into the mirror at himself, and laughed. But his lips soon stopped him laughing; he threw himself on his bed, and pressed his face into the pillows. He lay there half-dressed throughout the night, and when he rose, soon after dawn, he had not made his mind up what to do. The only thing he knew for certain was that he must not meet Antonia.

At last he penned the following:

'I have had a sleepless night with toothache, and think it best to run up to the dentist at once. If a tooth must come out, the sooner the better.'

He addressed it to Mrs Dennant, and left it on his table. After doing this he threw himself once more upon his bed, and this time fell into a doze.

He woke with a start, dressed, and let himself quietly out. The likeness of his going to that of Ferrand struck him. 'Both outcasts now,' he thought.

He tramped on till noon without knowing or caring where he went; then, entering a field, threw himself down under the hedge, and fell asleep.

He was awakened by a whirr. A covey of partridges, with wings glistening in the sun, were straggling out across the adjoining field of mustard. They soon settled in the old-maidish way of partridges, and began to call upon each other.

Some cattle had approached him in his sleep, and a beautiful bay cow, with her head turned sideways, was snuffing at him gently, exhaling her peculiar sweetness. She was as fine in legs and coat as any race-horse. She dribbled at the corners of her black, moist lips; her eye was soft and cynical. Breathing the vague sweetness of the mustard-field, rubbing dry grass-stalks in his fingers, Shelton had a moment's happiness—the happiness of sun and sky, of the eternal quiet, and untold movements of the fields. Why could not human beings let their troubles be as this cow left the flies that clung about her eyes? He dozed again, and woke up with a laugh, for this was what he dreamed :

He fancied he was in a room, at once the hall and drawing-room of some country house. In the centre of this room a lady stood, who was looking in a hand-glass at her face. Beyond a door, or window, could be seen a garden with a row of statues, and through this door people passed without apparent object.

Suddenly Shelton saw his mother advancing to the lady with the hand-glass, whom now he recognised as Mrs Foliot. But, as he looked, his mother changed to Mrs Dennant, and began speaking in a voice, neither his mother's nor Mrs Dennant's, but a voice that was a sort of abstract of refinement. '*Je fais de la philosophie*,' it said; 'I take the individual for what she's worth. I do not condemn; above all, one must have spirit!' The lady with the mirror continued looking in the glass; and though he could not see her face, he could see its image—pale, with greenish eyes, and a smile like scorn itself. Then, by a swift transition, he was walking in the garden talking to Mrs Dennant.

It was from this talk that he awoke with laughter. 'But,' she had been saying, 'Dick, I've always been accustomed to believe what I was told. It was so unkind of her to scorn me just because I happen to be conventional.' And her voice awakened Shelton's pity; it was like a frightened child's. 'I don't know what I shall do if I have to form opinions for myself. I wasn't brought up to it. I've always had them nice and second-hand. How am I to go to work? One must believe what other people do; not that I think much of other people, but, you do know what it is—one feels so much more comfortable,' and her skirts rustled. 'But, Dick, whatever happens'—her voice entreated—'do let Antonia get her judgments second-hand. Never mind for me—if I must form opinions for myself, I must—but don't let her; any old opinions so long as they *are* old. It's dreadful to have to think out new ones for oneself.' And he awoke. His dream had had in it the element called Art, for, in its gross absurdity Mrs Dennant had said things which showed her soul more fully than anything she would have said in life.

'No,' said a voice quite close, behind the hedge, 'not many Frenchmen, thank the Lord! A few coveys of Hungarians over from the Duke's. Sir James, some pie?'

Shelton raised himself with drowsy curiosity—still half asleep —and applied his face to a gap in the high thick osiers of the hedge. Four men were seated on camp-stools round a folding-table, on which was a pie and other things to eat. A game-cart, well adorned with birds and hares, stood at a short distance; the tails of some dogs were seen moving humbly, and a valet opening bottles. Shelton had forgotten that it was 'the first'. The host was a soldierly and freckled man; an older man sat next him, square-jawed, with an absent-looking eye and sharpened nose; next him, again, there was a bearded person whom they seemed to call the Commodore; in the fourth, to his alarm, Shelton recognised the gentleman called Mabbey. It was really no matter for surprise to meet him miles from his own place, for he was one of those who wander with a valet and two guns from the twelfth of August to the end of January, and are then supposed to go to Monte Carlo or to sleep until the twelfth of August comes again.

He was speaking.

'Did you hear what a bag we made on the twelfth, Sir James?'

'Ah! yes; what was that? Have you sold your bay horse, Glennie?'

Shelton had not decided whether or no to sneak away, when the Commodore's thick voice began:

'My man tellsh me that Mrs Foliot—haw—has lamed her Arab. Does she mean to come out cubbing?'

Shelton observed the smile that came on all their faces. 'Foliot's paying for his good time now; what a donkey to get caught!' it seemed to say. He turned his back and shut his eyes.

'Cubbing?' replied Glennie; 'hardly.'

'Never could shee anything wonderful in her looks,' went on the Commodore; 'so quiet, you never knew that she was in the room. I remember sayin' to her once: "Mrs Lutheran, now what

169

do you like besht in all the world?" and what do you think she answered? "Music!" Haw!'

The voice of Mabbey said:

'He was always a dark horse, Foliot. It's always the dark horses that get let in for this kind of thing'; and there was a sound as though he licked his lips.

'They say,' said the voice of the host, 'he never gives you back a greeting now. Queer fish; they say that she's devoted to him.'

Coming so closely on his meeting with this lady, and on the dream from which he had awakened, this conversation mesmerised the listener behind the hedge.

'If he gives up his huntin' and his shootin', I don't see what the deuce he'll do; he's resigned his clubs; as to his chance of Parliament——' said the voice of Mabbey.

'Thousand pities,' said Sir James; 'still, he knew what to expect.'

'Very queer fellows, those Foliots,' said the Commodore. 'There was his father: he'd always rather talk to any scarecrow he came across than to you or me. Wonder what he'll do with all his horses? I should like that chestnut of his.'

'You can't tell *what* a fellow'll do,' said the voice of Mabbey— 'take to drink or writin' books. Old Charlie Wayne came to gazin' at stars, and twice a week he used to go and paddle round in Whitechapel, teachin' pothooks——'

'Glennie,' said Sir James, 'what's become of Smollett, your old keeper?'

'Obliged to get rid of him.' Shelton tried again to close his ears, but again he listened. 'Getting a bit too old; lost me a lot of eggs last season.'

'Ah!' said the Commodore, 'when they oncesh begin to lose eggsh——'

'As a matter of fact, his son—you remember him, Sir James, he used to load for you?—got a girl into trouble; when her people gave her the chuck old Smollett took her in; beastly scandal it made, too. The girl refused to marry Smollett, and old Smollett backed her up. Naturally, the parson and the village cut up rough; my wife offered to get her into one of those reformatory what-d'you-call-'ems, but the old fellow said she shouldn't go if she didn't want to. Bad business altogether; put him quite off his stroke. I only got five hundred pheasants last year instead of eight.'

There was a silence. Shelton again peeped through the hedge. All were eating pie.

'In W——shire,' said the Commodore, 'they always marry—haw—and live reshpectable ever after.'

'Quite so,' remarked the host; 'it was a bit too thick her refusing to marry him. She said he took advantage of her.'

'She's sorry by this time,' said Sir James; 'lucky escape for young Smollett. Queer, the obstinacy of some of these old fellows!'

'What are we doing after lunch?' asked the Commodore.

'The next field,' said the host, 'is pasture. We line up along the hedge, and drive that mustard towards the roots; there ought to be a good few birds.'

Shelton rose; and, crouching, stole softly to the gate.

'On the twelfth, shootin' in two parties,' followed the voice of Mabbey from the distance.

Whether from his walk or from his sleepless night, Shelton seemed to ache in every limb; but he continued his tramp along the road. He was no nearer to deciding what to do. It was late in the afternoon when he reached Maidenhead, and, after breaking fast, got a London train and went to sleep. At ten o'clock that evening he walked into St James's Park and there sat down.

The lamp-light dappled through the tired foliage on to those benches which have rested many vagrants. Darkness had ceased to be the lawful cloak of the unhappy; but Mother Night was soft and moonless, and man had not quite despoiled her of her comfort.

Shelton was not alone on the seat, for at the far end was sitting a young girl with a red, round, sullen face; and beyond, and further still, were dim benches and dim figures sitting on them, as though life's institutions had shot them out in an endless line of rubbish.

'Ah!' thought Shelton, in the dreamy way of tired people; 'the institutions are all right; it's the spirit that's all——'

'Wrong?' said a voice behind him; 'why, of course! You've taken the wrong turn, old man.'

He saw a policeman, with a red face shining through the darkness, talking to a strange old figure like some aged and dishevelled bird.

'Thank you, constable,' the old man said; 'as I've come wrong I'll take a rest.' Chewing his gums, he seemed to fear to take the liberty of sitting down.

Shelton made room, and the old fellow took the vacant place.

'You'll excuse me, sir, I'm sure,' he said in shaky tones, and snatching at his battered hat; 'I see you was a gentleman'—and lovingly he dwelt upon the word—'wouldn't disturb you for the world. I'm not used to being out at night, and the seats do get so full. Old age must lean on something; you'll excuse me, sir, I'm sure.'

'Of course,' said Shelton gently.

'I'm a respectable old man, really,' said his neighbour; 'I never took a liberty in my life. But at my age, sir, you get nervous; standin' about the streets as I been this last week, an sleepin' in them doss-houses——Oh, they're dreadful rough places—a dreadful rough lot there! Yes,' the old man said again, as Shelton turned to look at him, struck by the real self-pity in his voice, 'dreadful rough places!'

A movement of his head, which grew on a lean, plucked neck like that of an old fowl's, had brought his face into the light. It was long, and run to seed, and had a large, red nose; its thin, colourless lips were twisted sideways and apart, showing his semi-toothless mouth; and his eyes had that aged look of eyes in which all colour runs into a thin rim round the iris, and over them kept coming films like the films over parrots' eyes. He was, or should have been, clean-shaven. His hair—for he had taken off his hat—was thick and lank, of dusty colour, as far as could be seen, without a speck of grey, and parted very beautifully just about the middle.

'I can put up with that,' he said again. 'I never interferes with nobody, and nobody don't interfere with me; but what frightens me'—his voice grew steady, as if too terrified to shake—'is never knowin' day to day what's to become of yer. Oh, that's dreadful, that is!'

'It must be,' answered Shelton.

'Ah! it is,' the old man said; 'and the winter comin' on. I never was much used to open air, bein' in domestic service all my life; but I don't mind that, so long as I can see my way to earn a livin'. Well, thank God! I've got a job at last;' and his voice grew cheerful suddenly. 'Sellin' papers is not what I been accustomed to; but the *Westminster*, they tell me that's one of the most respectable of the evenin' papers—in fact, I know it is. So now I'm sure to get on; I try hard.'

'How did you get the job?' asked Shelton.

'I've got my character,' the old fellow said, making a gesture with a skinny hand towards his chest, as if it were there he kept his character.

'Thank God, nobody can't take that away! I never parts from that;' and, fumbling, he produced a packet, holding first one paper

172

to the light, and then another, and he looked anxiously at Shelton. 'In that house where I been sleepin' they're not honest; they've stolen a parcel of my things—a lovely shirt, an' a pair of beautiful gloves a gentleman gave me for holdin' of his horse. Now, wouldn't you prosecute 'em, sir?'

'It depends on what you can prove.'

'I know they had 'em. A man must stand up for his rights; that's only proper. I can't afford to lose beautiful things like them. I think I ought to prosecute, now, don't you, sir?'

Shelton restrained a smile.

'There!' said the old man, smoothing out a piece of paper shakily, 'that's Sir George!' and his withered finger-tip trembled on the middle of the page: ' "Joshua Creed, in my service five years as butler, during which time I have found him all that a servant should be." And this 'ere,' he fumbled with another—'this 'ere's Lady Glengow: "Joshua Creed——" thought I'd like you to read 'em since you've been so kind.'

'Will you have a pipe?'

'Thank ye, sir,' replied the aged butler, filling his clay from Shelton's pouch; then, taking a front tooth between his finger and his thumb, he began to feel it tenderly, working it to and fro with a sort of melancholy pride.

'My teeth's a-comin' out,' he said; 'but I enjoys pretty good health for a man of my age.'

'How old is that?'

'Seventy-two! Barrin' my cough, and my rupture and this 'ere affliction'—he passed his hand over his face—'I've nothing to complain of; everybody has something, it seems. I'm a wonder for my age, I think.'

Shelton, for all his pity, would have given much to laugh.

'Seventy-two!' he said; 'yes, a great age. You remember the country when it was very different to what it is now?'

'Ah!' said the old butler, 'there was gentry then; I remember them drivin' down to Newmarket (my native place, sir) with their own horses. There wasn't so much o' these here *middle* classes then. There was more, too, what you might call the milk o' human kindness in people then—none o' them Amalgamated Stores, every man keepin' his own little shop; not so eager to cut his neighbour's throat, as you might say. And then look at the price of bread! Oh dear! why, it isn't a quarter what it was!'

'And are people happier now than they were then?' asked Shelton.

The old butler sucked his pipe.

'No,' he answered, shaking his old head; 'they've lost the contented spirit. I see people runnin' here and runnin' there, readin' books, findin' things out; they ain't not so self-contented as they were.'

'Is that possible?' thought Shelton.

'No,' repeated the old man, again sucking at his pipe, and this time blowing out a lot of smoke; 'I don't see as much happiness about, not the same look on the faces. 'Tisn't likely. See these 'ere motor-cars, too; they say 'orses is goin' out;' and as if dumbfounded at his own conclusion, he sat silent for some time, engaged in the lighting and relighting of his pipe.

The girl at the far end stirred, cleared her throat, and settled down again; her movement disengaged a scent of frowsy clothes. The policeman had approached and scrutinised these three ill-assorted faces; his glance was jovially contemptuous till he noticed Shelton, and then was modified by curiosity.

'There's good men in the police,' the aged butler said, when the policeman had passed on—'there's good men in the police, as good men as you can see, and there's them that treats you like the dirt—a dreadful low class of man. Oh dear, yes! when they see you down in the world, they think they can speak to you as they like. I don't give them no chance to worry me; I keeps myself to myself, and speak civil to all the world. You have to hold the candle to them; for, oh dear! if they're crossed—some of them, they're a dreadful unscrup'lous lot of men!'

'Are you going to spend the night here?'

'It's nice and warm to-night,' replied the aged butler. 'I said to the man at that low place, I said: "Don't you ever speak to me again," I said, "don't you come near me!" Straightforward and honest's been my motto all my life; I don't want to have nothing to say to them low fellows'—he made an annihilating gesture—'after the way they treated me, takin' my things like that. To-morrow I shall get a room. I can get a room for three shillin's a week, don't you think so, sir! Well, then I shall be all right. I'm not afraid now; the mind at rest. So long as I can keep myself, that's all I want. I shall do first rate, I think;' and he stared at Shelton, but the look in his eyes and the half-scared optimism of his voice convinced the latter that he lived in dread. 'So long as I keep myself,' he said again, 'I shan't need no workhouse nor lose respectability.'

'No,' thought Shelton; and for some time sat without a word.

'When you can,' he said at last, 'come and see me; here's my card.'

The aged butler became conscious with a jerk, for he was nodding.

'Thank ye, sir; I will,' he said, with pitiful alacrity. 'Down by Belgravia? Oh, I know it well; I lived down in them parts with a gentleman of the name of Bateson—perhaps you knew him; he's dead now—the Honourable Bateson. Thank ye, sir; I'll be sure to come;' and snatching at his battered hat, he toilsomely secreted Shelton's card amongst his character. A minute later he began again to nod.

The policeman passed a second time; his gaze seemed to say, 'Now, what's a toff doing on that seat with those two rotters?' And Shelton caught his eye.

'Ah!' he thought; 'exactly! You don't know what to make of me—a man of my position sitting here! Poor devil! to spend your days in spying on your fellow-creatures! Poor devil! But you don't know that you're a poor devil, and so you're not one.'

The man on the next bench sneezed—a shrill and disapproving sneeze.

The policeman passed again, and seeing that the lower creatures were both dozing, he spoke to Shelton:

'Not very safe on these 'ere benches, sir,' he said; 'you never know who you may be sittin' next to. If I were you, sir, I should be gettin' on—if you're not goin' to spend the night here, that is;' and he laughed, as at an admirable joke.

Shelton looked at him, and itched to say: 'Why shouldn't I?' but it struck him that it would sound very odd. 'Besides,' he thought, 'I shall only catch a cold;' and, without speaking, he left the seat, and went along towards his rooms.

Chapter 33

THE END

HE reached his rooms at midnight so exhausted that, without waiting to light up, he dropped into a chair. The curtains and blinds had been removed for cleaning, and the tall windows admitted the night's staring gaze. Shelton fixed his eyes on that outside darkness, as one lost man might fix his eyes upon another.

An unaired, dusty odour clung about the room, but, like some

God-sent whiff of grass or flowers wafted to one sometimes in the street, a perfume came to him, the spice from the withered clove-carnation still clinging to his buttonhole; and he suddenly awoke from his queer trance. There was a decision to be made. He rose to light a candle; the dust was thick on everything he touched. 'Ugh!' he thought, 'how wretched!' and the loneliness that had seized him on the stone seat at Holm Oaks the day before returned with fearful force.

On his table, heaped without order, were a pile of bills and circulars. He opened them, tearing at their covers with the random haste of men back from their holidays. A single long envelope was placed apart.

'MY DEAR DICK (he read),

'I enclose you herewith the revised draft of your marriage settlement. It is now shipshape. Return it before the end of the week, and I will have it engrossed for signature. I go to Scotland next Wednesday for a month; shall be back in good time for your wedding. My love to your mother when you see her.

'Your affectionate uncle,
'EDMUND PARAMOR.'

Shelton smiled, and took out the draft.

'This Indenture made the   day of   , 190-, between Richard Paramor Shelton———.'

He put it down, and sank back in his chair, the chair in which the foreign vagrant had been wont to sit on mornings when he came to preach philosophy.

He did not stay there long, but in sheer unhappiness got up, and, taking his candle, roamed about the room, fingering things, and gazing in the mirror at his face, which seemed to him repulsive in its wretchedness. He went at last into the hall and opened the door, to go downstairs again into the street; but the sudden certainty that, in street or house, in town or country, he would have to take his trouble with him, made him shut it to. He felt in the letter-box, drew forth a letter and with this he went back to the sitting-room.

It was from Antonia. And such was his excitement that he was forced to take three turns between the window and the wall before he read; then, with a heart beating so that he could hardly hold the paper, he began :

'I was wrong to ask you to go away. I see now that it was breaking my promise, and I didn't mean to do that. I don't know why things have come to be so different. You never think as I do about anything.

'I had better tell you that that letter of Monsieur Ferrand's to mother was impudent. Of course you didn't know what was in it; but when Professor Brayne was asking you about him at breakfast, I felt that you believed that he was right and we were wrong, and I can't understand it. And then in the afternoon when that woman hurt her horse, it was all as if you were on her side. How can you feel like that?

'I must say this, because I don't think I ought to have asked you to go away, and I want you to believe that I will keep my promise, or I should feel that you and everybody else had a right to condemn me. I was awake all last night, and have a bad headache this morning. I can't write any more.   'ANTONIA.'

His first sensation was a sort of stupefaction of relief which had in it an element of anger. He was reprieved! She would not break her promise; she considered herself bound! In the midst of the exaltation of this thought he smiled, and that smile was strange.

He read it through again, and, like a judge, began to weigh what she had written, her thoughts when she was writing, the facts which had led up to this.

The vagrant's farewell document had done the business. True to his fatal gift of divesting things of clothing, Ferrand had not vanished without showing up his patron in his proper colours; even to Shelton those colours were made plain. Antonia had felt her lover was a traitor. Sounding his heart even in his stress of indecision. Shelton knew that this was true.

'Then in the afternoon, when the woman hurt her horse——' That woman! 'It was all as if you were on her side!'

He saw too well her mind, its clear rigidity, its intuitive perception of that with which it was not safe to sympathise, its instinct for self-preservation, its spontaneous contempt for those without that instinct. And she had written these words considering herself bound to *him*—a man of sentiment, of rebellious sympathies, of untidiness of principle! Here was the answer to the question he had asked all day: 'How have things come to such a pass?' and he began to feel compassion for her.

Poor child! She could not jilt him; there was something vulgar in the word! Never should it be said that Antonia Dennant had accepted him and thrown him over. No lady did these things! They were impossible! At the bottom of his heart he had a queer, unconscious sympathy with this impossibility.

Once again he read the letter, which seemed now impregnated with fresh meaning, and the anger which had mingled with his first sensation of relief detached itself and grew in force. In that letter there was something tyrannous, a denial of his right to have a separate point of view. It was like a finger pointed at him as an unsound person. In marrying her he would be marrying not only her, but her class—his class. She would be there always to make him look on her and on himself, and all the people that they knew and all the things they did, complacently; she would be there to make him feel himself superior to everyone whose life was cast in other moral moulds. To feel himself superior, not blatantly, not consciously, but with subconscious righteousness.

But his anger, which was like the paroxysm that two days before had made him mutter at the Connoisseur, 'I hate your d——d superiority,' struck him all at once as impotent and ludicrous. What was the good of being angry? He was on the point of losing her! And the anguish of that thought, reacting on his anger, intensified it threefold. She was so certain of herself, so superior to her very longing to be free from him. Of *that* fact, at all events, Shelton had no longer any doubt. It was beyond argument. She did not really love him; she wanted to be free of him!

A photograph hung in his bedroom at Holm Oaks of a group round the hall door; the Honourable Charlotte Penguin, Mrs Dennant, Lady Bonington, Halidome, Mr Dennant, and the stained-glass man—all were there; and on the left-hand side, looking straight in front of her, Antonia. Her face in its youthfulness, more than all those others, expressed their point of view. Behind those calm young eyes lay a world of safety and tradition. 'I am not as others are,' they seemed to say.

And from that photograph Mr and Mrs Dennant singled themselves out; he could see their faces as they talked—their faces with a peculiar and uneasy look on them; and he could hear their voices, still decisive, but a little acid, as if they had been quarrelling:

'He's made a donkey of himself!'

'Ah! it's too distressin'!'

They, too, thought him unsound, and didn't want him; but to

178

save the situation they would be glad to keep him. *She* didn't want him, but she refused to lose her right to say: 'Commoner girls may break their promises; *I* will not!' He sat down at the table between the candles, covering his face. If she would not free herself, the duty was on him! She was ready without love to marry him, as a sacrifice to her ideal of what she ought to be!

But she hadn't, after all, the monopoly of pride!

As if she stood before him, he could see the shadows underneath her eyes that he had dreamed of kissing, the eager movements of her lips. For several minutes he remained, not moving hand or limb. Then once more his anger blazed. She was going to sacrifice herself and—him! All his manhood scoffed at such a senseless sacrifice. That was not exactly what he wanted!

He went to the bureau, took a piece of paper and an envelope, and wrote as follows:

'There never was, is not, and never would have been any question of being bound between us. I refuse to trade on any such thing. You are absolutely free. Our engagement is at an end by mutual consent.

'RICHARD SHELTON.'

He sealed it, and sitting with his hands between his knees, he let his forehead droop lower and lower to the table, till it rested on his Marriage Settlement. And he had a feeling of relief, like one who drops exhausted at his journey's end.

1904.